SUSPICION OF MURDER

Frowning, Matt riffled through his reports again. There was nothing to suggest that Warren's death wasn't what it seemed, nothing to prove that he wasn't in league with the thieves, except . . .

He'd missed something, he was sure of it. Stopping at random, he read again a report of the earliest theft. Ten paintings had been taken in all, all carefully removed from their frames, which had then been stacked neatly on the floor. Matt was about to go on when a thought struck him, making him go back to the very first report on Warren's death, one he had written himself. And there it was. In that case the painting stolen had been cut from the frame, which was left on the wall.

Matt sat back, tapping at his teeth with the end of his pencil, his thoughts racing. Why would the thief have deviated so from his former methods? Panic? If so, why steal a painting at all? The man who had wielded a knife with precision enough to stab a man through the heart didn't seem the type to panic. But to cut a painting out of a frame, as if that were his main intention . . .

Matt sat very still, fingertips resting on the edge of his desk, while his brain made a great leap in logic. Of course. Whoever had killed Warren hadn't cared about the painting, not if he had cut it, and damaged it. Thus, he hadn't been one of the thieves, but someone with another purpose, using the painting only as a cover. Matt didn't yet have the facts to support his theory, but of one thing he was deeply, completely certain.

Joseph Warren had been murdered.

Books by Mary Kruger:

DEATH ON THE CLIFF WALK
NO HONEYMOON FOR DEATH
MASTERPIECE OF MURDER

Published by Kensington Publishing

MARY KRUGER

Masterpiece of Murder

A Gilded Age Mystery

KENSINGTON BOOKS
KENSINGTON PUBLISHING CORP.

http://www.kensingtonbooks.com

KENSINGTON BOOKS are published by

Kensington Publishing Corp.
850 Third Avenue
New York, NY 10022

First Kensington Hardcover Printing: December, 1996
First Kensington Paperback Printing: September, 1997
10 9 8 7 6 5 4 3 2 1

Printed in the United States of America

To my brother, Thomas Kruger. Thank you for encouraging me to go for my dream.

Prologue

New York, April 1896

Late night, and the Manhattan Museum of Art was dark and quiet, all visitors gone, all staff left for the day. Joseph Warren, assistant director and curator of the paintings department, paced impatiently along the second floor gallery, lighted only by the reflected glow from the offices at the far end. In the gloom, shadows played off the stiff pleats of the burgundy draperies; light glinted on a gilded frame, while leaving another in darkness. It was unusual for Warren to work late, but his position in the museum precluded questioning. If he were to illuminate the gallery, though, the watchman would take heed, and that must be avoided. At all costs, there must be privacy for this meeting.

It was a mess, all of it, the whole sorry business, and he wished he'd never gotten involved. Too many people were asking questions; too many wondered if the disappearance of paintings from the museum's collection was as random as it seemed. Warren stopped pacing for a moment, standing with hands in pockets and glaring sightlessly at a Turner landscape. It hadn't seemed like such a bad idea at the time, but now it was all crashing down on him. After tonight he'd have no more of it. Anything would be better than living in this constant hell of anxiety, of fear that his actions would be discovered. Never mind the scandal, or the likelihood that he'd go to prison. After tonight he'd confess to what he'd done, and face the consequences like a man.

A footfall at the far end of the gallery made him turn. "There you are," he said, his voice pitched low as the figure, backlit by the electric glow from the offices, approached him. "Why did you want to meet me here, when I could—hey! It's you."

Warren's companion took a cigarette from his pocket and lit it with quick, practiced motions, waving out the match. "You were expecting someone else?"

"Yes, dammit. Put that thing out. Smoking damages the paintings."

"Ah, your beloved pictures. I've heard of them."

Warren went still. "What have you heard?"

The cigarette dropped to the parquet floor and was ground out by a hard leather heel. "Enough to know you're holding out on me," his companion whispered, and flicked out a knife.

"What are you doing with that?" Warren said sharply.

"Getting what's owed me." And with that the man lunged.

It was over in a moment. Warren was quick on his feet for so large a man, but not quick enough; the long, thin blade pierced him just under the ribs and traveled up, up. He grabbed his assailant by the arms, clutching, his eyes bulging; and though he opened his mouth to speak, only a gurgle emerged. Hard fingers loosened his desperate grip and his knees gave out. He was dead before he had completely slumped to the floor.

His assailant stood a few feet away, looking dispassionately down at the still figure, its muscles contracting and twitching in the aftermath of death, blood flowing in a thin river along the varnished floor. It had been a peaceful death, all things considered; no noise to alert the watchman or anyone else who might be in the building. Rather a neat piece of work. With thumb and forefinger extended, the murderer reached down to remove the knife, wiping the blade carefully on a snowy-white handkerchief. Then, still dispassionate, almost casually, he turned away, flicking his knife along the edges of a painting chosen at random, cutting it from its frame. Many paintings were missing from the museum; this would be just one more.

With the canvas carefully folded within the pages of a newspaper and the knife returned to an inner pocket, the killer at last moved away, treading quietly through the gallery. The lighted offices that belonged to the museum staff posed one potential obstacle; the great south lobby on the first floor, another. Both were deserted. The museum doors opened quietly and closed with a soft snick, and all was peaceful again.

And as the carriage drove along Fifth Avenue, the killer, safely inside and now distant from the crime, had no idea of the one crucial mistake that he had made.

1

Matt let his carpetbag drop to the parquet floor with a thud. "Good God."

"What is it?" Brooke looked up from pulling off her gloves, tinted gold to match her traveling ensemble of tan trimmed with gold braid, and drew in her breath. "Oh, my."

"Oh, my, indeed," Matt said, glaring about him with his hands on his hips. They were home, and about time, too, as far as Brooke was concerned. Their honeymoon in Europe had been eventful and wonderful, and very long. Much as Brooke had enjoyed being alone with Matt for three months, she had lately had the feeling that their real life together wouldn't begin until they were home, at the apartment in the Dakota, across from Central Park. The apartment that her aunt Winifred had so generously offered to decorate for them, even if she did disapprove of their living there.

"Dear heavens. I should have expected something like this," she said, gazing around. The entrance hall, where they stood, was a good-sized room in itself, but the decorations made it appear small, almost claustrophobic. In the one corner Aunt

Winifred had put together an altogether astonishing array of furniture and decorations, starting with a red plush settee curving along the wall, scattered with cushions in every hue of the rainbow. Scarlet velvet curtains draped the settee like a tent, while a small table covered with a cloth of East Indian design held a Turkish lamp, some Japanese carvings in ivory, and a statue of the Buddha. Set at right angles to this Turkish nook was, incongruously, that staple of every home's hallway, a combination umbrella-and-hat stand in dark oak, with a large plate glass mirror set into it. More velvet draperies, these royal blue, cascaded to the sides. Brooke briefly closed her eyes. "It can't all be this bad, can it?"

"Knowing your aunt, it's worse," Matt said, and turned toward one of the doorways that opened off the anteroom. Ignoring the butler who held out his hand for Matt's bowler hat, as well as the maid in proper black and white who curtsied, they went into the parlor. The Oriental carpet was good, its jewel colors glowing even in the gloom, but otherwise the decorations were disastrous. A tufted sofa and club chairs of gold panne velvet competed for attention with a Steinway grand piano draped with a fringed paisley shawl and weighted down with silver picture frames, while the dark gold brocade draperies blocked any possibility of sunlight even entering the room. Any free wall space was taken up with paintings in heavy frames; Brooke was relieved to see that most of these were decent, though the standing electric lamp was so befrilled and furbelowed that it appeared to be wearing a very fussy hat. "Oh, dear," Brooke said inadequately, and turned, to see that Matt had stalked from the room. Bracing herself, she followed.

The library, down the hall from the parlor, wasn't quite so bad. Evidently this was meant to be a masculine room, for it was furnished with burgundy leather armchairs and a huge desk, and the drapery was minimal. The bookshelves lining the walls were actually handsome, filled with volumes bound in Morocco leather of red and blue and green. Almost passable, except for the huge bearskin rug. Matt took one look at that and turned on his heel, snorting; once again Brooke followed, her lips twitching.

The dining room, across the corridor, continued the pattern. The table and sideboard of dark, curved and curlicued mahogany were massive and ugly. The purple velvet upholstery of the chairs and the matching cloths covering everything only made matters worse, while the marble mantelpiece was obscured by yet another silk shawl. "The sideboard looks like an altar in Lent," Brooke murmured, and Matt, snorting again, stalked out. Her lips twitching even more, Brooke followed him. Surely the bedroom couldn't be any worse than what they'd already seen.

It was. Scattered across the fine Aubusson carpet were chairs and a vanity table in white and gold, the seats tufted in velvet of pale pink and blue. Upon a platform so high it required stairs to ascend, stood their bed, in solitary majesty under a canopy of white satin, which cascaded to either side from a crown molding above the head of the bed. Upon the molding was an insignia. Brooke frowned at it, and then bit her lips. "That's— Napoleon's seal," she said, her voice shaking as she pointed at the emblem.

Matt looked up. "What?"

"Napoleon's seal. Oh, Matt!" At last she gave way to the merriment that had been building within her through the tour of the apartment. She collapsed onto the bed in a fit of giggles and promptly slid off the slippery satin counterpane. "Royal blue, royal purple, and now this. Did you ever see yourself as an emperor?"

He glared at her. "It's not funny, Brooke."

"Of course it is." She sat up, wiping at her eyes. "It's so deliciously awful, it can't be anything but." And thank heavens her aunt wasn't here to witness their reactions to what she doubtless believed was a fashionable decorating scheme.

Matt stood, arms akimbo, a reluctant smile creeping onto his face. "At least she had the sense not to put twin beds in here."

"Matt." Brooke tilted her head toward the open doorway. They had servants to consider now, the butler, maid, and cook that her aunt deemed the very minimum of household staff. It meant that she and Matt would have to get used to a certain lack of privacy.

"I'll have nightmares in this room." Matt ambled over to a window and pulled back the mauve brocade drape, staring absently out at Central Park, across the street. "Makes me wish I'd stayed at Mulberry Street."

Brooke rose, removing her hat and then patting at her hair to make sure it was neat. "You could go back. It's still early in the day."

"You heard TR," Matt said, and this time he was the one to smile. " 'Enjoy yourself, my boy,' " he quoted. " 'Plenty of work for you tomorrow. Dee-lighted to have you back.' "

"I think he meant it, Matt."

Matt shrugged, reaching up to massage his neck muscles as he looked out again. "If so, he's the only one."

"That will change," she murmured, coming up behind him to massage his neck for him. When their ship had docked, Matt's eagerness to find out what had happened at police headquarters, particularly in the special squad to which he was assigned in the detective bureau, was obvious. For he was every inch a policeman, like his father before him, and proud to be a member of the force recently dubbed "the Finest." Proud that he'd been hired by Theodore Roosevelt, the president of the police commissioners, and more than a little concerned that his extended absence would cause problems. And so Brooke had firmly told the driver of their hansom cab to stop first at police headquarters at 300 Mulberry Street before proceeding to the Dakota. Matt had put up only a token argument.

The hansom cab pulled up before headquarters, located in the midst of tenements and saloons, and even a whorehouse across the street, its stoop enclosed by a board fence. It was a tall, drab marble-faced building, enlivened by tattered and faded awnings shading the windows from the fierce July sun, and by the constant human cavalcade. As Matt leaned forward to speak to the driver, Brooke looked out at a scene that was new yet familiar: immigrant women, shawls draped around their heads, scurrying toward the shabby brick or rickety wooden tenements where they lived; a peddler selling, of all things, toy police whistles and celluloid dentures; newly arrested miscreants descending from a paddy wagon and stumbling up the stairs of the building, prodded by the business end of a patrolman's club. On the sidewalk a man with a notebook talked with a patrolman who had pushed his bucket-shaped leather helmet back on his head, while across the street more men lounged on the steps of another, equally drab building, apparently at ease, but their eyes sharp, alert. Police reporters, Brooke guessed, waiting for the next big story. New York City's police headquarters was different, and yet essentially the same, as the smaller Newport police station where Brooke had spent time growing up, the proud daughter of a cop.

Matt turned to her. "I just want a word with Captain O'Neill," he said, referring to the head of the detective bureau. "I'm not expected back until tomorrow, so this shouldn't take long—"

"But I'm coming with you," she said sweetly. "I don't feel safe in this neighborhood."

The look Matt gave her was suspicious. "There are enough cops around if you need help."

"And enough criminals." She glanced out again, and he followed her gaze, to see a small, wizened-faced man with thumbs tucked into the pockets of his black-and-yellow checked vest, catching hold of one of the lampposts that flanked the staircase and swinging himself to the sidewalk. Apparently this time he had escaped the law. "Besides, I'd like to see inside," she said, and pushed past him to the door of the cab. "Would you help me down, please?"

Matt muttered something under his breath, but he jumped down to the cobbled street, turning to help her down. Instantly the aroma of New York in the summer assaulted her, a mixture of dust and horse droppings and the dank, fetid smell that was unique to the tenements clustered so close together. Raising her handkerchief to protect her face from the dust that likely as not contained powdery dried manure, Brooke placed her hand on Matt's arm as he led her up the stairs. "This isn't necessary, you know," he grumbled.

"Oh, come now, Matt. Aren't we partners?"

"If we should ever run up against a body on the Cliff Walk or an ocean passenger missing overboard again, yes. In my job, no. And I don't expect," he went on, opening one side of the double door, "that we'll encounter that kind of crime again."

Brooke made a little face as she passed him. Partners they were, equals in both their marriage and, when the opportunity afforded itself, detecting, and yet Matt sometimes seemed to forget that. And while it was true that she couldn't don a blue wool uniform and police the streets, she knew deep down that had she been born male, she, too, would be a cop.

Inside the headquarters the foyer was dim and stuffy, the warmth enriched by the scents of overheated wool and overheated, overfrightened civilians. To the right was a staircase;

tucked in behind that was the metal cage of the elevator shaft. The sergeant at the high desk to the left glanced up incuriously at their entrance, and then looked again. "Devlin," he said, his voice carefully neutral. "So ye're back from yer honeymoon, are ye?"

Matt nodded crisply. "Yes, Sergeant. Is Captain O'Neill in the detective bureau?"

"Himself's out. Workin'. If ye'll wait, I'll see if there's anyone else for ye to talk to—just a minute." This as the telephone on his desk emitted a shrill ring. He raised the cone-shaped receiver with the same bored, incurious look with which he'd greeted them, while beside her Brooke could feel Matt's muscles tight and bunched with strain. He was, she guessed, very angry.

"Yes, sir," the sergeant said, suddenly sitting up straighter, his walrus mustache bobbing up and down as he nodded. "No, sir. Yes, sir, I'll tell him. Ye're to go up," he said to Matt, replacing the receiver. "Mr. Roosevelt wants a word with ye."

"Thank you. This is more like it," Matt muttered, taking Brooke's arm and leading her over to the stairs, for he still distrusted elevators.

"Well, of course," Brooke said serenely. "What did you expect?"

Matt raised his eyebrows, but said nothing. If she hadn't noticed the coolness of the reception, he had. Not that it was unexpected. Here he was, on the force for less than a year, and yet he'd gone on a three-month honeymoon. With all the efforts being made to reform the police, such a long leave didn't look good. Probably, he thought gloomily as they reached the second floor, Roosevelt was going to reprimand him. Even if he had approved Matt's request for leave.

Theodore Roosevelt's arrival at Mulberry Street the previous year had blown a wide, wild wind through the force. In the light of revelations of widespread corruption among the police, politicians and citizens alike had clamored for reform. Roosevelt, known to nearly everyone simply as "TR," had passed up the chance to be mayor of New York, but he gladly accepted the job as police commissioner. With the other three members of the board, he was a whirlwind of activity, holding hearings on officers accused of dereliction of duty or worse, and meting out suitable punishment; bringing in his own men to replace those gone either through forced resignations or retirement; and checking up on errant patrolmen himself in what he liked to call midnight rambles. He had met with some success. He had also made enemies, among them two of the other commissioners, with whom he was currently engaged in a struggle for power. If TR were forced out of office, as Matt knew was possible from reading whatever New York newspaper he could find in Europe, all his efforts would be for naught.

TR's secretary, Miss Kelly, smiled and told Matt and Brooke to go into Roosevelt's office. Another innovation of TR's, Matt thought, returning the smile, installing a young woman as his secretary, and an attractive one at that. Doubtless she was a great deal easier to look at than the pair of men who had served as assistants to the commissioners before.

Brooke's fingers bit into his arm. "And will you be seeing her very often?" she whispered.

"No," he answered, straight-faced, as he opened the office door for her. "Maybe once a day."

The look Brooke gave him was expressive, but she had no opportunity to say anything more. Roosevelt was rising from behind his desk to greet them, his large white teeth, so beloved by caricaturists, bared in a wide grin.

"Matt Devlin. Dee-lighted to have you back," he boomed, reaching over to shake Matt's hand. "And Mrs. Devlin. Dee-lightful to see you again. Saw you arrive, you know," he went on, indicating the window behind him with a jerk of his head as he sat, and they took chairs facing him. "Eager to get started again?"

"Of course," Matt said, still straight-faced.

"Well, we could use you, my boy, we could use you." His face turned serious. "Things aren't good around here, you know. Everything I've been trying to do is being blocked."

"Yes, sir, so I've read. And I don't imagine having a detective go on a three-month honeymoon has helped."

Beside him he sensed Brooke giving him a sharp look, but Roosevelt was speaking again. "No, I took some criticism for that, but I approved your leave myself, my boy." He turned his toothy grin on Brooke. "Besides"—he grinned, his eyes behind his nose glasses glinting—"I heard you managed to take care of some crime yourself while you were gone."

"Yes, sir. But that was something we stumbled into." Matt leaned forward in his chair. "I thought I'd check in with Captain O'Neill. See what he'll want me working on."

"There's plenty, my boy. Too much going on in this city. Murders are up this year, not to mention the rest of the vice in this city. But at least we've got the Bend cleared out," he went on, referring to Mulberry Bend, not far distant from headquarters. It had once been one of the worst neighborhoods in the city, with dark, dirty tenements crowded with newly arrived immigrants, all poor, all desperate. "It's a park now."

"But that's wonderful progress," Brooke said, smiling so broadly at Roosevelt that Matt gave her a suspicious glance. "Perhaps now people will see the need to clean up the rest of the slums."

"I wish more people felt as you do, Mrs. Devlin." Roosevelt gave her a toothy smile. "Then we wouldn't have the problems we do."

"I was wondering." Brooke's tone was artless, as if something had just occurred to her. After seven months of marriage, Matt already knew better. "When we left, Mr. Warren of the Manhattan Museum had just been found dead. Whatever happened in that case?"

Roosevelt shot Matt a look. "You were working on that case, weren't you, Devlin?"

Matt nodded. "Yes, sir." He was no longer surprised at Roosevelt's knowledge of such small details. "He was killed during a robbery at the museum."

"Yes." Roosevelt frowned. "Far as we know, that's all it is. Looks like Warren caught the thief in the act and paid for it. Hard to admit, my boy, but that case is still open."

Matt nodded again. He wasn't really surprised; nor did he imagine anyone was actively working the case. It was, after all, three months old, and, as Roosevelt himself had said, there was too much going on in the city. "Thank you, sir," he said, rising. "I'll call Captain O'Neill later to let him know I'm back."

"Do that, my boy. Dee-lighted to have you on the force," he said, and Matt and Brooke rose to leave the office.

And now they were home, and Matt's muscles under Brooke's fingers were tighter than they had been just a moment before. "Matt?" she said softly.

He jumped. "What?" he said, and blinked, as if surprised to find himself in the rococo atmosphere of what was supposed to be their bedroom.

She'd have to do something about the decor, she thought, and sighed. "Solving crime seems like so much more fun."

Matt turned to her. "It isn't." His voice was short. "Not the type of crime I usually see. And don't think it's going to be easy for me there, Brooke, because it isn't."

"But Mr. Roosevelt is glad you're back—"

"Yes, well, he's probably the only one. Didn't you notice?"

"What?"

"Never mind," he muttered, swinging away from her. "Where's the telephone in this godforsaken place?"

Brooke followed him into the dark, narrow corridor that linked the rooms together and was one of the disadvantages of apartment living. "Matt, you've proven yourself time and again."

"And don't think that won't cause problems," he shot back. "Getting my name in the paper for solving a crime on a luxury liner isn't going to make me popular with the other detectives."

"You needn't snap at me, Matt," she said, striving to keep her tone even. "I'm on your side, remember?"

"Dammit. Yes." He ran a hand through his hair and smiled at her crookedly. "I know you are. It's just all this"—he waved his hand to indicate the apartment—"isn't real."

"Must life be dirty and drab to be real?" she retorted.

"Sometimes, yes. Now, where's that telephone?"

Brooke let out her breath and gave up. "I don't know. I'll ask the butler. Whatever his name is," she tossed over her shoulder as she went down the corridor. For the life of her, she would never understand why he felt he had to prove himself in an area where he excelled. He was, she knew, a very good cop. And where that left her, she didn't know. Or, rather, she very much feared that she did.

While Fuller, the butler, showed Matt to the telephone in the hallway off the kitchen, Brooke stood in the middle of the parlor and glanced slowly around. Home, sweet home, and while Matt went every day to work that meant something, she would be spending her time in trivial pursuits. The apartment would have to be redecorated, no question about that, and she would have to find a tactful way to tell Aunt Winifred. And after that, what? Driving in her carriage to pay morning calls and leaving her card at the homes of people she didn't even like; attending long, tedious dinners or balls; taking tea with other society matrons. *Matrons*. The word made her scowl. It was not something she particularly wished to be. It didn't look, though, as if she had much choice.

Brooke let out her breath again, lifting the strand of hair that never would stay tucked into her chignon, and turned away, to get more fully acquainted with her home. What she wouldn't give for a good, juicy murder, she thought, smiling at her foolishness. The smile quickly died though. For without something to give purpose to her days, her future stretched before her, bleak and meaningless.

By morning Brooke's mood had improved. Matt, tense yet eager to get started, had gone off to work, catching the Eighth Avenue trolley to bring him downtown. She had enough to fill her life: a husband who saw her as more than just an ornament, interests of her own, and, perhaps someday, children. It would have to do.

The morning passed quickly as Brooke toured the apartment again, this time with an eye as to what could stay and what would have to go. She supposed the decor was smart and considered the height of fashion, but she hated it. If it were left up to her, she would get rid of everything and start fresh, since her taste differed so from her aunt's, but she knew that Matt would be shocked at the waste. Already it was a sore spot between them that her income paid the rent on the apartment. Buying new furniture would only make matters worse.

She would have to learn to live with the massive mahogany dining-room table and the enormous platform bed. She could dispose of the canopy, however, along with the assorted velvet and paisley shawls. And the Turkish nook in the entrance hall. She'd put light curtains at the windows, possibly lace, she thought, and maybe she'd paint the walls a light color too, as the apartment got the sun only in the morning and was dim the rest of the time. More than enough to keep her busy—and yet, as luxurious as the apartment was, what flashed into her mind at unexpected moments was an image of a square, workaday building set among tenements. Matt would not be spending his days contemplating the intricacies of interior design.

She was in the library, adding the bearskin rug to the list of items to be discarded, when Fuller knocked discreetly on the door. "A visitor, ma'am."

Brooke looked up, her face brightening. "Really? Who?"

"Her card." He handed across a black-banded square of pasteboard. "Shall I say you're not at home?"

"Goodness, no," Brooke said, looking at the card. Miss Linda Warren. "Please show Miss Warren to—well." She looked around and grimaced. "I suppose this room is the best of the lot. Show her in here, please."

"Yes, ma'am," Fuller said, and bowing, went out into the anteroom. In a moment he was back, followed by a tall, slender young woman dressed in black, a veiled hat sitting upon her elaborately piled coiffure of chestnut-brown hair. "Miss Warren, ma'am."

"Thank you, Fuller. Would you bring us tea, please?"

"No, that's quite all right," Linda Warren said, raising her veil to reveal large, serious gray eyes. "I don't mean to intrude, Brooke, when you've just returned home—"

"Nonsense, Linda, you're not." Brooke took Linda's arm, leading her over to a chair. "We're quite settled in, and I must say it's good to see old friends again. And I do want to say how sorry I am for your loss."

"Thank you." Linda sank, straight-backed, into one of the leather chairs. "It's been difficult."

"Yes, I can imagine."

"In fact, that's why I'm here. I wonder if—"

She broke off as Fuller came in with the tea tray. Brooke went through the ritual of pouring from the silver pot into fine porcelain cups, her mind working quickly. She and Linda Warren were old acquaintances, from the time when, bewildered by her parents' deaths, Brooke had come to live with her aunt and uncle. Linda was a serious girl, but today she was somber, grave, as if the events of the past three months had etched themselves upon her face. Why would she want to talk to Brooke about them?

Fuller at last left the room, and Brooke handed Linda her cup. "I was in London when I heard about your father. It was a terrible shock."

"To us too." Linda set her cup, untouched, upon the marble-topped table nearby. "Did you know they think he was responsible for the thefts?" she said abruptly.

"What? But that can't be."

"It's what they think. Well, you can understand why they would. So many paintings were stolen before, but there have been no thefts since my father died."

"I didn't know that." Brooke took a sip of her tea. The art world had been intrigued when the Manhattan had acquired several paintings reputed to be the works of long-dead masters; the entire city had been shocked when many of those paintings had been stolen in a series of thefts, along with other works of art. Brooke had learned from Matt that each time, a lock had been forced to admit the thieves entrance, but that the fact that they had taken just a few select works was suspicious, hinting that they were knowledgeable. The thefts had occurred at night; not once had the thieves been spotted by the watchman or any passersby. Not once had staff still working in the building heard so much as a whisper when the thefts occurred. Damned suspicious, Matt had said. The series of thefts might even have been an inside job, though there were few leads. The fact that the police had yet to catch the culprits hadn't enhanced the force's reputation.

None of which helped Linda. But, Brooke wondered, setting down her cup, could Mr. Warren have been the accomplice inside the museum? "Who believes that, Linda? The police?"

"Yes, the police, and I'm sure Mr. Owen, the director, too, as well as anyone else at the museum. But your uncle has been kind."

Brooke nodded absently and raised her teacup again; her uncle Henry was a trustee on the museum board. "Do they have any evidence to support the suspicion?"

"No!" Linda burst out. "How could they have? My father was innocent. He would never have taken those paintings, not when he went to such trouble to get them in the first place."

"What paintings? The lost masterpieces?"

"Yes."

"Heavens, I didn't know he was the one who'd acquired them." She frowned, tapping the rim of her cup with a fingernail. "What do the police think he did with them?"

"Sold them to a private collector, though we certainly haven't seen the money," she said bitterly. "We've had to sell our house."

"Oh, no. Where are you living now?"

Linda's eyes flickered. "In an apartment uptown. Nothing

like this."

"Oh," Brooke murmured, suddenly rather ashamed of the claustrophobic opulence of her apartment. "I am sorry. And I'd help if I could—"

"But you can," Linda interrupted, leaning forward, her hands tightly clasped. "You helped solve the Cliff Walk murders in Newport."

"Well, yes," Brooke said, mildly surprised. Apparently her role in that case was more well known than she'd thought.

"And then, with what happened on your honeymoon—I read about the case. I know you could do this."

Brooke frowned. "Do what, Linda?"

"Help me clear my father's name." She reached across to grasp Brooke's hands. "Please. Find whoever killed him."

2

Brooke pulled back, startled. "But I'm not a detective."

"Your husband's a policeman," Linda went on as if Brooke hadn't spoken. "He'd know where to start."

"But . . ." Brooke began, and then stopped. Of course Matt would know where to start, and in a case like this, already being handled by the New York police, he would be the one doing the investigating. Brooke's skin tingled. This was exactly the kind of case he thought they'd never encounter again, involving people from her world. It was the kind of case where she could help.

"Well." Brooke busied herself pouring another cup of tea. "Maybe we can do something."

Linda leaned forward. "Oh, do you think you could? It would mean so much to have his name cleared."

"I'm not promising anything, mind," Brooke said, sitting back against the soft leather chair. "It all depends on what my husband says and if his captain thinks he should pursue it. But I can try."

"The police have had three months to find his killer and they haven't done a thing."

Brooke nodded. "I know. Now." She set the cup down and leaned forward, intent. "Tell me everything you can about your father."

Captain Stephen O'Neill, in charge of the detective bureau, walked out of his office, Matt following behind him. "And you'll be busy soon enough," he was saying, continuing the speech he had begun the moment Matt had walked into his office. "Now that there's the Raines Law and saloons are calling themselves hotels so they can sell liquor on Sundays, we don't have to enforce Sunday closings as much, but we do have to keep an eye on them. Besides that, there's enough going on." He stood with fists on hips, surveying the large room that made up the detective bureau, furnished with old scarred desks and chairs. On this warm July morning it was nearly empty; those detectives doing paperwork at their desks looked up with some curiosity at Matt, and then away. "Enough to keep a special squad of detectives busy. Flynn will fill you in. Flynn!" he roared, and a man who sat at a desk in the back of the room looked up. "Come up here."

Tony Flynn rose, his movements unhurried, his face calm. His coloring and build belied his name; in appearance he favored the Italian ancestry of his mother, being of medium height and small frame, with black hair and deep brown eyes set in olive skin. His name was really Antonio, but no one called him by it. Not more than once, at least. "Yes, Captain?" he said when he reached the front of the room.

"You remember Devlin," O'Neill said.

Flynn's face was impassive, but his eyes flickered. "Barely."

O'Neill chose to take this as a joke, chuckling. "You two

worked well enough together before. Fill Devlin in on what's been happenin'. We could use him." He slapped Matt on the back, not gently. "Good to have you back."

"Thank you." Matt's voice was polite but otherwise without expression as he turned his attention to his partner. Flynn was studying him in return, his eyes shuttered. "Tony," he said, nodding.

"Devlin." Flynn's reply was equally terse. "So you decided to return after all. There was talk you wouldn't."

He was not going to let this get to him, Matt thought. He'd known he'd face resentment, even hostility, and he'd decided to keep calm, proving himself by his work. Easy to say in theory. In practice, however, it was much harder. "As you see," he said mildly enough, forcing his hands not to bunch into fists. "Does it bother you?"

Flynn shrugged and turned away. "Come on," he said, as somewhere in the office a telephone shrilled. "I'll show you which cases we're working right now."

"Flynn," O'Neill called, stepping out of his office.

Flynn turned. "Sir?"

"Man on Mott Street says his house has been broken into. You and Devlin go see him."

"Yes, sir. Come on," he said to Matt, and went out of the office without waiting for Matt to follow. "You might as well learn on the job."

Matt's hands did bunch into fists that time, but he had no chance, then or later, to express his anger. After interviewing the man who had been burglarized, there was the theft of a horse to be investigated, as well as the sudden death in her home of a woman who was, up until then, in good health. After that it was back to headquarters to write reports, followed by the investigation of yet another burglary, this one of a small dry goods shop on Bleecker Street. By the end of the day Matt was tired, but in a good way. Tomorrow would be much the same, he knew, and the day after as well, with too much work to do in too little time, but he didn't mind. It was good work, work that made a difference. And on the job it didn't much matter if his partner disliked and distrusted him.

Matt glanced up from the report he was writing. Across the room, in shirtsleeves, Flynn perched on the corner of a desk, talking to another detective. His hair, which had been slicked back that morning, was now unruly and wavy, and his celluloid collar was askew, but his gestures and bearing were those of a man who was alive and aware. Give Flynn his due, Matt thought, returning to the report. Whatever his personal feelings, on the job he was a total professional. But then, he'd been well trained. A New York policeman for nearly fifteen years, Flynn had started as a patrolman and worked his way through the ranks, becoming a detective under Thomas Byrnes, before that legendary cop became superintendent, before the investigation into police corruption forced his retirement.

Oddly enough, he and Flynn did work well together. Though they hadn't seen each other in three months, when conducting an investigation or interview they did so as long-time partners, each taking turns asking questions without being cued. Sometimes today it had seemed as if he and Flynn had known in advance what the other would ask, so that they only rarely worked at cross-purposes. Some of that came from experience, Matt knew, but not all of it. If Flynn would just get over his resentment, they might make a good team.

It was nearly six, time to quit. Matt stretched in his chair and then pulled on his suit jacket, since he wasn't on reserve tonight and thus could go home. After a cursory good-bye he stepped out into the corridor, nearly colliding with Detective Coughlin as he did so. "Done for the day, Devlin?" Coughlin asked.

"Looks that way. It'll all be the same tomorrow."

"Ain't that the truth. Me, I'm on reserve this week, so I have to sleep here." Coughlin shrugged a shoulder toward Flynn. "Worked out okay with him today?"

"Yes."

"Good. Thought it would. That Tony, he's a good guy, if a little hot-tempered. Know what I mean?"

"Not exactly," Matt said carefully.

"Well, look how things have worked out, and him hopping mad about it, too."

Matt's voice was very soft. "Was he now?"

"Didn't you know?" Coughlin looked surprised, an emotion Matt suspected was feigned. "Well, it's no secret. Just before you came back Tony asked to be assigned another partner."

It was nearly seven by the time Matt made it home, tired and sweaty after a long trip uptown. The trolley had been crowded with people making the same journey as he, from work to home; in the heat the car had been stifling, the smells of people crowded together nearly overpowering. He had had to stand the entire way, holding on to a strap and swaying with the motion of the trolley. Maybe tomorrow, he thought, stepping out of the elevator into the hall that served only the two apartments at this corner of the building and fishing in his pocket for his keys, he'd try making the trip by bicycle. At least he'd be out in the air.

The door to his apartment opened before he could turn the knob. "Good evening, sir," Fuller said

"Good evening," Matt muttered.

"May I take your hat, sir?"

"My hat—yeah. Thanks." He handed over his hat and pushed past Fuller, standing straight and dignified in a neat black suit and making Matt all too aware of how grubby and sweaty he was. A butler, for God's sake. He shook his head. What had his life come to?

"Matt." Brooke stood into the doorway to the parlor, looking deliciously cool in a soft gown of pale green. "Heavens, you look tired. Was it a difficult day?"

"No. Just hot." He walked into the parlor and stopped. "What's different in here?"

"The drapes are open, for one thing." She smiled. "And Katie and I spent a good part of the afternoon taking down every shawl we could find."

"Katie?"

"Our maid, Matt." Brooke studied him. Something was bothering him, something more than the heat. "You look like you could use a drink."

"A maid and a butler," he muttered.

"Excuse me?"

"Nothing." He turned toward her. "Yeah, a drink sounds good. Give me a minute to clean up first."

A few minutes later he was back, sitting beside Brooke on the gold velvet sofa that was more comfortable than it looked. With his jacket off and hair slicked back, and with a whiskey and soda in a frosty glass in his hand, he seemed more relaxed. Brooke tucked her legs up beneath her, arranging the folds of her tea gown just so, and studied him. "Tell me about your day."

He shrugged and took a sip of his drink. "Not much to tell. It went about how I expected."

"Who are you working with? And are you on anything interesting?"

Matt shrugged again. "Flynn. Nothing much interesting, a couple of burglaries and a woman whose death looks suspicious." He took another, longer sip of his drink. "Damn, that's good."

"Please don't swear," she said automatically, glancing away from him and frowning. There was something he wasn't telling her. A few months ago she might have tried to coax it out of him, but she'd since learned he'd tell her in his own good time. For some reason, he seemed to need to keep things to himself for a while. Though she was exactly the opposite, she thought she understood. "I had a visitor today."

"Who?" Matt asked without curiosity.

"Linda Warren."

"Who?"

"Joseph Warren's daughter."

That made him look at her. "What did she want?"

"She wants us to find whoever killed her father," she said calmly, and sat back, waiting for the explosion.

It didn't come. Instead, Matt gazed meditatively into his glass. "Why didn't I see this coming?" he asked rhetorically.

"Why should you have?"

"Because I know you, Brooke. I knew when you mentioned Warren to TR yesterday you were up to something—"

"I'm not up to anything! She came to me, not the other way around." She glanced away, lips compressed. In the silence the Eighth Avenue trolley rattling by outside sounded very loud. "You have to admit, Matt, it would be an interesting case."

"Dammit, Brooke!" Matt jumped to his feet and began pacing the room, the contents of his glass sloshing back and forth. "It's bad enough that they think I'm some kind of dandy at Mulberry Street. If I come to them with a case my wife found "

"Are you ashamed of me, Matt?" Brooke asked very quietly.

Matt stopped and returned her gaze, and for a moment tension crackled between them. "No," he said finally, dropping into one of the chairs that matched the sofa. "Of course I'm not. But, dammit, Brooke!" His voice was exasperated. "Why do you always seem to get involved with murders?"

Brooke ran her fingers along the arm of the sofa, back and forth, not looking at him. "Mr. Warren's murder is unsolved." Her voice was still quiet, reflecting the cold anger within her. "It was your case to start with. Don't you want to see the killer brought to justice?"

"Of course I do. If it's possible, after all this time." He made a face. "I'm just thinking of how it will look—"

"Look?" This time her voice blazed. "Since when did that matter to you, Matthew Devlin? Since when did it keep you from doing what's right? You know it is," she went on as he opened his mouth to speak. "And if you dare to say anything about 'your wife' again, I won't answer for the consequences."

"I was wrong," he said as quietly as she had spoken earlier, as if he were just now realizing the depth of her anger. "The problem is . . ."

"What?"

"I have to prove myself, Brooke."

"Oh, for heaven's sake! You've done that over and over again."

He shook his head. "No. Not in New York. You don't know what they think of me there, Brooke." He rose and began pacing again. "They know I came from a small town. They know I've been involved in two cases with you. And they know your background. No, hear me out," he said, holding up his hand as she began to protest. "I'm not saying it bothers me—"

"Though it does."

"—but it makes them look at me differently. Like I'm a society type dabbling at crime. Me!" He wheeled to face her, eyes black with anger. "Me, who's a cop's son, been a cop over ten years, worked for everything I've got. Yes, Brooke, I have to prove myself. And the only way I can think of to do that is to do the work I'm expected to do. Good, solid police work. Not some fancy murder case."

Brooke blew out her breath. "Would you investigate Warren's death if I weren't involved?"

Matt hesitated a fraction of a second too long. "Probably not. It's an old case. The trail's gone cold. No," he said with more conviction, "I wouldn't."

"I see." She glanced away, biting her lips. She'd expected an explosion when she told him about Linda's request, but not this. Never this. "What if the case didn't come from your wife?"

"What do you mean?"

"For heaven's sake, Matt," she said, sounding as exasperated as he had a moment earlier, "it was your case, wasn't it? No one would be surprised if you decided to look it over again. If you found something interesting, you'd be expected to investigate it. Think, Matt." She leaned forward. "It can't look good for the police not to have solved this crime. Can it?"

"No," he said slowly. "No, it's been a black eye for the force. So—"

"So look into it! That's all I ask."

Matt sat again, looking at her with narrowed eyes. "Is it?"

"Yes."

"And if I don't find anything, you'll leave it alone?"

"I promise I won't do anything to damage your reputation."

It wasn't quite the same thing, and from the look he gave her she knew Matt realized it, but he nodded at last. "All right. I'll be honest, it's been bothering me too. I'll see what I can find out." He ran a hand over his hair, his eyes averted. "Brooke, what I said before—it wasn't directed at you. I didn't mean it."

But he did, she thought, he did. In a way, she couldn't blame him. "For whom was it meant, Matt?"

"It doesn't matter." He looked up at her then, and his blue eyes were candid and clear as he held out his hand. After a moment she placed her own in it, and the last shred of her anger fled. "Not easy being married to a cop, is it?"

"Not easy being married to a socialite either," she retorted, but without heat. "Now. Do you want to hear what I have to tell you, or not?"

"Since you seem determined—"

"Wretch. Linda tells me that the police think her father was involved in the art thefts at the museum."

Matt lounged back in one of the tufted club chairs, seemingly at ease, though Brooke wasn't fooled. "I assume there's a reason for that."

"Yes. There haven't been any thefts since his death."

"Huh." He reached up a finger to rub at his mustache. "Doesn't have to mean anything. It could mean that the thief has decided to lie low. If Warren's blamed, then the real thief isn't in danger. Or"—he looked at her,—"Warren could be the thief."

She shook her head. "I doubt it. Not these paintings."

"Why? What's so special about them?"

"Don't you remember—never mind, I'll tell you." She leaned forward. "Mr. Warren was the curator for paintings at the museum and so he could acquire new ones. Not alone, of course, Mr. Owen—that's the director—is really the one responsible. But Mr. Warren did have some freedom. And a few years ago he came across something." She leaned forward, her eyes shining. "Paintings by the old masters—Van Dyck, Rembrandt, Vermeer, and more."

"So?"

"So these were works no one knew existed. Or they were works that were known about but presumed lost over the years."

"And he acquired them for the museum?"

"Yes."

"From where?"

She shook her head. "No one knows. He told no one."

Matt frowned. "Why not?"

"Well, think about it, Matt. When you use a source—what do you call them, stool pigeons?"

"Yes."

"You don't reveal who they are."

"Not quite the same thing."

"Of course it is. Whoever was dealing the paintings didn't want his name known."

"Are they stolen?"

"I don't know." Brooke frowned. "I asked Linda that, and she denied it. Strongly. Her father was a pillar of rectitude. He ushered at Grace Church, you know. Though that makes it strange that . . ."

"What?"

"Nothing. I'll get to that. I don't know. They may be stolen, though there's been no fuss raised in the art world. Linda thinks, and so do most people, that they were sold by someone who needed money but didn't want that known. Someone who has a reputation to maintain."

"Such as?"

"Impoverished European aristocrats. Well, think of it, Matt. They've huge estates to maintain, and little cash. Why do you think so many are marrying American heiresses?"

"True." He nodded. "All right. Let's forget about the source for a moment. How were the deals made?"

She shook her head. "Again, I don't know. Apparently they happened here, since Mr. Warren didn't go to Europe so very often."

"So there's someone here in the city who knows something about those paintings."

"Possibly. Possibly not. The museum hadn't acquired one for several months before Mr. Warren died. And that might have been because of the thefts."

"Were the paintings Warren acquired the ones that were stolen?" he asked sharply.

Brooke looked up in surprise. "Yes. How did you know?"

"A good guess. So." He stayed silent a moment, rubbing at his mustache. "Warren acquired some masterpieces. Which I assume didn't hurt him at all at the museum?"

"No, he was very highly thought of."

"Huh. So why steal the paintings? Yes, I see the logic. Or the illogic." He leaned forward, hands clasped between his knees. "Were any other paintings taken?"

"Oh, yes. The lost masterpieces were only a few of those taken."

"What happened to them?"

"No one knows." Her face was grave. "If they've been seen, Linda didn't know of it."

Matt tapped at his teeth. "They'd be difficult to get rid of. Wonder if there's a fence who deals in art? Must be," he said, answering his own question. "In this city there's probably a fence for anything and everything. All right." He nodded. "We'll assume Warren's not the thief. For now."

Brooke raised her eyebrows at that, but that was her only reaction. "Good. Did you have any theory about what happened to Mr. Warren?"

"No." He rose and began to pace again. "Before you and I left on our honeymoon, the investigation was just beginning.

That means we were interested in getting as much information as we could. But as I remember it, it looked as if he caught the thief in the act and was killed because of it."

Brooke nodded. "Linda tells me that's what everyone thought at first. She did too, except that only one painting was taken this time, a recent American one."

"Probably the thief got scared and took off when he realized Warren was dead."

"Yes, possibly. But—"

"That's probably what happened. If I look into this, I'll have to look at the thefts too. They usually happened at night, as I remember, after the museum was closed."

Brooke was frowning. "Yes."

"What was Warren doing there the night he was killed?"

"Working. He rarely worked late, but that night he did." Her frown deepened. "Matt, I wonder if—"

"If he was meeting up with the thief."

"Good heavens, why would he do that?" she exclaimed.

Matt shrugged. "I don't know. Just that it's a possibility."

"Not if he had nothing to do with the thefts."

"True. So he was working late. Probably he heard a noise and went to investigate. Huh."

"What?"

"Careless of the thief to pick that particular night."

"Or thieves. Matt, one person alone couldn't have carried out the earlier thefts. Too much was taken."

He nodded absently. "So even more of a risk for them, with someone in the building. More chances they'd be heard. And, as I recall, the gallery where Warren was killed isn't far from his office."

Brooke frowned again. "You do think he was involved, don't you?"

"Not necessarily. But either the thieves were careless and

didn't check to make sure the museum was empty, or something's wrong. And that I won't know until I look into it further."

There was a discreet knock on the door. "Excuse me, sir, ma'am," Fuller said deferentially, though his eyes were bright with interest. Brooke wondered how much of the conversation he had overheard. "Mrs. Fuller has dinner ready, but if you wish her to wait . . ."

"No." Matt shook his head and held his hand out to Brooke to help her up. "We'll eat now. Thank you." Fuller nodded and withdrew, Matt looking after him with a slight frown. "What did you say his name is?"

"Fuller. Matt, you will look into Mr. Warren's death, won't you?"

"Yes, but not now." He stretched out his arms. "It's been a long day. Tomorrow, Brooke."

Outside the rain hit the windows in intermittent sheets, the result of a late afternoon thunderstorm that had come after a day of miserable heat and stifling humidity. Matt glanced idly at the windows and then returned to the papers littered on the desk before him, reports from all the officers who had had anything to do with the Warren case. Life sometimes took strange turns, he thought. This time last year he'd been on the small Newport force, with his own office and humdrum crimes to handle. That had been before the Cliff Walk case had come along, however, with all its social and political ramifications, before he had realized that he could no longer work effectively in the town of his birth and had accepted the job here. Sometimes he wondered if he was mad.

The windows had been closed against the rain; a mixed relief, since it shut out the fetid smell of the tenements, but also kept in the still, suffocating air. Forcing himself to concentrate in spite of the presence of other men in the detective bureau, Matt bent his attention to the reports before him. Most were handwritten; some, a very few, had been produced on a typewriter. None were dated earlier than the previous April. Still, there were enough references to the series of thefts that had taken place at the Manhattan that he didn't have to resort to those reports. Not yet, at least. For now he had quite enough to go on.

Warren had been found, dead, lying in a pool of his own blood by the Manhattan Museum's night watchman. According to the autopsy report, he had been stabbed through the heart and had died instantly. A painting had been stolen as well, cut from its frame. In light of the previous thefts, the clear inference was that Warren had come across the thief while in the act of stealing the picture, and had been killed because of it. Matt frowned. It took skill and nerve to slip a knife through someone's ribs. This was no panicked thief stabbing out at random; this was someone who knew what he was doing. Warren clearly had come up against more than he could handle. The question now was, who?

Paging through the reports, ignoring the curious glances that Tony, across the room, and the other detectives threw him, Matt began to piece together the history of the thefts from the museum. They had begun the summer before, a shocking event, when several of the newly acquired masterpieces had been taken, along with lesser works. The first theft had taken place late at night; a window in a door fronting onto Central Park had been broken, and the door opened that way. No one had heard anything; no one had seen anything until the theft was discovered the following morning.

The museum's staff immediately stepped up security, putting bars on all windows that looked onto the park and adding a watchman. A reward was offered for the return of the paintings, in vain. Thus the second theft, in late summer, came as a shock. Again a selection of paintings was taken, including a few more of the lost masterpieces; again, no one heard or saw anything. This time, however, access had apparently been gained through a small, unlocked lavatory window.

And finally came the most shocking theft of all. On Thanksgiving Day the thieves came in, not through a forced door or a carelessly unlocked window, but through a service door that showed no signs of having been tampered with. For the first time a hidden suspicion was spoken aloud: someone in the museum was connected with the thefts. No wonder then if, after Warren's death, suspicion had fallen on him.

Frowning, Matt riffled through the reports again. There was nothing to suggest that Warren's death wasn't what it seemed, nothing to prove that he wasn't in league with the thieves, except . . . He'd missed something, he was sure of it. Stopping at random, he read again a report of the earliest theft. Ten paintings had been taken in all, all carefully removed from their frames, which had then been stacked neatly on the floor. Matt was about to go on when a thought struck him, making him go back to the very first report on Warren's death, one he had written himself. And there it was. In that case the painting stolen had been cut from the frame, which was left on the wall.

Matt sat back, tapping at his teeth with the end of his pencil, his thoughts racing. A small thing, but a curious one. Why would the thief have deviated so from his former methods? Panic? If so, why steal a painting at all? The man who had wielded a knife with precision enough to stab a man through the heart didn't seem the type to panic. But to cut a painting out of a frame, as if that were his main intention . . .

Matt sat very still, fingertips resting on the edge of his desk, while his brain made a great leap in logic. Of course. Whoever had killed Warren hadn't cared about the painting, not if he had cut it, and damaged it. Thus, he hadn't been one of the thieves, but someone with another purpose, using the painting only as cover. Matt didn't yet have the facts to support his theory, but of one thing he was deeply, completely certain. Joseph Warren had been murdered.

3

Captain O'Neill swiveled his chair away from his big rolltop desk, frowning at Matt. "You're certain of this?"

"Yes, sir." Matt, though standing, was at ease, hands tucked in trouser pockets. It was the following morning, and he'd spent a good part of it reading. "I've checked back through all the reports of the thefts, and found that in each case the paintings were removed from the frames, not cut. Yet this one time, a painting was."

The captain's frown deepened; he was too seasoned a cop not to notice the significance of the change in method. "What else do you have?" he asked finally, wearily.

"Warren wasn't in the habit of working nights. Yet that night he told everyone to go home, that he'd lock up the offices."

"Yes, so?"

"So his secretary wondered why. Apparently there hadn't been any more work than usual to justify it."

"You think that Warren was waiting to meet someone?"

"I think it's likely, sir."

"Very well. How did the killer get in and out without being seen?"

"That I won't know, sir, unless I investigate." He paused. "If I investigate."

O'Neill rubbed tiredly at his eyes. "It's the devil of a thing," he said. "This case has been hanging over us for three months now, and the papers keep on harpin' on it, making us look like fools. Warren looks guilty, you know, guilty as sin, but with what you tell me . . ." His voice trailed off. "It might be worth following up."

"Yes, sir, I agree."

"Flynn!" O'Neill roared suddenly, making Matt jump.

"Sir?" Tony poked his head into O'Neill's office.

"Get in here, and close the door."

"Yes, sir." Tony cast a curious glance at Matt. "What is it?"

"Devlin here has some ideas about the Warren case. I want you both to work on it, see what you can find. You got some problem with that?" he added sharply, and out of the corner of his eye Matt could see that Tony's face was twisted up.

"No, sir."

"Good." O'Neill glared at Tony for a moment, and then looked back at Matt. "I'll give you two days. If you don't turn up anything new, we'll drop it."

Matt's lips tightened. "And if we do?"

"Depends what it is. Go on, get out of here." He waved toward the door. "You've got work to do."

"Yes, sir," Matt said, and went out, Tony preceding him. "Flynn," he said, his voice low but firm, and Tony turned. "Do you have a problem with it? If so, I want to know."

Tony gazed back at him, dark eyes unreadable. "I've always thought there's more to the Warren case than it seems."

"That's not what I mean, and you know it."

"Captain told us to work on it, Devlin." He turned away,

crooking his finger to lift his jacket from the back of a chair. "Come on. If we have only two days we'd better get on it."

Tony sauntered out of the detective bureau, his gait deceptively slow, and Matt, after a moment, followed. This wasn't the time, he told himself, shrugging into his jacket, but someday the right moment would come. The dislike between him and Flynn was growing daily. Someday soon he and Tony would have it out.

Brooke adjusted the tilt of her black straw hat trimmed with violet ostrich feathers one last time as she stood before the massive umbrella stand. Reflected in the mirror she could still see the Turkish nook of divan and drapes. The sight made her shudder, though she could do little about it just now. Housekeeping might be important, but murder took precedence. Though Matt had not asked for her help solving the mystery of Warren's death, neither had he expressed any opposition to it. Thus she was about to start her phase of the investigation. Under the guise of a condolence call, she was about to interview Sylvia Warren, Joseph Warren's grieving widow.

Fuller came into the entrance hall, bowing slightly. "Your carriage is waiting in the courtyard, madam."

"Thank you, Fuller."

"I shall call for the elevator. Would madam care for an escort?"

Brooke, engaged in pulling on her gloves, glanced up at him, startled. There it was, that same avid gleam she'd noticed in his eye yesterday. "No, thank you, Fuller. I'm just going to pay a condolence call."

"Of course, madam. But madam should know that I am quite an aficionado of detective stories. If I can assist in any way . . ."

"Thank you, Fuller, I'll keep you in mind," she said, and swept out into the hallway, where the elevator awaited her. Dear heaven, an amateur sleuth, she thought, and then smiled a bit. Now she understood how Matt felt when she insisted on assisting him. But that was different. She knew what she was doing.

The Devlins' carriage, a smart victoria, stood before the fountain in the center courtyard. With the assistance of the coachman, Brooke climbed into the carriage and settled against its buttery-soft leather cushions. The carriage had been a wedding present from her uncle Octavius, a practical gift, especially since the Dakota maintained stables for its residents at Broadway and West 73rd Street. Matt, however, hated it, refusing to use it for traveling to and from work. This morning he'd chosen to take his bicycle. She supposed she couldn't blame him. The trappings of wealth could be suffocating if a person wasn't used to them, as she well knew. Really, he was being remarkably good about things. He had yet to say a word in protest about the carriage. He just wouldn't drive in it.

The carriage turned out onto 71st Street and then onto Central Park West, heading north. The view grew progressively rural as they proceeded uptown, though New York had grown alarmingly in the past decade and there were still squatters living in shacks in the park, beyond the low stone wall and the fine, leafy trees. The Dakota had received its name from its location, so far from the center of things when it was built in 1884 that a wit had commented that it might as well be out west. Since then the city had grown up around Central Park and points north, with even more apartment buildings and fine private homes going up on the West Side. Farther north the former village of Harlem had become a bustling middle-class suburb, while Morningside Heights, where she was heading, was a pleasant residential section. It was a strange place to find the Warrens, pillars of society that they were, Brooke thought as the carriage pulled up before the modest clapboard building where Sylvia and Linda Warren now lived. Brooke gave a card to the coachman, printed with her name alone to indicate that she was visiting without her husband, and then sat back, awaiting results. Chances were very good Mrs. Warren wouldn't receive her. The trip wouldn't have been wasted, however. At least contact would have been established.

Within a few moments John, her coachman, was back, helping Brooke to alight. Mrs. Warren would see her after all. Holding her skirts so that they wouldn't drag in the dust, Brooke went into the building and ascended the three flights of stairs to the Warrens' apartment, arriving breathless. The Warrens had come down in the world, she thought, raising her hand to knock on the door. Mrs. Warren was from an old Georgia family; her late husband's stock, while of more recent origins, had considerably more wealth, and the Warrens had been much seen in society. Sylvia had at one time been intimate with *the* Mrs. Astor herself. Surely if she had decided to leave her grand house on 37th Street for the convenience of an apartment, she could have chosen a more stylish location. Which made Brooke wonder what the real reasons were for the move.

"Brooke, dear," Sylvia said, rising, as a maid showed Brooke into what was evidently the parlor. It was a small room, filled to bursting with furniture suited to a larger residence: huge plush maroon sofa, grand piano swathed in silk shawls, an enormous gilt-framed mirror hanging over the ornately carved, but mass-produced, chimney piece. "How kind of you to visit. So many young people these days don't seem to remember their manners."

Brooke brushed her cheek against Sylvia's. "I would have come earlier, Mrs. Warren, but I was on my honeymoon."

"Yes." A small frown puckered Sylvia's face. "Please, dear, do sit down. I receive so few visitors nowadays. You ran into some unpleasantness at sea, I understand."

"Yes," Brooke said, not wanting to get into the story of the crimes and the subsequent investigation she and Matt had encountered on their honeymoon. "I am so sorry for your loss, Mrs. Warren."

"Thank you, dear." Sylvia sat back as the maid, a sturdy girl in a gray gabardine skirt and crisp white shirtwaist, served tea from a fine mahogany tea trolley. The china was good, fine porcelain; the tea service wasn't. Evidently the Warrens' silver tea service had not made the trip uptown. Brooke's suspicions deepened. "I so rarely see people nowadays," Sylvia went on, pouring the tea with assurance, quite as if she held the silver teapot to which she was accustomed, rather than ordinary crockery. "I believe people think they're bein' kind, lettin' us accustom ourselves to our loss. But I do welcome the diversion. Time does hang heavy without my dear Joseph."

"I'm sure it must," Brooke murmured, sipping at her tea and regarding Sylvia carefully over the rim of her cup. She was a dumpling of a woman, tiny, all soft curves in a tea gown of dove gray that had unmistakably come from Worth. Her soft brown hair was fading to the same shade of dove. Nothing harsh or hard about the widow Warren, including her speech, which bore traces of her native Atlanta. "Linda isn't at home today?"

"Dear me, no. That girl does like to keep busy. Why, do you know she decided to take a position at Home Life Insurance as a typewriter? It's not necessary, of course, but she's lonely too. I just shudder to think of her in a skyscraper, ridin' an elevator up and down, but it helps to fill her time, I suppose."

"I'm sure it does." Brooke filed away the fact that Linda had actually taken a job, a startling thing for a young woman of her station to do, along with all the other evidence. Worth gown and fine porcelain notwithstanding, the Warrens had not removed to this small, distant apartment for the sake of convenience. They had done so because they lacked money, and that was a curious circumstance. "Did you know that Linda came to visit me yesterday?" she said, deciding to be blunt.

Sylvia took a sip of her tea before answering. "She did tell me, yes. The poor dear. She misses her father so. But then, we all do."

"She told me that he's suspected of being involved in the thefts at the museum."

"Now that's just wrong!" Sylvia set her cup down on the saucer with a clatter. "As if my Joseph would ever have done such a thing! Anyone who knew him knows better."

"Of course," Brooke murmured, again using her cup to shield her face. "He had no reason to be involved."

"Of course not! My dear, I believe you mean well, but such a statement is an insult. Why, I do believe my Joseph must be turnin' over in his grave at the thought."

"My apologies, Mrs. Warren. I meant nothing by it."

"I should hope not! Why, if I didn't know you better, Brooke, I would think you actually believed such a thing."

"Heavens, no." At least, not without proof. "But you must see, Mrs. Warren, that it's a suspicion that must be laid to rest if we're ever to find out what happened to him."

"If my Joseph were involved in such a thing, we certainly never saw the proceeds of it," Sylvia said with just a touch of bitterness, and then looked up at Brooke. "What do you mean, to find out what happened?"

"Linda asked me to, ma'am."

"Oh, that girl." Sylvia sighed. "She's taken this hard, the poor dear, but to carry things this far . . . Well. I suppose she meant well, but, really, dear, we know what happened. My

Joseph tried to stop a thief and suffered for it. The act of a hero, I do believe."

"Er, yes. But, Mrs. Warren, don't you want the thief caught?"

"Well, of course I do, dear. I do want to see my dear Joseph's name cleared. But please, Brooke." She reached across the space separating them to lay her hand on Brooke's. "Please don't go stirrin' things up. It won't help."

Brooke frowned. "I'm not sure I understand."

"It won't change anything, dear. My Joseph will still be gone. And all the talk . . ." Her face twisted. "I just can't bear to hear all the talk again. You understand, I'm sure, dear."

"I know it's difficult to be the object of gossip," Brooke said, picking her words carefully. "But when it's in a good cause—"

"You're young, dear." Sylvia patted her hand. "When you reach my age you'll know there are some battles that just aren't worth fightin'. And I just don't know if I could take it, dear." Her fingers fluttered near her breast. "Not with my heart."

"I see." Brooke nodded, conceding defeat for the moment. Like Sylvia, her aunt Winifred resorted to a heart complaint when matters threatened to become inconvenient. "I won't bother you about it anymore, then," she said, and rose, drawing on her gloves.

"Thank you, dear. I knew you'd understand."

Brooke walked to the door, Sylvia by her side. "There is just one problem."

"What is that, dear?"

"I mentioned Linda's visit to my husband last night. He was the detective who originally looked into Mr. Warren's death." She let the words hang. "If he decides to pursue the case, I can't stop him," she said, and went out, leaving Sylvia to stare at her openmouthed.

The sky was growing dark and ominous as Brooke climbed

back into her carriage. Another summer storm was brewing; it would be welcome after the heat that had her removing her gloves and fanning herself with them. She really shouldn't have talked to Mrs. Warren so, she thought as the carriage turned and headed back downtown. The woman had obviously been through a great deal; beside being widowed, she had lost both her fortune and her social standing. Yet she seemed to bear up well, something Brooke had to admire. She well knew how it felt to lose everything one held dear, and to be thrust into a strange new world, as she had been after her parents' deaths.

Sitting back in the carriage, Brooke glanced out as they drove along Broadway, catching occasional glimpses of Riverside Park, with the Hudson sullen in the dull light and the Palisades beyond, shadowed; the new buildings of Columbia University, quiet and brooding in the summer heat; and the skeletal structure of what one day would be the Cathedral of St. John the Divine, begun just a few years past. Yet she saw little of anything. What, she wondered, would Matt make of the information she'd garnered? It had raised her own curiosity. Joseph Warren had been born into a family that had made its fortune in the China trade; he had then married well, and had lived at the very top echelons of New York society. Yet his wife was now reduced to living in a rented flat in Morningside Heights. What had happened to Warren's money? With that one question, the mystery surrounding him had just deepened.

Matt caught up with Tony just past the front desk. "Slow down," he commanded. "This isn't something we can just rush into."

Tony waited impatiently near the door, rocking back and

forth on his heels. "Crime's crime, no matter who it happens to. Ask the same questions, get the same lies in return."

Matt actually began to smile before he caught himself. Last year he'd felt much the same. The wealthy and powerful had to answer for their crimes, just like any other person. While he still believed that, his methods had changed. Barging in on any of the people connected with Warren would only cause antagonism. "Regardless, we've got to go slowly with this."

"Should've known," Tony muttered, turning away.

"What?"

Tony resumed that rocking motion, but now his hands were balled into fists. "That you'd side with the rich. What'd they do, get you your job?"

Only by using great willpower did Matt keep from exploding. "I will personally arrest and bring in anyone with evidence of crime against him, whether it's J. P. Morgan or Mayor Strong himself," he said, his voice low, fierce. The cocksure, belligerent expression on Tony's face began to flicker and then to fade, to be replaced by uncertainty. "These people have power, Flynn. If they close ranks, they can make our lives difficult. I've been studying the case files," he went on, turning on his heel. "You can bring me up-to-date on what's happened." He paused, looking back over his shoulder. "Coming?"

Tony muttered something in Italian, fortunately too low and too fast for Matt to catch. "Yeah," he said, and followed Matt back into the detective bureau.

The first skirmish was over, Matt thought, sitting at his desk, and on the whole he thought he'd done well. He also could guess now why Tony resented him. His money—correction, his wife's money. It was almost funny. He, a son of Newport's Fifth Ward, being accused of favoring the rich.

"Now," he said when Tony was seated across from him, the files spread across the desk. This was his case, and he was in control. "Tell me what's happened in the last three months."

"With Warren? Not much," Tony said, and went on to relate all that Matt had already read in the various reports, his hands fluid and fluent. "You gotta admit it doesn't look good for Warren," he finished. "Three months, and no thefts since."

"There were gaps of nearly that long before," Matt said absently, stroking his mustache.

"But what would the thieves have to gain? This way the heat's off them, if we think Warren did it."

"Thieves? You think there was more than one?"

"With what was taken each time? Sure. Don't you? Some of those canvases were big. I've wondered sometimes how they got the frames down without making noise. And how they got the paintings out. But they knew what they were going for. None of the French salon for them, or the Impressionists."

"Do you know much about art?" Matt asked, genuinely curious.

"Some. Probably not as much as you."

This time Matt did laugh, and he was aware of curious glances from the other detectives. "Give over, Flynn. I didn't have any more money growing up than you did, and you know it."

"Yeah. But you married it."

"Yes." Matt's voice was suddenly crisply cool. "You interviewed everyone involved, didn't you? Staff at the museum and such?"

"Yeah," Tony said after a moment. "Everyone from the director down to the janitor. And Warren's widow."

"Who do you like for it?"

Tony's face was expressionless. "Who says I think anyone's guilty?"

"You've been a cop too long not to have some opinion."

Tony hesitated again, and then nodded. "Yeah. You want to know the truth, I'm not too sure of Owen. Chandler Owen, the director."

"Why not?"

"Got the feeling he was lying when he answered some of my questions. I couldn't prove it, of course. But there was something."

Matt nodded. He himself had often felt the certainty that someone he questioned was lying, a sense honed over years of experience. Sometimes the lie was trivial, having nothing to do with the case; sometimes it wasn't. "All right, then. We'll go to Owen first. We'll have to, anyway, to get permission to talk to the staff. But, maybe . . ." His voice trailed off. Maybe with two detectives present, Owen would be more forthcoming. "Tell me everything you can about him."

The rain was letting up when Matt and Tony at last ascended the entrance stairs at the red brick Manhattan Museum of Art. They had traveled from headquarters by cab, a few miles in distance, but far in spirit, Matt thought, from the mud and the muck and the mire of Mulberry Street. Here were massive, palatial homes facing onto Fifth Avenue; here was the gem of a park designed by Frederick Law Olmsted. Altogether it was a more genteel, more refined world, and the guard who stood near the turnstiles in the museum regarded the two detectives suspiciously. "He don't think we're good enough for this place," Tony muttered.

Matt frowned. Not too long ago he might have felt the same way. "We have a job to do," he said crisply, approaching the guard. The man frowned when Matt addressed him, and then pointed to the right, past several galleries, to a staircase. There they would find Mr. Owen, upstairs in his office. Whether Mr. Owen would see them was another matter.

For a rainy afternoon, Statuary Hall, the large gallery just past the entrance, was remarkably full of people looking at statues by Hiram Powers or W. W. Story or others who Matt couldn't immediately identify. Most were obviously upper class, judging from their clothes, but some, dressed more humbly, were not. "I came here with my wife once," Matt remarked as they trod through a gallery containing antiquities from Egypt and Cyprus and Greece.

"Just once?"

Matt glanced over his shoulder at the sarcasm in Tony's voice. If Tony didn't relax, working with him would be impossible. "And on the investigation," he said, his voice hardening as they reached the stairs at last and began to climb.

"Yeah. Three months ago."

That almost did it. Matt nearly spun around on the landing to face his partner, to get to the root of the hostility and tension between them, even if it meant coming to blows. After a moment, however, he went on. This wasn't the place. Better to let any confrontation wait until they were back at headquarters. But, by God, if Flynn hindered the investigation, Captain O'Neill would hear about it.

After a tense walk through more galleries, they at last reached the museum's offices. "Maybe I should go first," Tony said, his first words since his jibe at Matt. "I've been here more recently."

"Three months ago," Matt retorted.

Tony stared at him for a moment, and then, to Matt's surprise, grinned. "All right, you take it." He opened a door marked DIRECTOR. "And see if you do any better than I did."

Frowning, Matt entered a small anteroom, where a man, sitting at a typewriter, looked up at them with just the faintest hint of distaste. His center-parted hair was slicked back with brilliantine, and his white linen collar was stiff, even in this heat. "I believe you're in the wrong place, gentlemen," he said, laying just the faintest ironic stress on the last word. "These are private offices."

Matt produced his badge, the shield of a detective sergeant. "Police."

The man's eyebrows rose. "Police? Well." He studied the badge for a moment and then looked up at Matt. "Have you finally done something about finding our paintings?"

"It's another matter. You are—?"

The man's eyebrows rose again. "Charles Seaton. Mr. Owen's secretary."

Matt nodded in acknowledgment. "If we might see Mr. Owen, please."

"Well . . ." Seaton frowned. "He's in the building somewhere, but where—oh, here he is," he broke off as the door to the office opened again and Chandler Owen came in. He was a tall man, thin except for a paunch, with silvery hair, an aristocratically high forehead, and a long, thin nose. His suit, though conservative, was of excellent cut, Matt noticed, and his face was very red. "Did you take the stairs again, sir?" Seaton said reprovingly.

"You know I don't like elevators," Owen said mildly, looking at Matt and Tony. "And you are?"

"Police, sir. About Mr. Warren."

"Oh? Well, if you'll excuse me a moment, I have some things to do, and then I'll see you." With that, he disappeared into his office. A few moments later the telephone on Seaton's desk rang. The secretary answered it, glanced at the two policemen, and then nodded.

"He'll see you now," he said, setting down the telephone. "And remember, he's a very busy man."

Matt nodded. "We'll remember," he said, and with Tony in tow at last went in to interview Chandler Owen.

Joseph Warren's killer set down the receiver to the telephone and stared at his steepled fingers. So. The police were snooping around again. He frowned, just for a moment, and then his face quickly lost all expression. It wouldn't do to show fear. Not even fear, really, not when he'd so carefully covered his tracks; not when he had people willing to warn him of what was coming. But he'd thought the investigation done with, finished. At least, he'd been assured that it was. Everyone thought that Warren had been killed by a thief, and, since that thief was still at large, so was the killer. An investigation might turn up things that were better left alone, unless it was stopped.

It would have to be. He had power enough to do so if he chose. If that didn't suffice, there were other methods. More direct, brutal methods. The killer leaned back in his leather chair and permitted himself a very small, very cold smile as he again lifted the telephone receiver. One way or another, the police would be stopped. He would see to it.

4

At the same time that Matt and Flynn were entering Owen's office, the Devlins' carriage pulled up outside the museum on Fifth Avenue. "Thank you, John," Brooke said to the coachman as she descended. "My, the rain didn't cool things down, did it?"

"No, ma'am. If you ask me, it's even more steamy."

Brooke nodded, looking up at the redbrick Gothic building. "I don't know how long I'll be. Probably not above an hour. Find someplace to keep dry."

"Yes, ma'am. I'll be here when you need me."

"Thank you," Brooke said again, and strolled to the imposing south entrance of the museum.

The storm had caught them not long after she had left the Warrens' apartment and had continued throughout the journey downtown. Their progress was slow, hampered by muddy streets and pedestrians dashing for shelter, but at last they had reached the Dakota. And there, Brooke changed her mind. The thought of going into the apartment, gloomy on such a day, made her flinch with revulsion. Really, she would have to do something about redecorating it. Yet if she didn't go in, what else could she do? There was no one else she could think of to talk to about Mr. Warren's death or the mysterious thefts of paintings, no one who would have any information. This was going to be more Matt's case than hers, she thought gloomily, and straightened. Oh, no, she was not going to let that happen. Matt might hold the advantage of being a policeman, but there were things she knew that he didn't. For one thing, she knew art. "No, I'm not going in," she said to the coachman, who stood outside in the Dakota's courtyard, holding an umbrella for her. "Take me to the Manhattan Museum."

And so now here she was, about to enter the first gallery, Statuary Hall. The same guard who had earlier glared disapprovingly at Matt tipped his hat as she passed through the turnstile. "Good afternoon, Mrs. Devlin. Good to see you here again."

"Thank you," she said, though she didn't recognize the man.

"Devlin," he went on musingly, as she would have walked away. "Where've I heard that name? Oh, yeah. The cop."

Brooke stopped. "What about him?"

"Came through here not ten minutes ago, wanting to see Mr. Owen."

"Oh." So Matt was here. Interesting, and a bit annoying. "Thank you," she said again, and at last moved on.

Dutifully she wandered through Statuary Hall, the great glass ceiling arching overhead, though to her eye the groupings were static and mundane. Nor did the antiquities from Cyprus in the next gallery interest her. She had come to view what remained of the lost masterpieces Mr. Warren had acquired. As she recalled, most of them were hung in a second floor gallery, making her head for one of the stairways.

Here it was quieter. Only a few people browsed among the paintings, giving her ample opportunity to study them. Doing

o took some concentration, for the paintings were hung from
loor to ceiling on a red-cloth-covered wall, and were draped
about by stiffly pleated curtains of burgundy twill, creating a
fussy, overpowering effect. Worse, genuine gems nestled with
more mediocre works, the result of the museum's struggle to
obtain adequate funding, and the acceptance of donations of
large private collections. Gems they were, though, and Brooke,
who had been well trained by her artist uncle and who had
some aspirations herself, was entranced. There was a Rubens,
The Return of the Holy Family from Egypt, and a Vermeer in
glowing jewel colors, *Young Woman with a Water Jug.* In another gallery were sketches and drawings by old masters, too
many of which had turned out to be merely copies, and in yet
another more modern American works, by Gilbert Stuart or
Charles Wilson Peale. Brooke could happily have stayed there
all afternoon, studying the ways different artists used light and
color and brushwork.

At last, however, she turned away. She wasn't here for her
own edification. Giving a Rembrandt portrait one last look, she
began to walk away, hearing as she did a tapping noise behind
her, as of a footfall, loud and sharp on the heavily shellacked
parquet floor. Puzzled, she turned, but saw no one. The galleries
were growing increasingly deserted as the afternoon advanced,
and yet there was nothing unusual in that. Likely the noise had
been made by some person leaving, or by a staff member. Making a little face, she went on into the next gallery.

And here at last she found what she had sought: those few
of the so-called last masterpieces that were left to the museum. One was a Constable, a previously unknown work similar to many he had done, of rural England, and the luminosity
of the light in the painting held Brooke entranced. She could
almost understand why someone might want to take such a
thing as their own.

The sharp, short noise echoed again as Brooke moved to the next row of paintings, and this time she turned, frowning. Outside, thunder grumbled as the storm returned, and it was growing dark inside the gallery. Almost creepy, she thought, and instantly chided herself. Nonsense. The museum was a public place. Nothing would happen to her here.

Moving determinedly, not stopping now to admire paintings that caught her attention, she walked along the gallery that paralleled the museum's offices. When the lost masterpieces had been acquired, they had first been grouped together. Only since they had become the target of theft had they been separated, to hang in different galleries. The one she sought, a Rembrandt, was in a gallery on the park side of the building.

This gallery was deserted, testament to the storm and the lateness of the hour. The museum would be closing soon; she hadn't much time. Brooke glanced down as she approached the Rembrandt and saw a dark stain on the floor. She realized two things at once: this was the gallery where Joseph Warren had met his death, and the footsteps behind her, alternating with another tapping sound, had not stopped, but were coming on.

Later Brooke wouldn't be able to say what made her move except for a blind, unreasoning panic. Not stopping to think, she turned and scurried along the gallery, away from the offices and people, but toward the stairs that led down. Behind her the footsteps continued, staccato, urgent, unceasing; somehow menacing, though her view of whoever might be following her was blocked by successive doorways. She didn't particularly care. For some reason she had no desire to meet whoever it was that paced through the museum with such implacable steadiness. She had no desire to stay where murder had been done.

The stairs, at last. They led her to a point opposite where

she had begun, but there were more people here. She was safe. Not stopping to see if anyone still followed, she hurried along with those others who were leaving the museum—and ran straight into Matt.

Chandler Owen rose from behind his desk as Matt and Tony entered the office, appearing calmer than he had a few moments earlier. He had been the museum's director for several years, and most people agreed that under his stewardship the museum was making steady, if unremarkable, progress. The acquisition of the lost masterpieces had been counterbalanced by their subsequent thefts. Looking at Owen's chiseled, aristocratic features as he took a chair facing the desk, Matt wondered how the turbulence of the past year had affected Owen. It had been Warren who had acquired the masterpieces; Warren who had received the glory. Not for the first time, Matt wondered how Owen felt about that.

"So the police are finally giving Joseph's death some attention," Owen said, sitting down after they had shaken hands.

"Yes, sir," Matt said quietly, almost deferentially, and felt rather than saw Tony give him a surprised look. "Of course, we've never let it drop completely, but some new information has come to light."

Owen leaned forward, his brow puckered. "What is that?"

"I'm afraid I can't discuss it right now, sir. However, we thought we'd look in on you to assure you that we're still working on it."

"Good. Good." Owen leaned back in his big leather chair, and though his face had cleared there was something deep in his eyes, something in the set of his shoulders, that made Matt wary. Chandler Owen was, for some reason, very much on guard. "I'll be happy to cooperate with you in any way I can," he said, spreading his hands wide, "though of course I've already talked with many officers."

"Of course." Matt glanced up. "I'm curious about something, sir. Why did your secretary scold you for taking the stairs?"

Owen grimaced. "My family suffers under the misapprehension that I have a bad heart. I assure you, I am perfectly fine. I also do not like elevators."

"Me either. I don't trust them."

"It's not that. It's such a small space—but you didn't come here to talk about my health, did you?"

"No." Matt pretended to refer to his notebook. He could feel Tony's curious gaze on him, and yet he knew that the more he knew about the people involved in a case, the better the chances of solving it. "We would like to ask you some questions about the thefts you've had here."

"The thefts? But what do they have to do with Joseph—if you're thinking that he had anything to do with them, you might as well leave right now."

"No, sir," Tony put in smoothly. "We have no theories. Except that it seems that Mr. Warren might have caught the thief, or thieves, in the act."

"We believe there were more than one," Matt said as Owen relaxed just a bit. "With what was taken there would have to be. What puzzles us is that no one heard or saw anything."

Owen spread his hands again in that apparent gesture of openness. "It puzzles me too, gentlemen. As you may know, we stepped up security considerably after the first thefts."

"Yet they still got in," Tony said softly.

Matt nodded. "And there were no signs of a forced entrance in the last one."

"Who would have a key, sir?"

Owen had looked from one to the other during this exchange, like a spectator at a tennis match. "I assure you, gentlemen, we keep close watch on the keys. Only I and a few others have access to them."

"The watchmen, sir?" From Tony.

"And the curators?" Matt.

Owen frowned. "Yes, of course."

"What about your secretary?"

"Great God, are you accusing Seaton of having anything to do with the thieves?"

"Heavens, no," Matt said, adopting Brooke's best wide-eyed stare. "Just trying to clarify matters."

"You see, sir," Tony put in, "if we know who has keys, we might be able to narrow things down."

"You're still saying someone here, on my staff, is involved in the thefts! Well, I won't have it, gentlemen, and if you are going to continue in this way, I must ask to you leave—"

"You'll have to forgive Mr. Flynn," Matt said, his voice apologetic. "I'm afraid he sometimes gets carried away."

Tony cast Matt a resentful look, though up close Matt saw that his eyes gleamed. "Yeah. Sorry," he muttered.

"I should hope so," Owen said, regarding them both warily. "I assure you, no one in the museum had anything to do with the thefts, or with Warren's death."

"We're not accusing anyone, sir. Is there a chance, though, that someone could have come from outside and gotten a key somehow? Maybe made a wax impression to have a copy made."

"No. After the first theft I made certain there were no loose keys around. After the last one"—his face turned grim—"we had the locks changed. I assure you, gentlemen, that only a few people have keys and that they keep them on their person, as I do. No one from outside could get a key."

"But before the locks were changed, they could have?"

Owen hesitated. "Possibly," he said finally. "I'm not quite sure how things were done when my predecessor was here."

Matt nodded and flipped a page in his notebook; he'd learned all he could on that subject. "Tell us about the paintings that were taken."

Owen relaxed, leaning back in his chair. "What can I tell you, gentlemen?" he said, spreading his hands wide again. "They were a great loss to our collection."

"They were"—Matt referred to his notebook again—"recent acquisitions?"

"Some were, yes. The newspapers have taken to calling them the lost masterpieces."

Matt sat, pencil poised above his notebook. "How were they acquired, sir?"

"Joseph was in charge of that." Owen shifted in his chair. "I've already answered this question over and over."

"Yes, sir, I know, but they want us to do things this way," Matt said apologetically, though he didn't explain who "they" were. "How did Mr. Warren acquire the paintings, sir?"

"He worked through an agent who was selling them for someone else, I believe."

"And the agent was—"

"I don't know."

"Yeah," Tony muttered. "A thing like that, and you don't know?"

"It does seem strange," Matt put in before Owen, red-faced again, could explode. "You're the director, and yet you don't know who sold Warren the paintings."

Owen spread his hands again. "I assure you, gentlemen, that I don't know. The owner of the paintings wanted complete secrecy. Joseph didn't even know who he was."

"You did, I assume, have the paintings authenticated?"

Owen stiffened. "What are you implying?"

Matt looked up, startled at this reply. "Nothing, sir. I would just think that you would want to be sure that paintings acquired in such a way were genuine."

"They are," Owen said, still stiff. "Joseph saw to that."

"Mmm-hmm." Matt nodded. "And has the owner approached the museum since Warren's death?"

"Unfortunately, no." Owen glanced at his watch and rose. "I wish I could help you gentlemen further, but that is really all I know."

Tony stayed sitting, frowning, but Matt got up. "Thank you, sir," he said, holding out his hand. "We appreciate your time. Flynn?"

Tony looked up. "Yeah?"

"Let's go."

"Yeah." Tony got to his feet. "But we'll be back, Mr. Owen. We're going to find out who killed Warren, one way or another," he said, and sauntered out of the office.

In the corridor outside the offices Tony clapped his bowler hat onto his head. "He didn't tell us much."

"More than he realized." Matt fell into step beside him, heading for the stairs. "He knows something, I'd bet on that."

"Yeah, I thought so too."

Matt glanced at him as they reached the stairs. "You did well in there."

"Yeah, well, someone had to be tough with him. You weren't."

Matt shrugged. All things considered, the interview had gone rather well. If they still didn't know who had killed Warren, they did know that Owen was somehow involved, judging by his reactions to the questions. He had not acted like an innocent man, for all his protestations of wishing to help. More important, Matt thought, he and Tony had acted as a team, trading off on the questioning with only the slightest cue, and instinctively falling into the best strategy for bringing an uncooperative witness out. "You've got to be careful with these people," he explained. They had reached the ground floor now, and were joining the exodus of people from the museum. "The wealthy, I mean. Mutts like we usually see, we can be tough on, but these people have power and they won't take that kind of treatment. It's a different world, Tony."

"Yeah, you'd know that, wouldn't you?"

Matt's good mood abruptly fled. He'd had enough of Tony's sniping and snide remarks. "Look, Flynn," he began, turning, when someone jostled him from behind. Startled, he whipped around, and to his astonishment saw Brooke.

"Matt!" she exclaimed. "I didn't think you were still here."

"What are you doing here?" he asked at the same time.

"Oh, it was a rainy day, so I thought I'd spend some time looking at the pictures," she said airily. She hadn't missed the fact that Matt hadn't explained his presence in the museum with a man who was obviously another policeman. Apparently he didn't want her to interfere.

Matt took her arm, leading her away from the crush of people who were leaving. "Is everything all right?"

"Yes." She looked up at him. "Why wouldn't it be?"

"I don't know. You looked"—he frowned—"frightened."

"Frightened? Oh, that." She laughed, her fear of a few moments earlier now seeming foolish. "I thought someone was following me."

"Where?" Matt demanded, instantly alert, his eyes scanning the crowd behind her.

"In the galleries upstairs. Someone with a cane, of all things. Really, Matt, it was my imagination. When I realized I was in the gallery where Mr. Warren was killed, I'm afraid I let myself get spooked."

Matt frowned, still searching people's faces, and then looked down at her. "That's probably all it was," he agreed, but the look in his eyes told her he thought otherwise. It was the way he was, she thought, a cop, aware as no civilian could be of the underside of life. "You haven't met my partner yet, have you? Brooke, this is Tony Flynn. Tony, my wife."

For the first time, Brooke focused on the man standing next to Matt. They weren't at all alike; Flynn's coloring was dark, almost Mediterranean, while Matt was unmistakably Irish. Yet they were very much the same. With their sharp, observant eyes and the tense way they held themselves, they were, undoubtedly, cops. "Mr. Flynn," she said, holding out her hand. "How nice to meet you."

"My pleasure, ma'am," Tony said, and to Brooke's immense surprise bent over her hand with old world courtliness. "Matt didn't tell me he had such a beautiful wife."

"Why, thank you, Mr. Flynn."

"I understand you've helped Devlin in a few cases."

"Oh, no," she said quickly, feeling Matt tense. "I've simply had the misfortune of knowing people who were involved, and I've been able to tell Matt about them."

Tony's eyes actually twinkled. "Yeah. So you being here today has nothing to do with Warren's death."

"She's not a suspect, Flynn," Matt said.

"Well, I can't help being interested," Brooke said, shooting Matt a look. "Among other things, I've an uncle on the board of trustees. But, I assure you, I came for my own amusement today. I'm an amateur artist myself."

"And I'm sure you learned something today," Tony said with only the slightest trace of irony.

"How are you getting home, Brooke?" Matt interrupted, taking her arm and leading her toward the entrance.

"I've the carriage outside. Can I drop you anywhere?"

Matt shook his head, putting his hat back on as they

emerged into the drizzle. "We have to go back to Mulberry Street. I'll see you at home."

"Of course," she said, and let him escort her to the carriage, her curiosity bubbling inside her. What had Matt learned today at the museum?

Matt stood watching as the carriage, with Brooke inside, rolled safely away, and frowned. He didn't like what she'd told him. Brooke was sensible, not given to flights of fancy or to being, as she'd said, spooked. It was entirely possible that someone had been following her inside the museum. If so, who? "And why?" he muttered.

"What?" Tony said.

"Nothing. We'd better get back."

"Yeah." Tony strolled along beside him. "You know, I understand a bit more now."

"About what?"

"Just some things. Hey!" He held two fingers up to his mouth and let out a piercing whistle, at the same time waving frantically with his other arm. In the street, a hansom cab swerved to the curb. "Let's grab this cab while we can. Looks like the rain's getting worse again."

Matt nodded. The tension that had lain between him and Flynn was gone for the moment, but it would be back. He was certain of it. And when it returned, he thought, climbing into the cab and giving the driver their direction, he'd do something about it. He'd have to.

The air was rain-swept and fresh, the breeze cooling at last. Matt, in dinner clothes, stepped down from the hated carriage and turned to help Brooke descend. No need for all this ostentation, he knew, holding out his arm to her. At the Dakota they had the services of their own cook, or, if necessary, the building's private dining room. Matt had, however, discovered a previously unknown weakness for good food within himself. So, when Brooke had suggested dining out at Delmonico's, he'd agreed, even if it did mean forcing himself into this monkey suit.

Brooke smiled to herself as the maître d'hôtel led her and Matt to a round table covered with blindingly white linen, upon which fine crystal sparkled like ice. Just last year Matt would have hated Delmonico's, which had long been known for its exclusivity as well as for the excellence of its food. Glancing about the crowded dining room, she recognized a Vanderbilt here, a Van Schuyler there. And Matt, holding one of the large menus and reading the French with apparent ease, seemed to fit in here as well as anyone.

"What?" he said when the waiter had taken their orders and gone away.

"I didn't say anything."

"No, but you're staring at me." He shifted in his seat. "For God's sake, Brooke, is something wrong? Is my tie crooked, or—"

"No, silly." She smiled. "I was just thinking that I was surprised you agreed to come here."

He frowned, sitting back as the sommelier poured the first wine they had ordered, and nodding in approval as he sipped. "Why shouldn't I have agreed?" he said truculently. "Can't a man enjoy something like this once in a while?"

"Of course." She glanced around the room again, noting this time the fine wood in the coffered ceiling, the discreet glow of lights from the chandeliers, the silk wall hangings and draperies. Black-coated waiters bustled about quietly, only adding to the impression of hushed efficiency and excellence. Let Matt justify eating here as he wished. He'd admit the truth to himself sooner or later. "Was today so very bad?"

Matt sipped his wine again. "Not really. Just a lot of little things put together."

"Mr. Flynn seems quite pleasant."

"Huh."

"Well, he does." She sat back as their fish course, trout à la meunière, was served. "I called on Sylvia Warren today."

Matt regarded her without expression. "Did you learn anything?"

Brooke took a dainty bite of the trout. At least he hadn't exploded, as he would have in the past. Perhaps he really was becoming reconciled to her being a part of the investigation. "Quite a bit. Among other things, Mr. Warren apparently didn't leave any money."

"She told you that?"

"No, silly. It was obvious from the way she's living," she said, and went on to relate all she had seen and learned during her visit to the Warrens' apartment. When she finished, Matt sat back, looking thoughtful.

"So he left her penniless." He rubbed at his mustache. "Guess that means she didn't have any motive for killing him."

"Matt!" She stared at him reproachfully, only marginally aware of the waiter, come to take away their empty plates, who looked startled at this tidbit of conversation. "Surely you don't consider her a suspect."

He shrugged. "You know as well as I that when someone's killed, his nearest and dearest most likely did it."

"Well, if so, she's paying for it."

"So we're back with the theory that a thief killed Warren."

Brooke glanced up at his tone of voice. "But you don't believe that anymore, do you?"

"No. There's something very strange about those thefts. After Flynn and I left the museum—you got home all right, didn't you?"

"Of course," Brooke said, surprised. "I would have told you if anything happened."

"I was thinking of whoever followed you in the museum."

"Oh, that." Brooke waved her hand in dismissal. "I'm sure it was my imagination, Matt."

"Huh."

"Aren't you?"

His face was somber. "It just seems damned strange to me that just as I start investigating at the museum again, you thought someone was following you."

"You think it's connected?"

"I don't know. But I think that the answer to Warren's death is in the museum. Owen acted damned suspicious."

"My uncle thinks Mr. Owen is a decent man. Dull, but decent."

Matt frowned. "I wish your uncle were here. Since he's a trustee, I'd like to talk to him about the museum."

"Then let's go down to Newport."

"While I'm working? I can't, Brooke." He looked up at her. "But you'd like to, wouldn't you?"

"Why, yes," she said, startled both by his tone and by the longing his question evoked. Newport, which had been her home for so long, where her family was. But New York was her home now, she reminded herself. "Wouldn't you? It's so hot here."

"And get caught up in the social season? No, thank you. I'll take the heat." He paused. "But if you wanted to go . . ."

"Oh, nonsense, Matt. I'm perfectly happy here." Again they sat back as the waiter served their main course with a flourish, lobster à la Newburg for her and roast lamb for Matt, who didn't care for fancy sauces on his food. "Do you think Mr. Owen's involved?" she asked when the waiter had left.

"I don't know. I do know he wasn't honest with us today.

He's hiding something, Brooke. Might not be anything, but with what's happened, who knows?"

"You surely don't think he's involved with the murder!"

"I don't know. But there's something strange about those thefts." He leaned forward. "After we got back to Mulberry Street, I had a talk with Detective Kramer. He's been investigating the thefts."

"And?"

"And he thinks they were an inside job. That someone inside the museum was involved."

"Good heavens." Brooke patted at her lips with a napkin. "That would cause quite a scandal."

"Among other things. The first theft, a door was forced open. It was a back door, not much used, hidden from sight, so it could have been someone from outside. Except that they knew just what they wanted. They went to a certain gallery, and nothing else was touched."

"They probably looked the museum over beforehand."

"Maybe. Now, the second theft was different. By then there were more watchmen, and all doors like the one that was forced had bars on the glass."

"But they got in through a window, didn't they?"

"Supposedly. Kramer says that the window is so small, the thief is either a kid, or a midget."

"So?"

"So it looks like the window was broken to make it look like the way the thieves got in. By the way, the watchman heard nothing. The theft happened while he was in another part of the building. And how would the thieves know that unless they knew his routine? Then we come to the third theft," he went on, not giving her a chance to answer.

"And?"

"No signs of forced entrance anywhere. The watchman figures he went into the gallery right after the thieves left. They had a key, Brooke." He sat back, regarding her with a satisfied air. "They had to."

"Mmm." Brooke frowned at nothing in particular. "What does Detective Kramer think happened to the paintings?"

Matt shook his head. "He doesn't know. But he thinks it's possible some private collector has them and doesn't dare admit it. We might never know what happened to them."

"Unless we find the thieves."

Matt shook his head. "Even then. They might not know themselves."

"If they're in the museum, they very well might." Brooke stared down at her empty plate. She had consumed lobster and asparagus and wine without even noticing. "What are you going to do?"

"Go after Owen, find out what he's hiding. I'm willing to bet that once we do, we'll be able to solve this."

"Mmm-hmm." She gazed absently into space, barely aware of the waiter removing their plates. Matt was working in her world now, the world of society, the world of art. It was a world where he had no contacts, but she did. Quite possibly she could find out things he couldn't.

An image of Newport flashed into her mind, and was as quickly banished. "Tell me how I can help," she said, leaning forward.

The black maria was pulling up in Mulberry Street as Tony approached headquarters the following morning, whistling, hands tucked into his pockets. Yesterday's rain had washed clean even the streets here, and the customary smell was mercifully dampened. The day was fine, or, rather, it would be, if he didn't have to go inside that building and work with Devlin.

Tony didn't like Devlin, and he didn't really care who knew it. Tell the truth, a lot of the detectives were leery of him. He was TR's man. That in itself wasn't so bad, even if TR had made sure good cops like Clubber Alexander and Thomas Byrnes, who had been head of the detective bureau when Tony joined the force, had gotten the sack. Now that TR had been around for a year, most cops were beginning to appreciate just what he was trying to do by bringing in new recruits and by breaking the stranglehold politics had had on the force. Sure was a relief not to have to pay for a promotion, Tony admitted. Now the only way to get ahead was by merit. No, Tony couldn't fault TR for hiring Devlin. What he didn't like was Devlin's background.

It still rankled that Devlin was senior to him, at least on the Warren case. Sure, Devlin had solved some spectacular cases, but when you came down to it, who was he? Just some hick cop from a small town. Not only that, he'd used his wife's money to his advantage, taking all that time off for a honeymoon. When Tony had gotten married, he'd been glad that he and Angela had had a weekend alone together at Coney Island. No, he didn't like Devlin, and what made it worse was that the man was a good cop.

The doors to the black maria opened as Tony neared the headquarters building, and out spilled a sorry procession of humanity, mostly female, most in various stages of undress. Some wore stained wrappers over nightdresses or corsets; others had on filmy gowns that didn't cover much. All had on too much makeup, and the frowsy look of having been up all night. "What cathouse did you raid this time?" he asked the officer who stood by the paddy wagon, supervising the exodus.

"The one on Bowery and Stanton, sir," the patrolman said. Tony let out a whistle. "Horgan's place? That took guts." "Orders, sir."

"Yeah." Tony smiled. So they were going after Horgan again. Good. Of all the gang leaders in the city, from Monk Eastman to Frank Kelly, Frank Horgan was the worst. From his saloon on the Lower East Side, the Golden Harp, he controlled a vast network of crime, including liquor interests, gambling, and prostitution. With a gang of over one thousand men to back him up, and the cooperation of politicians who received handsome payments from him, he wouldn't be happy about any interference in his affairs. "It's about time. I—." He stopped in the act of turning away, as another woman, her hair an improbable shade of red, stepped down onto the street. "Maisie. Well, well."

The woman flinched as if she'd been struck. "Hello, Mr. Flynn," she said, her smile weak.

"Maisie. Well, well," he said again. His smile broad, Tony reached out and caught her arm. "I'll take care of this one myself, Sullivan."

Officer Sullivan shrugged, clearly bored. "Yes, sir."

Maisie didn't protest as Tony brought her into headquarters, down the corridor into the detective bureau. Nor did she say anything when he shoved her, surprisingly gently, toward a chair. "You have anything to eat this morning?"

"I'm not hungry," she whispered, her hands folded and head bent, the very picture of submissive womanhood. It was enough to remind Tony that she'd been an aspiring actress before linking up with Horgan.

"You will be," he predicted, sitting at his desk and regarding her coolly. "So, Maisie. It's been a long time."

"I don't know anything."

"What were you doing at Ma Meecham's academy?" He

grinned. Ma Meecham's formal name was Mrs. Meecham's Academy for Young Ladies. The women who worked inside, however, were frequently not young and very definitely not ladies.

"Working."

"What, you've been demoted? I thought Horgan had other uses for you." Maisie shrugged, and so he went on. "Tell me about him, Maisie. You know we're going to get him someday."

"I don't know anything. No, really," she protested before he could speak. "I ain't been around lately."

"Where have you been?"

"Madison Avenue. You don't believe me?" she challenged. "Well, I was, until he got himself killed."

"Your protector?" Tony laid ironic stress on the last word. "How'd he die?"

Maisie hesitated, glancing about the office. In the past she'd been of great help to Tony, feeding him information about Horgan's doings, always careful, never wanting to be caught. To do so would mean her death; Horgan did not forgive betrayals. In return, Tony had seen that she was well paid for her information, and that her identity was kept secret. Thus today's charade of his appearing to take her into custody. "I ain't no— I'm no snitch, no matter what you say."

"Never said you were, Maisie," Tony said easily, though inside he tensed. Now, why wasn't she answering his question? "Who was your protector?"

"No one you'd know."

"C'mon, Maisie. I know you're protecting someone. If he could set you up on Madison, then he had money."

"It doesn't matter."

"Satisfy my curiosity. Or do you want Horgan to know what you're doing here?"

Alarm flickered in Maisie's eyes, and then faded, replaced

by resignation. "You would, wouldn't you," she said, and it was not a question.

"Yeah, I would. So you might as well tell me everything."

She sighed and then shrugged. "All right, but I don't know what good it'll do you. Until April I was Joseph Warren's mistress."

5

Brooke stood in the middle of the parlor, William Eichhammer, the Dakota's painter, by her side. "It's too dark," she explained. "I want to keep what's in here—well, most of it—but we have to start with the walls."

Mr. Eichhammer nodded. "I told Mrs. Olmstead it would be," he said, looking around at the brown-and-gold-papered walls, "but she insisted."

"Aunt Winifred has very definite ideas about what she likes."

He nodded again. "I could do a nice fresco for you, or a French tint."

"I was thinking ivory."

"Ivory?"

"Ivory," she said, no less definite in her ideas than her aunt. If she was going to redecorate the apartment, she would do it right. "Though a French tint might be appropriate for the master bedroom." She smiled. "Have you seen it?"

"Indeed, I have. Ivory." He looked around the room again.

"It might work, at that. Maybe if you had some plaster mold-ings put in the ceiling . . ."

Brooke glanced up and nodded. "A fine idea, as long as they're not too ornate. I don't like fussiness, Mr. Eichhammer."

"No, ma'am. All right, I'll get on it. When would you want me to start?"

"As soon as possible, I'd think. I'd like to do the public rooms first."

"Yes, ma'am. Monday morning, then," he said, and went out.

Left alone, Brooke gazed about the room again, hands rest-ing on her hips. Yes. Ivory walls, no matter what Mr. Eich-hammer thought, and she'd hang lace curtains at the windows, so that the glorious view of the park wouldn't be obstructed. With those changes, the gold velvet furniture wouldn't loom so; in the dining room the mahogany table wouldn't seem quite so massive. The umbrella stand in the hall, however, would have to go.

Brooke smiled to herself. All in all, it had been a satisfac-tory morning. She'd finally made a start on the redecorating, and in an earlier telephone call from Alma Cartwright, an ac-quaintance of her aunt's, an old friend, she'd been asked to join the Voter Education League. Mrs. Cartwright had organized the group, consisting mostly of society ladies, to educate the poor about politics and government, and, not so incidentally, to work for women's suffrage. It wasn't the kind of good works her aunt would endorse, but Brooke found the idea appealing. Joining the league would give her days more of a sense of pur-pose.

Most important, however, was the letter she had written to Uncle Henry. At dinner last evening at Delmonico's, she and Matt had agreed that the best way she could help him was by finding out information about the museum and its staff that wasn't available to him. Her best source would be her uncle. Since it was summer, many of the people Brooke knew who were knowledgeable about art were out of town, in Newport or Bar Harbor. Having been a trustee of the museum for over ten years, Uncle Henry would probably know more about the staff. Now, if only her uncle Augustus were around, she could have made a good start.

Fuller came in at that moment, holding a silver tray upon which rested a card. "A visitor, madam," he said, his voice stiff. "Shall I say you're not at home?"

In the act of reaching for the card, Brooke stopped. "Why?"

"Well." Fuller hesitated, pushing his spectacles up on the bridge of his nose. "He isn't quite respectable, madam."

"In what way, Fuller?" she asked, curious as to what his criterion was.

"He has long hair, madam, and his coat." His nose wrinkled. "Definitely of European cut. A bounder, I'd say, madam."

"You intrigue me, Fuller." Brooke reached for the card at last, wondering who in the world who would be visiting who fit such a description, and let out a laugh. "For heaven's sake, Fuller, Mr. Low is my uncle! Please do show him in."

"Yes, madam," Fuller said woodenly, as if even the fact that Augustus Low was a relation didn't justify his appearance. Fuller was really a terrible snob, Brooke thought, lips twitching with amusement as she hurried to the parlor door. And there, in the entrance hall, stood her uncle.

"Uncle Augie!" she exclaimed, launching herself at him, and he laughed as he caught her up in an exuberant hug and twirled her around. He was a big bear of a man, tall, broad-shouldered and shaggy; not only was his coat European, it was also quite old, and his hair fell below his shoulders. About him hung the tangy scents of turpentine and linseed oil. No wonder Fuller had been suspicious. "I was just thinking about you."

"Were you?" Augustus set her down, his eyes twinkling. For the first time Brooke noticed the signs of aging in him, the gray in his hair and beard, but his deep brown eyes were as young as ever. "Then it's a good thing I'm here—good God." He stared blankly at the Turkish nook. "What is that?"

"Do you know, Matt reacted the same way? Fuller, would you please serve us madeira in the parlor?"

"Madeira, madam?"

"Yes, Fuller," she said firmly, taking her uncle's arm and leading him into the parlor. "I'm afraid the rest of the apartment is quite as bad, but don't worry. I'm redecorating."

"Quite a relief." He stood in the middle of the room, gazing about in blank astonishment. "Winifred's work, I'd guess."

"Yes. But Uncle Henry chose the books and the paintings."

"Good. And this rug is fine."

"Yes. But, oh, I don't want to talk about furniture with you!" She seized his hands, drawing him down onto the sofa. "Whatever are you doing in New York at this time of year?"

His smile was impish. "To annoy Octavius," he said, referring to his very proper and upright brother.

"Uncle Augie," Brooke chided. "Now, really, why are you here?"

"I'm not really sure." He shrugged. "Sometimes I get tired of Paris."

"How on earth does anyone get tired of Paris?"

"They're philistines, Brooke. No taste and no sense of the future."

"Oh." Which meant that Augustus's paintings were not, in all likelihood, selling very well. Not that he needed the money, but it must be a blow to his ego.

"Duveen said he might have a showing of my work."

"But hardly anyone's in town, Uncle."

"Maybe that's why." Augustus slouched down until his head rested against the back of the sofa, his hands tucked into his pockets and his face set into a pout. "I'm a failure, Brooke."

"Oh, nonsense," she said briskly, for she'd seen him in downcast moods before. As a child she'd taken them quite seriously but since then she'd learned he quickly bounced back. "What you need is to see your friends again, and perhaps to go to the Gaiety Theatre to see the Floradora Sextet."

"Brookie." His eyes twinkled again as he straightened. "That's a scandalous suggestion. As if any of those young ladies would interest me."

"Not even Miss Russell?"

"How do you know about Lillian and me—I doubt Diamond Jim would be pleased to see me," he said, recovering. "Besides, I'm too old for that kind of thing."

Brooke let out a laugh. "Nonsense, and you know it. Or," she said, suddenly struck by something in his eyes, "is it There's someone in your life, isn't there?"

Again he grinned. "It wouldn't be very discreet of me to discuss it, would it? Thank you." This to Fuller, who had come in bearing a cut-crystal decanter of madeira with goblets to match, set on a silver tray. "Good wine, Brooke."

"Mm-hm. Uncle Henry's doing, again." Brooke took a tiny sip from her glass, watching as Augustus refilled his with a free hand. He had a huge appetite, did her uncle, for food and life and love, and he lived as he chose. In the staid Low family that had sometimes led to scandal. It was entirely possible that his pursuit of whichever woman had caught his eye would do so again. "Actually, I'm glad you're here. Well, I am anyway, of course, but there are some questions I have that you might be able to answer. About the Manhattan Museum."

"Don't know anything about it," he declared, taking a large gulp of wine. "That's Henry's area."

"Yes, I know, and I've written to him. But you know art, Uncle Augie, and that's what I need right now. What do you think about the paintings the museum's acquired recently?"

"The lost masterpieces?" He looked at her sharply. "Are you interested in the thefts?"

"No."

"You are, aren't you?" He straightened. "Has Devlin got you involved in another investigation?"

"No. I involved myself. And it's not about the thefts, but about Mr. Warren's murder," she went on as he opened his mouth to protest. "Except that they seem to be linked."

"Dash it, Brooke." He rose, gulping the rest of the wine, and paced to a window without refilling his glass. "I like your husband, but I don't like it when you get involved in his work."

"Why? There's no harm in it."

"There could be."

"There isn't," she said firmly, and as she did so heard in her memory tapping on a polished parquet floor. Nonsense, no one had followed her yesterday in the museum. "Matt wouldn't allow it if there were. I'm just asking the questions he'd need answered, about the staff and the collections."

He glowered at her from the window. "If someone killed for those paintings . . ."

"You think someone did?"

"I don't know. Damn." He walked back to her, splashing wine into the goblet and sitting back, his long legs crossed at the ankle. "I don't like it, Brooke."

"You've always told me to go my own way."

"This is men's work."

"Not necessarily," she said, suddenly cool.

"Let your husband deal with it."

"He doesn't know anything about art. What do you know about the lost masterpieces?"

He gazed at her for a moment and then looked away, swear
ing under his breath. "Not much," he said, giving in. "I wen
to see them when they were first displayed, of course. They'r
fine works. But"—he looked at her over the rim of the glass—
"not as fine as I'd expected."

"Why not?" she said in surprise. "I saw a Constable yester
day that took my breath away."

"I don't know." He frowned. "No, I truly don't know why
Brooke. I just know that when I saw them I was disappointed
They're good, I'll admit that, but masterpieces? I don't know
For example." He sat up, clutching his glass in his hands. "Th
Vermeer—what was its name?"

"*Portrait of a Man*," she supplied.

"Yes. Well, I was disappointed in the colors. Not as glow
ing as I expected. Of course, they say it had been varnished an
the varnish had yellowed, but . . ." He shot her a glance. "Yo
know how the old masters painted? In thin layers of oils, ove
and over, until they got the right color and depth? I didn't hav
that feeling with this painting. The depth, I mean."

"Do you think it wasn't a real Vermeer? It was one of th
ones stolen, by the way."

"Maybe. Maybe it was by one of his students. But it woul
still have been painted in the same way."

"It was authenticated, Uncle."

He shrugged. "Then maybe it was a lesser work. I didn't stud
it closely, so I don't know."

"Mmm." Brooke ran a finger around the rim of the glass
"The police think the paintings have gone into the hands o
a private collector who paid to have them stolen. Have yo
heard—"

"Of anything like that? No. But someone who would do tha
would keep it quiet. He'd be the type who'd enjoy knowin

that he has something no one else has. It might be years before we see those paintings again, if ever."

"That's unusual, isn't it? That there haven't been any rumors?"

He shrugged again. "Not if the buyer wanted complete secrecy, and if he paid well enough. Now, if he didn't, someone might peach."

Brooke smiled at this piece of slang. "Well, no one's complained yet, so our mythical collector is safe. What about where they came from? Any talk about that?"

"Plenty. Most people think it's some impoverished aristocrat who doesn't want it known he needs money. I've heard everything from the Marquess of Dover to the Prince of Wales."

"Not really!"

"Well, he has an expensive lifestyle his mother doesn't approve of, you know." His teeth flashed in a grin. "Most people think it's a French *comte*, though, or a *vicomte*, though no one seems to know just who."

"And he hasn't had to sell any in nearly a year—heavens!" She abruptly straightened. "Which aristocrat recently married?"

"Why?"

"The Earl of Lynton was supposed to marry Julia Hoffman. She's an heiress. But with what happened on the ship taking her to England—"

"Right. Her father. Another case you were involved in."

"He needs money. The Duke of Marlborough married Consuelo Vanderbilt last year," she went on. "Did he sell anything from Blenheim, I wonder? And there must be others. I wonder . . ."

"You enjoy this, don't you?" Augustus said, looking at her shrewdly.

"Immensely." She smiled at him. "Sometimes I think should have been a cop."

Augustus let out a laugh. "Wouldn't that rile Octavius!"

"Not to mention Aunt Winifred. Seriously, Uncle. Do you think you could find out if any aristocrats have been selling of their family treasures?"

"I can try." His eyes glinted. "You've got me playing sleuth now, have you?"

"I have to keep you away from the Floradora girls," she said with an absolutely straight face.

"Ha. As if you could. All right, I'll see what I can find out.

Flynn laid down his cards and grinned. "Read 'em and weep gentlemen," he said, displaying a full house. All around the table a groan went up as Tony gathered in the pot he'd won Playing cards in the basement at police headquarters was a time-honored tradition, a way to keep cool for detectives, police reporters, and even a stray prisoner or two. Tony had participated in many a session here, to trade stories or simply to pass the time, and he was very good. For one thing, none of the reporters present, not Fischel of the *Sun* or Brisbane of the *World*, had any idea that he had any other purpose but to while away a drowsy Saturday afternoon.

Neither did Devlin. That thought turned Tony's grin wolfish as he dealt out the cards. Devlin had yet to be invited to sit in on a game. Maybe it was because the consensus was that he'd refuse; maybe because of the distance between him and them of which Tony was all too aware. In any event, Devlin was out trying to track down the whereabouts of the missing paintings while Tony had followed the investigation in another direction.

"A black maria brought Maisie in this morning," he said, rif fling through his cards and then arranging them neatly, and the man sitting next to him jumped. He was small, in a rusty black Prince Albert coat and a shirt with a stained, wilted collar; engaged in a small business, the numbers racket called policy. He was a numbers runner, a small fish. Ah, but his boss, his and Maisie's, there was a big catch indeed. Frank "Horse-Face" Horgan, and if Tony was right, the investigation into Warren's death led straight to him. "Seen her lately, Willie?"

Willie fiddled nervously with his cards. For a man in his occupation he gambled poorly, betting high on losing hands and cautiously on good ones, and he was apparently not comfortable in his surroundings. All the result of drink, Tony thought dispassionately, reducing a formerly nimble-fingered card dealer to this. But then, he'd seen the effects of drink before. "N-no. Not lately," he stammered.

"Maisie?" Brisbane asked. "Who's she?"

"Prostitute," Tony said briefly, discarding a card. "She was an actress once. Maisie Duncan."

"Never heard of her."

"Which is why she turned pro." And it had been as a pro that Maisie had first met Joseph Warren, in, of all places, the Golden Harp, Horgan's saloon. "She was at the Harp when you were, wasn't she?"

"I disremember," Willie said, feigning a lack of interest as poorly as he bluffed at cards.

"Sure, you do. When you were a dealer there? Before the drink got to you."

Max Fischel looked up. "Are you on to something here?" he asked.

"Nah." Tony looked at his cards and then slapped them, facedown, on the table. "Nothing for the *Sun*, anyway. Just talking. If you gents will excuse me, it's time for Willie here to go back to his cell."

"Maisie ain't been around lately," Willie chattered, suddenly voluble, as Tony had suspected he would be. "Took up with some swell. Heard he bought her a fine house on Madison Avenue."

"Anyone we know?" Brisbane asked, looking up with interest.

Willie blinked. "Don't think so. Gee, Mr. Flynn." He turned huge, pleading eyes on Tony. "If you've got a drink on you, I'd be mighty grateful—"

"No drinking at headquarters, Willie. You know that." Tony rose and dragged Willie to his feet. "Another day, gentlemen," he said, and walked away, Willie in tow.

"But, gee, Mr. Flynn," Willie went on, lagging behind as much as he could. "Do I got to go back? You know how I hate that cell."

"You have to, Willie," Tony said patiently, holding open the cell door, set with a grate in its top half. "What do you think TR would say if he learned you were out, and him death on gambling?

"But it's small, a man can't breathe—gee, Mr. Flynn, if you could just get me a drink—"

"Do you remember the name of the swell Maisie took up with?"

"N-no."

From his inside coat pocket Tony took out a slim metal flask. "You're sure?"

Willie licked his lips. "Well—it might have been Warren."

"Oh?" Flynn toyed with the cap of the flask, Willie's eyes following his every movement. "How'd she meet him, Willie?"

"At the Harp, o'course. Mr. Flynn, if you'd just let me have a sip—"

"Where, Willie?" Tony said, the steel in his voice no longer quite hidden by his false affability.

"Gambling, Mr. Flynn. I—"

"Upstairs, Willie?"

"Yeah. Yeah, upstairs in one of the private rooms. Lucky Baldwin was there, too, and even Bet-a-Million Gates, and me dealing, and Mr. Horgan, he had some of the girls come up to keep them company."

"Did he, now." So far what Willie had said tallied with Maisie's story.

"Yeah. Maisie was pretty, then."

"I'm sure." Tony unscrewed the cap of the flask. "Did Warren go there often?"

"Yeah." Willie licked his lips again, his eyes avid, and then suddenly looked up at Tony. "If I tell you, will you give me a sip? Just a little teeny sip?"

"Depends on what you tell me." Tony raised the flask to his lips, pretending to take a long swallow. "Damn, that's good. Not much left, though," he said, and all at once Willie broke, seeming to crumble before Tony's eyes.

"I'll tell you, Mr. Flynn, I will. Mr. Horgan, he don't like us tellin' his business, but this ain't no secret. Warren came to the Golden Harp a lot and he was about as good a gambler as I am now. I was good once." He held out his hands, wrinkled and trembly. "Could palm a card or ring in a cold deck with the best of 'em. I swear to you, Mr. Flynn, I wish I'd never taken a drink in my life."

"I believe you," Tony said, and for once was absolutely sincere. "So Warren lost?"

"Uh-huh. A lot, and always thought he could make the losses good. He never did, though. Always just lost more."

"Did he pay Horgan back?"

"Nope. At first he did, but not later. Horgan even sent some men to rough him up, but it didn't do him no good. 'Course, Warren had to stop going there."

"When was that?"

"I disremember—last year sometime? Yeah. Last year, in the winter. Ain't seen him since."

Last year. *Damn*, Tony thought. The connection between Warren and Horgan wasn't recent. Still, if Warren had died owing Horgan money, that left something for Tony to look into. "Here," he said, and shoved the flask at Willie, because he was, at heart, a kind man. "But don't tell anyone where you got it."

"No, Mr. Flynn, that I won't. You're all right, for a bull," Willie said as Tony, stopping before Willie's cell, gestured to the jailor. "I won't forget this, Mr. Flynn, that I won't."

"Neither will I, Willie." Tony turned away, heading for the stairs, and only when he was well away did he allow a broad grin to cross his face. Some money lost at cards, some spent on cheap booze. Small investment, for what it had paid off. Joseph Warren had not been the upright citizen he'd appeared, and wasn't that interesting? And with this tie-in to Horgan, he thought, the captain might just be interested too.

Grinning, Tony took the stairs to the first floor two at a time to talk with Captain O'Neill and go on with the investigation. And what made today's discoveries even better was that he'd stolen a march on Devlin.

Sunday was quiet. Matt and Brooke attended services at All Souls' on Madison Avenue, and then took a drive by the river. Neither one, by unspoken agreement, discussed the case. On Monday Matt went off to work and Brooke got busy with the redecorating, when Mr. Eichhammer and his men came in to start painting the apartment. And on Wednesday, Uncle Henry's reply to Brooke's letter, asking about the museum's other trustees, finally arrived. "Essentially he's told me to mind my own business," she told her uncle Augustus that afternoon as they ambled along a gallery in the Manhattan Museum. "That what I want to know is not my concern and I shouldn't be investigating crime anyway."

Augustus was bent over, peering at a small canvas hanging among several larger ones. "Uh-huh."

"Uncle Augie, have you been listening to me?"

"Henry's getting stuffy," he said absently, fumbling in his inside jacket pocket for his glasses and then putting them on. "Not the best Millet's ever done." He leaned over the brass railing that ran along the wall at waist height to protect the paintings. "You can see his point."

"Who?" Brooke said, confused. "Millet?"

"No. Henry."

"I thought you were on my side in this."

"Maybe. You have to admit, Brooke, that what you're doing isn't done."

"Not done," she echoed.

"Not for a woman, or one of us."

"One of us! Honestly, Augie, you sound just like Aunt Winifred!"

Augustus straightened with a start. "I do, don't I?" he said guiltily. "I'm sorry, Brooke. I didn't mean to."

"I think you're more conventional than you let on."

"Shh! Don't let anyone hear you say that." He glanced around the gallery as if it were filled with his numerous acquaintances. "I have a reputation to maintain."

"Then help me, Uncle Augie. Do you know anything about the museum's trustees?"

"Those pillars of rectitude? No. Unless"—he glanced about—"you want to know who's keeping a mistress."

"Oh, for heaven's sake! That's not what I meant at all. I—"

"Because I heard something the other day, Brooke."

"What?"

"I heard a rumor that Warren had a mistress."

Brooke stared at him. "You're not serious."

He shrugged as they moved on to examine another painting. "It's nothing new."

"Yes, but since he was murdered, why haven't we heard about her before?"

"You're thinking like a cop, Brooke." He leaned forward, peering at the painting. "Try to remember that most people don't want their secrets known."

"I have to think like a cop," she said impatiently, secretly pleased at his comment. "It's the only way I'll find anything out."

"I suppose," he said, and with an apparent lack of interest moved on to another painting. "Now, this is worthwhile."

"What do you know about Mr. Warren you're not telling me, Uncle?"

"Nothing. At least, nothing that isn't already known." He glanced over at her. "Did you know that he painted once?"

"No," she said, genuinely surprised. "Was he any good?"

Augustus snorted. "If he had been, he'd have been an artist, not a curator."

"Oh. I suppose that's true. But I'd think that his training would have helped him in his work."

"I imagine it did. He made some fine additions to the collection. Nothing outstanding, but good, solid work."

"Do you know what works he acquired? Beyond the lost masterpieces, I mean."

"Some. The drawings in there"—he indicated an inner gallery—"were his acquisition. They were offered to the museum, true, and they're copies rather than the real thing, but he was the one to accept them and catalogue them. And a few other works. Manet, for one."

"I like his work," Brooke said. "So he was valuable to the museum?"

"Probably. It's possible Owen resented him for it." He glanced at her. "Not much of a motive for murder."

"You'd be surprised." Brooke stopped in front of a painting. "This is the Constable I told you about, Uncle. Look at the way he used light. It's just—"

"I've seen this painting before," Augustus said abruptly.

"Oh? Then you've been here already?"

"No, not here. Where?" His brow furrowed, and then his face cleared. "So that's what it is," he said softly.

"What?"

"Brooke, I saw this painting in a studio right here in New York."

"What? Then it was never really lost?"

"It never existed. I saw it being painted."

Brooke stared at him. "Do you mean—"

"Yes." Augustus's tone was grim as he turned back to the painting. "It's a forgery."

6

Coat slung over one shoulder by a fingertip, Matt trudged up the stairs at 300 Mulberry Street, ignoring the shouted questions from the police reporters across the street as well as the catcalls from the prostitutes who worked nearby. It had been a profitless day, spent with such noted agents of art as the Duveens and Mitchell Samuels of French and Company, none of whom claimed any knowledge of the lost masterpieces. All admitted to wishing they'd handled the works; but if they knew where the paintings had come from or where they'd gone, they weren't saying. It looked as if this avenue of the investigation was at an end.

The day was warm, though without the humidity of earlier days. Still, Matt was looking forward to going home, where there would be cool breezes from the park and he could relax. And if Flynn considered him a snob for such thoughts, let him. He didn't know where the hell Flynn had been all day, anyway. They'd both been present at morning roll call, but then Flynn had disappeared, to where, no one knew. So much for the feeling of partnership he'd felt with Flynn yesterday at the museum. If things kept on this way, he'd talk to the captain about a reassignment.

The detective bureau was, as usual, bustling. At one desk an officer sat, interviewing someone, whether a suspect or victim or offender, Matt didn't know. Another detective, tongue between his teeth and pen gripped firmly, was writing a report, while still others were grabbing their hats and rushing out to handle some recent crime. Flynn stood st the door of Captain O'Neill's office, and the sight made Matt frown. "Devlin," O'Neill said when he spotted Matt. "Come here."

"What?" Matt said, approaching them.

"In my office. Flynn's been tellin' me some interestin' things," he went on, sitting at his desk. "And close the door."

"What did you find out today?" Tony put in before Matt could say anything.

"Damn all." Matt ran a hand down his face. "I spoke with the art dealers I told you about, sir, and none of them know anything about the missing paintings. So they say."

"Forget about that for now," O'Neill said brusquely. "We might be dealin' with somethin' else."

"Oh?"

"Hear of a feller named Horgan? Horse-Face Horgan?"

"Yes, of course I have."

"Warren owed him money," Tony said softly. "Big money."

Matt stared at him. "How d'you know that?"

"My sources. When you've worked here as long as I have, you get to know people."

Matt's hands slowly clenched. "I see. So you've been investigating today."

"Yeah." Flynn tilted the legs of his chair back, thrusting his thumbs under his suspenders. "Found out some interesting things. Warren liked to gamble, and guess where?"

"The Golden Harp."

"Bull's-eye."

"You have proof?"

"Eyewitnesses."

"Who?"

"Can't tell you that." Tony pretended to look remorseful, without success. "I promised I'd protect them. Sorry."

"Associates of Horgan's?"

"Maybe. I also found out Warren kept a mistress."

Matt leaned forward. "Who?"

"A sometime actress who is now a prostitute for—guess who—Horgan."

"We want to get Horgan," O'Neill said before Matt, glaring at Tony, could say anything. "This just might do it."

Matt looked back at the captain. "I thought the idea was to catch Warren's killer."

"I think we have," Tony said.

Matt stared at him, his fists tightening. This was too much. He'd known Tony resented him, but to be made to look like a fool in such a way went beyond mere resentment. "Sir. With all due respect for Mr. Flynn's abilities, I'd like to request another—"

"Another day? You've got it." O'Neill rose. "I want Horgan. You two are going to get him."

"But—"

"And quickly. Well? What are you waiting for? Get to work."

Matt rose, looking at the captain for a moment, aware of Tony smirking beside him. "Yes, sir," he said, and turning on his heel, strode out of the room.

Tony sauntered behind him, grinning, hands tucked in trouser pockets. "Looks like we've got some work to do, partner."

"Partner?" Matt turned, lips compressed, hands knotted. "Since when the hell are we partners?"

Tony's eyebrows rose in mock surprise. "Since the captain assigned us to each other."

"Yeah?" Matt's eyes narrowed. For too long he'd held in his anger, hoping that Tony's resentment would ease, hoping they'd somehow become a team. With what had happened today, however, he had to face the fact that that would never happen. "Not what you wanted, was it?"

Tony's smile faded. "You want the truth? No. It's not what I wanted."

"Fine." Matt turned again, starting toward O'Neill's office. "Let's just tell the captain and get this over with—"

"And who do you think he'll assign this case to, Devlin? Who found out that Horgan's involved? Not you."

Matt stopped. "Dammit," he said, his voice low, for he was aware of the other detectives watching them. "This is my case."

"Mine too." Tony glared at him, his fists bunched as well. "And I'm not going to let some fancy society cop tell me how to do my job."

"Fancy society—hah." Matt's laugh was bitter at that, the last thing he'd ever expected to be accused of. "I know my job, Flynn. If you doubt it, just watch me."

"You can't solve this case without me, Devlin, and you know it."

"And you can't solve it without me," Matt retorted.

For a moment there was tense, tight silence as the two men glared at each other, their shoulders hunched and their faces thrust forward. "Hey, you gonna take it outside?" one of the other detectives called, anticipating a fight, and Matt stirred. "I'll work with you on this one," he said, his voice hard, and had the satisfaction of seeing angry color stain Flynn's face. "But after this I'm requesting a new partner."

"Fine by me," Tony said as Matt turned and stalked out of the detective bureau.

Behind him Matt heard Tony say something more, followed by raucous laughter, and his shoulders hunched again. He wanted nothing more than to go back into that room and plant a good one on Flynn's nose, but he knew that would only make things worse. Dammit, he didn't need this. He and Flynn would never work well together, that much was clear. When Matt asked to be reassigned, however, it would look as if he were the one with the problem, and not Flynn. Ordinarily such things wouldn't bother him, but on a force that had so recently been rocked by scandals and changes in leadership, how he was viewed by others mattered. He was the new man among a veteran force, and he had to prove himself.

One thing he knew though, he vowed, swinging down the steps of the building into the steaming, sweating street. This case was his. He would solve it if it killed him.

"Good evening, sir." Fuller had the apartment door open before Matt had even stepped off the elevator. "Mrs. Devlin and Mr. Low are in the library."

Matt made a face. He was tired and hot and grubby after his long bicycle ride uptown; discouraged, as well. The last thing he wanted was to face one of his in-laws. "Which Mr. Low?"

"Mr. Augustus, sir. May I take your hat?"

Matt paused as he pulled off his hat, and then shrugged. Augustus wasn't a bad sort. Not a worker, but then, with his income, he didn't have to be. At least he, unlike the other Lows, hadn't been shocked when Brooke had chosen to marry a policeman. "All right, Fuller," he said, resigning himself to his fate. "Tell them I'll be there in a moment."

"Yes, sir. And, sir?"

Matt, already heading down the hall toward the master bedroom, turned. "Yes?"

"A whiskey and soda, sir?"

For the first time in what felt like years, Matt's spirits lifted. "Good idea, Fuller," he said, and turned away.

A few minutes later, feeling marginally more human with his suit coat off and his hair slicked back, Matt walked into the library, being used instead of the parlor, which was being painted. At least, he noted, the bearskin rug was gone.

"Matt." Brooke rose from a leather chair and handed him a short crystal tumbler sweating with condensation. "You look as if you could use this."

"I could." Matt tossed back half the contents of the glass at one gulp, and then sank down into another chair, his legs stretched out. "Augustus," he said, nodding to his relative by marriage.

Augustus smiled, as if enjoying a joke he alone knew. "Matthew. Hard day?"

Matt shrugged, watching Brooke as she tucked her legs beneath her. There was something about her tonight, a kind of suppressed excitement, that made him suspicious. What had she been up to? "About the same as usual," he said, taking another sip.

"What's happening with the case?"

Matt shook his head. "Not much." Now was not the time to talk about his confrontation with Flynn. Damn, he'd been looking forward to telling Brooke about it, rehearsing in his mind all the way home what he would say. Not with Augustus there though. "It's possible that Warren's death isn't connected with the museum at all."

Brooke glanced at Augustus, who had suddenly begun to grin. "Do you want to tell him?"

Augustus waved his hand. "No, dear girl. He's your husband."

"But you discovered it."

"Tell me what?" Matt said, watching both of them from under half-closed lids.

"Matt, we found something out today." Brooke untangled her legs and leaned forward. "We were at the Manhattan, looking at the works Mr. Warren acquired, and Uncle Augie recognized one of them."

Matt finished his drink, the ice cubes clinking in the empty tumbler. "So?"

"Don't you understand? It's a painting no one knew existed before, but—"

"He recognized it?" Matt said, sitting up suddenly and staring at Augustus as the implications of what Brooke was saying hit him. "How?"

"I saw it being painted. And not by Constable."

"Holy God." Matt set down his glass on the marble-topped table. "Are you saying it's a forgery?"

Augustus's eyes gleamed. "It looks that way."

"A forgery." Matt rose, paced to the windows, and spun around. "Are you sure?"

Augustus shrugged self-deprecatingly. "I do know something about art, Matthew, and I do remember seeing this particular work in progress."

"Where?"

"In a studio in Greenwich Village."

"Greenwich—by who?"

"His name's James Carter Earle. He added the Carter when he started painting portraits, and moved to Washington Square. He's beginning to make a name for himself."

"How did you happen to see it?"

"Earle and I are old acquaintances, studied in Paris together. When he moved into the studio in Greenwich Village, I went to see it. This was last year sometime. Of course I looked at his works, and I saw this particular one. Very different from what he usually does, a landscape instead of portraits. But Earle has an unusual talent." Augustus leaned forward. "When we were students we would often have to copy paintings, to learn different types of brushwork and other techniques. Earle proved to be good at it."

"How good?"

"He could copy just about anything set in front of him, and you'd have a hard time telling it from the original. His own work wasn't so good. He never could seem to establish any style for himself."

Matt braced his hands on the back of the chair. "Do you think he could produce a work that wasn't a copy, but seemed to be by some other painter?"

"I'm sure of it. I understand the portraits he does are in the style of Sargent. John Singer Sargent, you know."

"Yes, I know. This painting you saw, the one that appears to be by—who is it?"

"Constable. English landscape painter. I was being nosy. I am sometimes, you know." Augustus shrugged. "There were several canvases stacked on the floor, and I looked through them. The one we're talking about was at the back, only partly finished. I made some sort of comment about it not being Earle's usual thing, and he got upset."

"Upset, how?"

Augustus shook his head. "I thought for a minute he was going to throw me out, he looked so angry. But then he got control of himself, said it was something he'd started as an exercise and put aside. He told me he had an appointment not long after that though, so I left."

"The same painting you saw today?"

"The very same."

"You'd testify to that?"

Augustus glanced at Brooke, his eyes twinkling. "Wouldn't that annoy Octavius? Yes. I'd testify to it."

"Holy God." Matt sank down into his chair again. "What about the other paintings?"

"We looked at them, Matt, but we just don't know," Brooke said. "But it looks suspicious, doesn't it?"

"Damned suspicious," Matt agreed, and suddenly grinned. "This is good work. I should put you both on the payroll."

"Of course, we'll have to find out more about Earle. We don't know what his connection was with Mr. Warren."

"Or that Warren knowingly bought forged works. But since the source of the paintings has been so hard to figure out . . ."

Augustus stretched. "It's easy enough to ship paintings to Europe and then send them back, if one wanted to."

"Is it." Matt looked at him. His grin had faded, though inside he was still filled with glee. This part of the case was his alone. Flynn had no part in it. "Could you see what you can find out about that?"

Augustus raised his eyebrows and regarded Matt over the top of his steepled fingers. "You're asking me to work, dear boy?"

Matt grinned. "Yes, Augustus. I'm asking you to work. Brooke."

Brooke looked up. "What?"

"I think it's time you had your portrait painted, don't you?"

"At a studio in Washington Square?"

"Yes."

Brooke's eyes gleamed. "Definitely."

"Upon my soul," Chandler Owen said, wiping his high forehead with his handkerchief. "Are you saying we have forged paintings in our collection?"

Matt nodded crisply. It was the afternoon after he'd learned about the forgeries, and he'd been quite busy since then. James Carter Earle had an apparently spotless record, at least so far as the New York police were concerned. What his reputation was in other cities was another matter; Earle had studied in Paris and had worked in Chicago and Philadelphia before coming to New York. If necessary, however, Matt would contact the police in those cities. Combined with Warren's death, the circumstance of a forged painting being found at the museum was simply too suspicious to be ignored. And, Matt thought, it was his lead alone to follow, since Flynn was busily investigating Horgan. "I know it must be a shock," he said, for Owen had gone first pale and then an alarming red, reminding Matt that he had a bad heart. "But I have a source who can identify one of the paintings acquired by Warren as a forgery."

"Upon my soul," Owen said again, and rose, pushing his office window open farther and taking a deep breath before turning back to Matt. "With all that has happened, we don't need this, but . . ." He straightened. "If there are forgeries in this museum, they must be removed."

Matt took out his notebook. "You must have methods of authenticating paintings, to avoid this kind of thing."

"Of course we do." Owen had recovered some of his composure as he sat back in his burgundy leather chair. "Besides having a highly trained staff, we have outside consultants to call on should we suspect a painting's provenance. History," he explained at Matt's questioning look. "Where it has been since it was painted."

"I see. And everything about the provenance of the lost masterpieces was in order?"

Owen shifted in his seat, clearly uncomfortable. "Well, er, no. The ones that truly were lost, the paintings everyone knew about, those we could authenticate. But the unknown works . . ."

His voice trailed off. "But the styles are quite distinctive. Our experts had no trouble agreeing on the artist in question. Now, see here, Devlin." Owen straightened again. "Doesn't that militate against forgeries? The different styles, I mean."

"Not if the forger is clever. So." He glanced at his notebook. "Some of the paintings weren't fully authenticated."

"Well . . ." Owen looked down at his hands. "No."

Matt nodded as he noted that down. "But Warren was satisfied?"

"We all were, Devlin. Even now you've offered no proof of what you've said."

"Who sold the museum the paintings?"

Owen's lips firmed. "I've told you before, no one knew that except Warren."

"So they didn't come through a reputable dealer. Look," Matt said as Owen hesitated. "Duveen and the other dealers have all denied dealing in those paintings, though they wish they had. And they all deny knowing the source."

Owen pursed his lips. "That doesn't surprise me. These dealers are all very competitive, you know."

"I realize that. But I don't think they were keeping things back from me."

The silence dragged on for a moment. "You're asking if I knew the paintings were forged. If they were."

Experience kept Matt from showing his surprise. He hadn't made such an accusation; for Owen to say such a thing implied a guilty conscience. "No, sir, I am not."

"No?"

"No. And I wouldn't expect you to tell me if you did. Yet." He allowed himself a brief smile, and had the satisfaction of seeing Owen shift in his chair again.

"I trusted Joseph's judgment in these matters," he said defensively. "He was the curator for paintings."

"I'm aware of that. But the entire museum is your responsibility, isn't it, Owen?" he said softly. "So if there are any irregularities, it would be on your head." And he wouldn't want them known, either.

"I've told you, Devlin." Owen's lips had set in that firm line again. "I know nothing of any forgeries. Now, unless you've proof of what you say, I am quite busy—"

"Are you acquainted with a painter named Earle? James Carter Earle."

"Earle?" Owen appeared perplexed. "Vaguely. He paints portraits of those aspiring to enter society, I believe. Candy-box portraits."

"Excuse me?"

"Unduly flattering ones, Devlin."

"And doing well at it."

Owen shrugged. "So?"

"Has he ever done any work for the museum?"

Owen frowned. "Such as?"

"Cleaning paintings, for example—"

"Oh, no, we have a firm to do that. No, I don't believe Mr. Earle has ever been employed by us in any capacity."

"Huh." Matt flipped his notebook closed. He could look at employment records, but he doubted he'd find anything. Earle wouldn't be listed for the simple reason that his work would have been secret. "Has he ever been in the museum?"

"I've no idea. I wouldn't know the man if I fell over him. Now." Owen rose. "I do have a lot to do, so if you'll excuse me?"

Matt looked at him a moment and then nodded, getting to his feet. "Rest assured that I am looking into this," he said gravely, and walked out of the office knowing that he had just unsettled Owen further. Good. Because something wasn't right here, and he was determined to find out what it was.

The outer office was empty. Matt collected his hat from the

hat stand and was about to leave, when Seaton came in. "Oh Mr. Devlin. You're still here?"

"Just leaving." Matt turned in the doorway. "Where would I find the records for people who have worked here?"

Seaton appeared shocked. "Oh, I couldn't let you see those sir. Not without asking Mr. Owen."

"Doesn't matter. I don't expect to find what I'm looking for anyway."

"What are you looking for, Detective?"

Matt paused in the doorway again and glanced at Owen's closed door. What he would ask was hardly a secret. "Whether a man named Earle has ever been employed here."

Seaton glanced quickly at Owen's door. "What did Mr Owen tell you, sir?"

"That he wasn't." Matt studied Seaton closely. "Was he?"

"Well . . ." Seaton looked at the inner office door again, and then rose. "I have some papers to bring to the statuary department, so if you'll excuse me."

Matt followed him out. "I have the feeling you know something you're not saying."

Seaton closed the outer office door. They were now in the gallery that adjoined the museum's offices. Here and there people wandered, studying the different groups of paintings "Look. Mr. Owen is my employer and I have to be careful what I say."

"So?"

His voice dropped. "I didn't want him hearing me telling you that Earle did work here."

"Did he. When?"

"Within the last year. But you won't find that in any records Detective."

"Why not?"

"Because none were kept on him."

Matt stared at Seaton, whose face was as devoid of expression as his own. "Owen told me Earle's never worked here."

"Then Mr. Owen lied, sir." Seaton looked directly at Matt. "Makes you wonder why, doesn't it?"

The following morning Matt walked into headquarters, carefully attired in one of his suits from Brooks Brothers, with a fob upon his watch chain and a malacca cane in his hand. The ensemble provoked some looks and a whistle or two when Matt walked into the detective bureau. He merely grinned and raised the walking stick in reply, his humor too good to take the catcalls seriously. After spending some time closeted with Captain O'Neill, he strolled out again, more purposeful. Let Flynn investigate whatever he wished. Matt had a lead of his own.

"Devlin," a voice called as Matt reached the front desk, and Matt turned. Flynn was walking toward him, his cuffs rolled back and the garters on his sleeves pushed up. By the look of his eyes, rimmed with red, he'd had little sleep the previous night, which probably explained his untidy appearance. "Hold on a minute."

Matt waited as Flynn approached. "What's up?"

"That's what I was going to ask you." Tony stopped near him, his voice low. "You looking into something on the case?"

"Could be."

"What?"

Matt shook his head. "Can't tell you that yet."

Tony's face darkened. "Dammit, Devlin, I'm your partner—"

"Are you?" Matt said, and the two men glared at each other. "I don't have time for this." He turned away from the desk. "If anything pans out, I'll let you know."

"Devlin." Tony's voice was hard, and Matt turned from

the doorway. "We both know this should have been my case."

"But it's not. So do yourself a favor. Stick to what you're doing, and leave me to my work." Matt turned and strode out the door. Behind him he heard Tony say something in Italian, bringing a grim smile to his face. Let Flynn have a taste of his own medicine. Maybe it was petty, but Matt was rather enjoying it.

Outside headquarters the victoria, which Matt usually hated using, waited. He climbed in and sat facing Brooke. "Well?" she demanded.

"The captain didn't like it, but he finally agreed it's worth a try."

"I should hope so! It shows that something was going on at the museum."

He shook his head as their carriage moved along Bleecker Street, toward Broadway. "You can't blame him too much, Brooke. Flynn's developing a theory that involves gangsters, and here I am, going after a society painter. If I were him, I'd prefer Flynn's ideas. Causes a lot less trouble."

Brooke regarded him steadily. "You've changed, Matt."

"Have I?"

"Yes. This time last year you would have been angry about the captain."

"Yeah?" Matt glanced out the window as the carriage turned onto Broadway and came to an abrupt, jolting stop. Traffic going in the other direction, carts and drays and cabs, was moving, if slowly, and the clanging of the trolleys was incessant. "Wonder what the holdup is? Yeah." He turned back to Brooke, shrugging. "I suppose I would have been. Guess I've learned a thing or two."

"Still, if Mr. Earle has something to do with the murder of

the thefts, he'll have to be investigated, Matt. No matter whose portraits he paints."

Matt grinned. "Now who's changed?"

"I'm only saying—"

"Last year you found it hard to believe that anyone in society could be involved in crime. That's better," he added as the carriage started again, though slowly.

"Not hard to believe. Just unlikely." She sighed. "I suppose I've learned some things, too. Oh, dear, look at that."

"What?" Matt glanced out again, to see a horse collapsed on the street, a not uncommon sight in New York in the summer. The driver of the wagon was standing over it, prodding it to get up. "That horse has had it."

"Yes. It hasn't always been fun, Matt."

"What? Oh. Getting involved in investigating, you mean. No, I know that." He held his hand out to her. "I meant what I said the other day. Spotting the forgeries was good work."

"Uncle Augie did that, not me."

"Maybe. But if you hadn't kept snooping around at the museum, we wouldn't know it."

"We still don't, Matt. Why would Mr. Earle put his career in such danger when he's becoming popular?"

"Money, Brooke. What do you think? I'm willing to bet that if we looked into his finances, we'd find he went through some hard times." He glanced out the window of the carriage. They were on Waverly Place now, leagues away in atmosphere from Mulberry Street. Washington Square itself provided a welcome spot of greenery in a congested area, and the great white marble arch dedicated to George Washington and designed by Stanford White was impressive. This section of the city wasn't quite as fashionable as it once had been, with many of the city's wealthy moving farther uptown, yet still it had a certain solidity and style. On the east side was a tall office building, housing, among other things, some of the classrooms of New York University; on the south side, a church. Graceful old brick houses lined the north side of the square, and it was in front of one of these that their carriage stopped. "Earle must be doing pretty well," Matt commented, glancing up as he stepped out. The top floor of the house had been renovated, with a window several times larger than the others dominating. Most likely it provided light to Earle's studio.

"He's become very popular," Brooke agreed as Matt helped her down. "If John Singer Sargent isn't available, that is."

"Are you saying Earle's second choice?"

Brooke nodded as they climbed the stairs of the house. "Yes, and that if you wish to be truly fashionable, you don't have your portrait painted by him. Though he actually does rather nice work. Flattering."

Matt let the brass door knocker fall once, twice. "Too much so?"

"No, he gets a good likeness, but—well, you'll see."

The front door was opened by a butler, who looked at them inquiringly. "Mr. and Mrs. Devlin," Matt said, handing him a card. "I believe we are expected."

The butler bowed. "Yes, sir. If you'll please come this way.'

"You did that well," Brooke whispered as they followed the butler up the stairs to Earle's studio.

"I do know how to ape my betters."

"Matt."

"Just joking." He smiled at her, though his face quickly turned serious again, reminding her of the purpose of this visit. Playacting as they were was rather fun, but Matt had apparently not lost sight of their real reason for being there. In the past year he had changed, picking up more of the manners and social graces that society demanded, and wearing his well-tailored clothes with a careless, almost insouciant air. One thing about him remained the same, however, and always would. He was a policeman, and everything else was secondary.

"Mr. Earle," the butler said, opening the door to the studio and releasing into the hall the distinctive odors of turpentine and linseed oil. "Mr. and Mrs. Devlin, sir."

A man clad in baggy trousers and paint-spattered smock stood before a huge canvas, large enough for a life-sized portrait. To the side a young woman stood on a platform, and behind the artist a man, probably her husband, lounged back in a chair, watching the proceedings.

"A moment, Gerard," he said, frowning. "No, come in, come in." This to Matt and Brooke. "I'm running late, but if you don't mind looking around for a few minutes, I'll be right with you."

"Oh, no, of course not." Brooke's voice was breathless, making Matt glance sharply at her. "I've always wanted to see a real artist's studio."

"And suppose he knows who you are?" Matt whispered as they strolled through the room, viewing canvases in various stages of completion. Most were portraits; here and there were a landscape or a still life that even to Matt's untrained eye appeared mediocre. Doubt flared within him. How could this man be the clever forger they suspected?

"He probably does. I'll just tell him I've never seen Uncle Augie's studio." She cast him a quick look, her eyes sparkling. "And it's quite true. Aunt Winifred calls it a den of iniquity and wouldn't allow me to go there."

"Is it?"

"Uncle Augie lives the way he chooses. Look." They had stopped across the room from Earle, still busily adding the final touches of his work, and they had a good view of it. The rather plump young woman standing on the platform, garbed in a gown of rich ivory satin, looked both uncertain and bored. "Do you see what I mean? About his style."

"Yes," Matt said after a moment. Earle had indeed captured a good likeness, and yet the portrait was subtly wrong. Gown and headpiece and jewels had been caught in precise detail, but the subject of the portrait appeared taller and slimmer than she actually was, and the slight sallowness of her complexion had been enlivened to appear fresh and flawless. Matt quickly revised his opinion of Earle's work, formed only a moment before. The man knew what he was doing. "He's not what I expected."

"Why? Doesn't he look like an artist?"

"I'm not really sure what an artist is supposed to look like anymore." But it was certain that Earle did not fit the popular conception of a man consumed by his art. He was a robust man apparently in his early thirties, tall, with broad shoulders and a barrel chest. Matt supposed some women would consider him attractive, with his full face and thick, dark hair. "I can see why he's so popular. Especially with the ladies."

Brooke cast a quick glance at him; he had the distinct impression she was biting back a smile. "Not your usual method of investigating, is it?"

"Shh." He looked at Earle, but the artist appeared oblivious, absorbed in getting the last detail of the portrait right. "I don't want him to know who I am yet."

"I'm aware of that, Matt."

He glanced at her, and then shrugged. "Sorry. I'm not used to playacting."

"This is hardly playing, Matt."

"No, not for me," he agreed, and out of the corner of his eye saw Brooke give him an annoyed look. "Looks like Earle is nearly ready for us."

Earle had stepped away from the canvas and was regarding it intently, his arms folded. A moment later he was joined by the subject of the painting and her husband, who proceeded to praise the portrait enthusiastically. After more conversation in the same vein, they allowed themselves to be escorted to the door by Earle. Hands on hips, he watched them leave, a small, scornful smile on his face. "New money," he muttered.

Matt cleared his throat, and Earle started, turning toward him and Brooke. "Mr. and Mrs. Devlin." His smile smoothed out as he crossed the room to them. "Do forgive me for keeping you waiting. *Enchanté*, madame," he murmured, raising Brooke's hand to kiss it.

Brooke didn't have to pretend to be flustered, though Matt had seen her handle far more intricate situations with aplomb. But then, this wasn't quite the usual social circumstance. "I'd like a portrait of my wife," Matt said directly. "We're told you're the man to see."

Earle shrugged self-deprecatingly. "I do what I can. But, come, madame. On the platform. We shall see what pose suits you best, no?"

Brooke took Matt's hand as she stepped up onto the platform. "Are you French, sir?" she asked.

"What?" Earle, studying her, frowned. "No. But I studied in Paris and I fear I picked up some of the mannerisms. Eh, *bien*." He shrugged, very Gallic, and it was all Matt could do to hold back a snort. If ever he'd seen a faker, this man was one.

"I do so admire your work," Brooke went on. "I couldn't help noticing that you sometimes choose different styles."

"Yes. I think we'll have you seated for the portrait. Yes. Holding a rose, I think. Like this." Pulling a rose from a crystal vase, he thrust it into Brooke's hand and then stepped back, studying the effect. "Yes, quite lovely. Have you thought about your ensemble?"

"I have an outfit from Paris, haven't I, darling?" Brooke beamed at Matt. "A divine pink gown."

"Mmm. Yes, that would do," Earle said, and in that moment Matt's estimation of his wife rose, while his respect for Earle, already low, faded. Not only did Brooke detest pink; it didn't suit her. "Mr. Devlin. Have you any thoughts?"

Matt cleared his throat. "Just so she looks pretty."

"Of course, of course. I will make a few sketches first. If you will sit there, madame?"

Brooke sank gracefully onto the tufted velvet ottoman, letting the rose droop across her clasped hands. "Like this?" she asked as Earle took up his sketch pad.

"Mmm. Yes. Like that."

"Am I allowed to talk?"

"Mmm. Until I tell you not to."

"Oh, good." She glanced quickly at Matt, who shrugged. This part was more her responsibility than his. "As I said, sir, I do admire your work. Particularly that you work in different styles. I saw one painting that quite reminded me of Gainsborough."

"Did you? No, turn your head the other way. There, that's good."

"Do you often do such work?"

"It is a talent of mine," Earle said absently, his fingers quickly creating a charcoal portrait of Brooke. He wasn't bad, Matt admitted, looking over his shoulder. The likeness was good, though he hadn't captured the essence that made Brooke more than just another society matron, her independence or her humor or her intelligence. "Since the time I began studying art, when we were set to copying the masters, I found I could mimic their different styles."

"But that is wonderful!" Brooke clapped her hands. "Darling, that painting I saw, that I liked so?"

Matt stiffened, alerted by something in her voice. "Which one was that, dear?"

"The landscape with the huge clouds—oh, surely you remember? It was at the Manhattan, an English artist. Not Reynolds—oh, I can't remember."

"Turner?" Earle said.

"No, no. I believe it began with a C, but I just can't think . . ."

"Constable?"

"Yes! Constable. Yes, that's it." She beamed at Earle, and Matt saw at last where she was going. "How clever of you to know."

"It is my job, madame."

"Yes, my wife quite admired that painting," Matt said. "Said it would look good over our mantel."

Brooke made a little face. "Well, it would."

"And I told you that we can't afford it."

Brooke pouted, making Matt want to laugh. She was quite good at this. "Well, I think it's mean of you, when you know I don't ask for very much. Unless." She brightened. "Mr. Earle, do you think you could paint something similar?"

"A landscape in the style of Constable?" Earle frowned absently. "Certainly. I've done so before."

Brooke shot Matt a look. "Oh, have you? But that would be lovely."

"I told you, dear," Matt said, trying to act the part of the heavy-handed husband, "that we can't afford such things on my salary."

"Oh, I believe you'd find me quite reasonable," Earle put in. "There. What do you think?"

Matt gazed down at the sketchbook. "You've earned your reputation, sir."

"Thank you." There was no trace of modesty in Earle's voice. "By the way, what is it you do?"

"For a living? Didn't I say?" Matt smiled. "I'm with the police."

7

"Did you see his face?" Brooke chattered as their carriage set off from Washington Square, retracing the route to Mulberry Street. "When you said you were with the police, he looked terrified."

Matt frowned. "Suspicious, maybe, but not terrified."

"Terrified." Brooke sat back, folding her hands on her lap in a satisfied manner. "And if that doesn't show he has a guilty conscience, I don't know what does."

"It's not proof, Brooke."

"Oh, proof." Brooke waved that off, still giddy from the last hour spent playing her role. "He's capable of painting in different styles, and he's done work for the museum. It looks clear to me. He's the forger."

"I agree with you, Brooke. He probably is. But until we have proof he actually forged those paintings and sold them to the Manhattan—"

"What kind of proof?"

"I don't know. Bills of sale, witnesses, small things like that." His voice was dry. Playacting had been rather fun, he admitted, but now that it was over, what did he have to show for it? "Things that can be admitted as evidence in court. Or would you care to see me arrest an innocent man again?"

Brooke quickly sobered. The year before, Matt had arrested her uncle Henry for murder, on insufficient evidence. It had been a bad time for both of them. "No, of course not. But now you've a suspect, Matt, that you didn't have before."

"Mmm. I know." And Owen too. "Why did Owen lie about Earle working at the museum?"

Brooke's eyes grew wide. "Do you think Owen is involved?"

"I think it's possible, yes. And I think we've just warned both of them that they're suspects."

Brooke sat back, pulling idly at the finger of her glove. "That might not be such a bad thing."

"Unless they destroy evidence."

"Matt, do you really think there'd be such a thing as a bill of sale for forged paintings?"

"Well . . . no. But there might be something on paper." He frowned. "I'll put men on both of them, Earle and Owen, to watch them. But I can't watch them inside their own homes."

"And after today they'll know I'm involved in investigating too."

"That probably wouldn't have stayed a secret for very long." He looked at her. "It means you'll have to be careful."

"Of course I will."

"I mean it, Brooke. If Earle's involved, he's already proved he won't hesitate to kill."

"If he's the killer." She paused. "Do you think he is?"

"I don't know."

"I don't either."

"There's something going on in this case. Flynn . . ."

"What about him?" Brooke asked when Matt didn't go on.

"Nothing."

Brooke glanced out as the carriage turned from Broadway onto Bleecker Street, and the tenements rose up to either side. "Matt, the other day, when Uncle Augie was at our apartment, you were upset about something."

"Nothing important."

She leaned forward, touching his knee. "Are you sure?"

"I'm sure, Brooke."

Brooke left her hand on his knee for a moment, and then sat back. "You're doing it again."

"What?"

"Shutting me out."

"It has nothing to do with the case."

"What is Flynn working on, Matt?"

"Something else."

"Even though he's your partner?"

"Yes, dammit!" Matt glowered at her, and then let out his breath in imitation of her mannerism. "Sorry. It's not you. It's . . ." He frowned out the window, crushing the brim of his brown felt bowler in his hands. "He's got his own work."

"What does Captain O'Neill say?"

Matt shrugged. "That it's a good lead and Flynn should follow it."

"And it doesn't include you."

"I don't have the sources Flynn does."

"Sources?"

"Let it go, Brooke."

She leaned forward. "Who is he investigating?"

"A gangster." Matt continued to look out the window, as if he didn't care very much. "Flynn has sources of information. He's been on the force a long time."

"But, Matt, you're good at what you do—"

"I told you I'd have to prove myself, Brooke." Matt frowned at his mangled hat and then put it on as the carriage came to a stop before police headquarters. "And I'm damned if I won't!"

"You will." She held out her hand to him as he rose, opening the door to the carriage. "Don't forget. You have sources, too."

Matt glanced down at her and grinned. "Yeah. Better than Flynn's."

"I should hope so!" Brooke sat back, watching through the carriage window as Matt took the stairs at headquarters two at a time. She should be going in there too, she thought, and then sighed. Her fight for acceptance in such a case would be even harder than Matt's. "I might as well forget about it," she muttered, and tapped on the roof of the carriage to signal the driver to move on. Matt might officially be the policeman in the family, but she was not going to let herself be left out.

Nothing of much importance appeared to happen in the next few days. Crime continued rampant, keeping the detective bureau busy, but not with Warren's murder. The men Matt had watching Owen and Earle reported nothing irregular; the two men apparently went about their daily routines as if nothing were amiss. Matt, hoping for some sign of guilt from either Earle or Owen, was disappointed but not discouraged. He was still working. So far he'd found no one but Seaton who could place Earle in the museum, and nothing had shown up in Warren's papers about Earle. Still, the connection was there, somewhere. And if Flynn was having any better luck with his own investigation, it didn't show. Something from outside was going to have to break for there to be progress made on the case.

It was well after midnight, several days after the visit to Earle's studio, when the telephone rang in the apartment at the Dakota. Matt, awakened by a rumpled, sleepy-eyed Fuller, pulled on a robe with alacrity and ran to the telephone; Brooke, struggling with her wrapper, was close behind, her heart in her throat. A telephone call at this time of night could mean only bad news.

"This is Devlin," Matt was saying into the speaker when Brooke reached him, his hair standing on end and the receiver grasped in his hand. "Who is this—Flynn?"

"Flynn?" Brooke said, startled.

Matt turned quickly to her, shaking his head for silence. "What? Yeah, I had men watching him. Why?"

"Watching whom?"

"He did? I'll be—why did he call you?" Matt listened for a moment. "Hell, I know, but this is my witness . . . No, I'll talk to him . . . Yes, dammit, I'm sure. Go back to bed," he said, and slammed the receiver onto the hook.

"Matt?"

"Earle tried to run." Matt pushed past her, into their bedroom, and she followed.

"What?" Brooke sat on the bed, watching as Matt hastily began to pull on a brown gabardine suit. "Where?"

"Don't know yet, but he was at Grand Central Station. He claims he had an important commission out of town, at"—he consulted his watch—"dammit, quarter past two in the morning? Looks damned suspicious."

"Yes." Brooke sat with her arms wrapped around her bent knees. "You're not going out now?"

"Of course I am." Matt ducked into the dressing room that adjoined their bedroom. "If Earle tried to run, it means we've scared him."

"But the time—"

"I know." He came out, smoothing down his freshly slicked-back hair. "Policemen have to keep odd hours."

"Will Flynn be there?"

Matt grunted, standing before the mirror to tie his tie. "Yeah. The man I had following Earle claims he didn't know how to get in touch with me, so he called Flynn."

"Well, at least Mr. Flynn called you."

"Yeah. Because he doesn't know anything about Earle." He shrugged into his jacket. "And he wants to find out."

Brooke followed him as he went out of the room again. "Let Fuller call for the carriage—"

"What, and wake someone else up? No. I'll walk."

"At this time of night? You will not. Fuller—"

"Yes, madam. I paged downstairs, and there's a cab waiting," Fuller said in the hallway.

"Thank you, Fuller," Brooke said, restraining herself from throwing Matt a triumphant glance. "You may go back to bed now."

Fuller cleared his throat. "If you'd like, sir, perhaps I could be of help?"

Brooke glanced quickly away, for fear she'd laugh at the blatant eagerness in Fuller's voice and the corresponding surprise on Matt's face. "No, thank you, Fuller," Matt said with admirable gravity. "Make sure everything's all right here."

"Yes, sir, that I can do," Fuller said, and stepping out into the vestibule, pressed the button to summon the elevator.

"Thank you." Matt gave Brooke a quick kiss. "Go back to bed," he said, and stepped onto the elevator.

"Back to bed. Heavens. As if I could sleep after that," Brooke said as the elevator door closed behind Matt.

"Is police work always so exciting, ma'am?"

"No, Fuller." Brooke turned, walking down the hall that led to her bedroom. "Very often it's just boring."

"If you say so, ma'am."

"I do say so," Brooke said, and let out her breath. "Oh, bother. I might as well try to sleep. You too, Fuller."

"If you're sure, ma'am?"

"I'm sure. Good night." Brooke closed the bedroom door behind her and walked to the bed. No, police work was rarely this exciting, and that was just as well; late-night telephone calls were nerveracking. She doubted, too, that she'd go back to sleep. Matt didn't appear to be facing danger, but that was always a possibility. Still, she couldn't help wishing, as she settled back against the pillows, that she, too, were on her way to Mulberry Street to question a suspect in a murder.

The heat of the day had abated, but it had left behind clamminess and an intense miasma of odors surrounding headquarters. The tenements were dark and quiet, leaving the neighborhood ghostly and strange. Inside wasn't much better, the gas lights giving off harsh, bright light and casting shadows everywhere. "Where is he?" Matt asked the desk sergeant.

"Down there." The sergeant jerked a thumb toward the stairs leading to the basement, making Matt grimace. If headquarters at night was unpleasant, the basement, where the cells were located, were likely to be unwholesome. "Flynn's with him."

"Oh, he is, is he," Matt said under his breath. "Thanks." He took the stairs at a lope. At the bottom he turned left, walking past the telegraph office, a hive of activity even at night, and the rooms belonging to the Third Precinct. From the cells, drunks and pickpockets, banco steerers and knockout-drop artists, and other miscreants, called out to him as he passed. Matt ignored them, focusing his attention, his energy, on the moment when he would confront Earle.

Earle was sitting in a chair in a room used to interrogate prisoners; the light from one electric bulb overhead was harsh and unforgiving. He looked up at Matt's entrance, his face blank.

Flynn, who perched on the corner of the table, one leg swinging idly to and from, was equally expressionless. "Well, Mr. Earle." Matt dragged a chair away from the table and dropped into it, legs crossed, gazing at Earle with great interest. "Planning to take a trip, I see."

Earle rose, planting his hands on the edge of the table. He was wearing a suit that Matt recognized as being of European cut, and he had yet to remove his homburg. "This is an outrage," he said, the Gallic mannerisms Matt had seen earlier gone. "I demand to know why I'm being held like this, like a common criminal."

"All in good time," Flynn said lazily. He glanced at Matt, and unspoken, unexpected communication flowed between them. "If I could have a word with you, Detective."

"Why? He giving you trouble?" Matt indicated Earle with a jerk of his head as he rose.

Flynn slid off the table and ambled over to the door. "Not yet."

"He'd better not, or we'll have to do something about it, won't we? What has he said?" Matt asked, the hard edge dropping from his voice as they reached the dimly lighted corridor.

"Nothing, yet. Claims he's got a commission out of town and that's why he was traveling. Devlin—"

"At two A.M.? Not bloody likely."

"Why are we holding him?"

Matt paused, and then made a quick decision. For better or worse, Flynn was his partner. He had to be informed as to what was going on. "There's evidence he's been forging paintings and selling them to the Manhattan," he said. Quickly he outlined what he had learned about Earle, and what he suspected about the museum's director. "I don't know if it had anything to do with Warren's death," he concluded, "but it looks damned suspicious to me."

Flynn let out a low whistle. "You sure do get around, Devlin. What'll we hold him on?"

"Material witness, to begin with. Possible fraud too. Based on that, we should be able to get a search warrant for his studio."

"Yeah. Not a bad idea." Flynn frowned. "I don't see how this links up with Horgan, though."

"Should it link up with Horgan?"

"I don't know." Flynn's voice lowered. "Maisie knows something, I'd swear to it, but she hasn't talked yet."

"And you haven't informed me of much of what she's said," Matt said dryly.

Flynn ignored that. "There's something there, though, Devlin. I think she's ready to spill."

Matt shrugged. "If there's a connection with Horgan, fine. It might be enough to get him off the street. But Earle's more likely to have to do with Warren. These aren't ordinary gangsters we're dealing with."

"Oh, I forgot." Flynn's face twisted. "This is a high-society crime."

To Matt's own surprise, he grinned at that. "Yeah. What I seem to keep running into. Come on. Let's go see what Earle has to say for himself. We'll go on as we started. He seems to like you more than me."

"Damn. I never get to be the bad guy."

"Huh," Matt said, and led the way back into the room, where Earle paced. "Sit down, Mr. Earle."

Earle glanced at him, eyes smoldering, but he sat at the table again. This time Matt perched on the corner of the table, leaning toward Earle, while Flynn sat with his chair tipped back and his legs crossed. "I demand to know why you're keeping me here against my will."

"Material witness to murder, for one," Matt said mildly.

"Murder! Hey, I've got nothing to do with that—"

"And fraud, Mr. Earle." Matt's voice had softened. "Specifically, forgeries."

Earle's mouth clamped tight. "I want to see my lawyer."

Matt didn't glance at Flynn, and yet he knew what he was thinking. Once a suspect asked for a lawyer, questioning him anymore was no good. "He wants a lawyer," he mused. "Must mean he's guilty."

The legs of Flynn's chair came down with a thud. "Now, Detective, we don't have proof—"

"If he's guilty, we've got to get it out of him, one way or another."

Earle had gone pale, but to his credit he sat straight and tall "If you lay a finger on me, I'll sue you—"

"Ha."

"—and how would that look to your society wife?"

Matt paused, genuinely angry. "My wife helped spot your forgeries," he said, his voice icy and controlled, somehow far more menacing than it had been a moment earlier. "You might as well tell us. We already know about it."

Earle crossed his arms over his chest. "I want my lawyer. I don't have to answer any questions without him. I know my rights."

"Hmm. Interesting. From experience?" Matt rose, a sardonic grin on his face. "All right, Earle, you'll get your lawyer. And we'll get the truth. Take him to a cell," he called over his shoulder to Flynn, and walked out of the room.

Flynn walked into the detective bureau a few minutes later "He's locked up," he announced, sitting down and stretching his arms out. The first light of dawn was beginning to penetrate into the large room, leaving it shadowy and ghostly "What are we doing here at this ungodly hour?"

"Earle tried to bolt." Matt was pacing back and forth, trying to think of ways to get Earle to talk, and not succeeding. "He knows something."

"I called his lawyer. We had to, you know."

"Yeah, I know." Matt stopped pacing and turned, gazing at Flynn across the room. The distance between them only emphasized their differences. "Are you with me on this? Because if you're not, I'll handle it alone."

Flynn tilted his chair back. "I'm with you. But I don't like being kept in the dark, Detective."

"Neither do I."

"Yeah? You've had every chance to go along with me on this one."

"It was my case to start with," Matt began, and then stopped, drawing a hand over his face. He was tired of the distance between him and Flynn, tired of the competitiveness. He wanted to prove himself, yes. But was working on his own the way to do it? "Seems if we share what we know with each other, we'd get this thing solved faster."

"Yeah?" Flynn's tone was frankly skeptical. "Mean to tell me you'd actually associate with someone like me?"

"What the hell does that mean?"

"Come off it, Devlin. Since you walked in, you've acted like you think you're better'n all of us just because of who you're married to. And you're not." The legs of Flynn's chair banged as he straightened up. "You didn't come on this force a cop walking the beat—"

"Not here, no."

"—and you didn't work your way up from the streets to make detective, neither. But here you are, some man brought in from outside, thinking you can just come in and take over, and you can't. You haven't earned it."

Oh, he'd earned it, Matt thought, but knew that he'd never convince Flynn. "If you feel that way," he said very softly, "then ask for another partner."

"Don't think I won't," Flynn shot back. "And don't think you'll get anyone else to partner with you, neither. You're not wanted here, Devlin." His gaze was steady, hostile. "Go on back to Fifth Avenue, where you belong."

Matt couldn't help it; he let out a laugh. If there was anyplace he didn't belong, it was in the mansions that lined Fifth Avenue. "Central Park West, actually," he said, knowing it would anger Flynn more, and had braced himself for a further outburst, when the door to the detective bureau opened.

"Flynn. Devlin. So you are here." Captain O'Neill stared at them from the doorway. "What the divil's goin' on? Got a hoity-toity lawyer outside, shoutin' about a false arrest."

Matt and Tony exchanged quick glances. "If we could go into your office, sir?" Matt said, crossing the room.

"All right, all right," he grumbled. "The divil of it is being told by a lawyer that the case is broken. Is it?"

"Not yet, sir." Matt and Tony stood together before O'Neill's desk. "The forger I told you about tried to bolt town last night, so we brought him in."

O'Neill leaned back in his chair. "He admittin' to forgery, then?"

"Not yet, but—"

"And Owen over at the museum doesn't know anything about him, does he?"

"No, sir," Matt said after a moment, startled by O'Neill's knowledge. "At least, so he claims."

"So you're saying Owen's a suspect too? A fine, upstandin' member of the community like him? Oh, sit down, sit down." He waved his hand at them. "Hurts my neck lookin' up at you. Now. You've made a thorough botch of it, both of you."

Matt and Tony both began to protest at once, and O'Neill held up his hand. "You, Flynn, haven't found anything linking the murder to Horgan."

"No, sir, but I'm close," Flynn began.

"And you." O'Neill glared at Devlin. "Arrestin' a society painter for travelin' to paint someone's picture. You know how that makes us look?"

"I told you about him, sir," Matt said with a calmness that was admirable under the circumstances.

"And no proof."

"Sir, if we got a search warrant—"

"On what grounds? No, Devlin, this arrest's shaky. Shaky. The entire case is."

"Sir, Earle looks suspicious," Flynn said, making Matt glance at him in surprise. "As far as Horgan goes—"

"No proof there either, is there, Flynn?"

"I'm working on it, sir."

"Not anymore, you're not."

Heavy silence fell over the room. "What do you mean?"

"I mean you're off the case. Both of you."

"What?"

"You can't take us off," Matt protested. "Not when we're making progress—"

"I can, and I will. Joseph Warren was killed by a burglar, but do I see you findin' the right man? No. All I see is you two goin' out on wild-goose chases, and I'm taking heat for it, that I can tell you."

"From whom?" Matt asked.

"We don't have the time to fool around with this anymore. There's other cases waitin' and people are wonderin' if we're just sittin' around scratching our backsides instead of workin'."

"But—"

"The commissioners want us to show results. These aren't

results, Detectives." The captain rose. "As far as I'm concerned, this case is closed."

"But—"

"It's closed, and that's final." O'Neill pulled some papers on his desk toward him. "Good day, gentlemen."

"Captain," Matt began, and O'Neill looked up.

"Out of my office, Devlin," he said very, very softly. Matt paused and then turned. There was no hope for it. As of this moment, he and Flynn were no longer investigating Warren's death.

8

"Someone got to him," Tony said bluntly.

"Strong accusation," Matt said mildly. Morning had come to Mulberry Street, and the tenements steamed in the warmth of the rising sun. Women hanging out laundry called across alleys to one another, while those who had spent the night in the basement cells were slinking away. Matt and Tony were sitting on the stairs of headquarters, drinking coffee from thick white mugs, and eating bagels from the bakery down the street. Matt had never had one before, and was finding it a novel experience.

Tony snorted as one of last night's detainees passed him, garbed in a purple satin gown and with a coiffure of jet-black hair that had apparently defied imprisonment. "Hey, Poochie," he called. "You in again?"

Poochie started and turned, and Matt saw, to his astonishment, the beginnings of a beard on his chin, incongruous among the powder and the rouge. "I'm just trying to make a living," Poochie complained, taking the skirts of his gown in his hands and spreading them. "This ensemble will never be the same."

"Tres attractive," Tony said, deliberately mispronouncing the French. "See you later, Poochie."

Matt stared after Poochie as he scurried away. "That was a man?"

"Yeah. He gets picked up for solicitation every now and then. Usually when one of his customers finds out he's not a woman." Tony shook his head, taking a sip of coffee. "And to think that we saw it on Mulberry Street."

"Yeah," Matt said blankly, and let out his breath, his mind returning to more important topics. "You really think someone got to O'Neill?"

Tony shrugged. "Only thing I can think of. And it wouldn't be the first time either."

"Huh. You're admitting there're problems in the New York force?"

Tony's dark skin reddened. "I've never denied there were some bad apples. I'm just not sure the problem's being solved by bringing in outsiders."

Matt waited a moment before speaking. "Meaning me."

Tony shrugged again and took a sip of coffee. "All I know is, you knew where you were in the old days. You knew who you were working with."

"Thieves and bullies." Matt rubbed his finger along his mustache. "At the moment, looks like you and I are the outsiders."

"Yeah." Tony looked down at the ground, his hands loosely clasped between his spread knees. "So what do we do now?"

"I don't want to drop it." Matt stared at him steadily. "Do you?"

"No." Tony frowned. "But, remember, I've been here longer'n you. I know how things work. If we go against the captain, we're asking for trouble."

"It's no different anyplace else."

"So—"

He was interrupted by the harsh sound of a window slamming open, followed by a high-pitched yell. "Hi-yi-yi! Come here, Jake, I need you!"

"TR in full war cry," Tony said as the window banged shut again, and he and Matt exchanged grins. Among TR's eccentricities was his habit of calling out the window like a cowboy to summon Jacob Riis or Lincoln Steffens, the two reporters who formed what had been called his Kitchen Police Board, from the press shack across the street. "Wonder what's up."

"That's it." Matt stood abruptly. "TR. Of course."

Tony peered up at him. "What are you talking about?"

"Don't you think he'd want to know what O'Neill's done, and why?"

"Hell, Devlin, we don't have any proof—"

"No, but you know as well as I it's damned suspicious. Solving Warren's murder was a high priority, and now it's not. Someone got to O'Neill."

Tony frowned, looking troubled, and then rose. "Yeah. Hate to admit it, but—yeah." He looked at Matt curiously. "So you want to stay on it?"

"Yeah. Don't you?"

"Yeah."

"Good. Let's go see TR, then."

"And this is our library," Alma Cartwright said, leading Brooke into a small, dusty room filed with crumbling leather-bound volumes. I'm afraid everything is old, but it's the best we can do."

Brooke nodded, glancing around the room. "With all the ladies who belong to the league, though, there should be more income."

"It's not the women who control the purse strings, Mrs.

Devlin, as you no doubt know. I'm afraid many of our city's leaders don't see any worth in what we're doing. Nor does Tammany Hall. Better for them if the voter stays uneducated and votes the straight Tammany ticket."

Brooke nodded, seeing the point. "And of course they don't support women's suffrage."

"Dear me, no! That's the worst heresy," Alma said, though she smiled. She was a small, plump woman with iron-gray hair and rimless pince-nez spectacles affixed to her nose. "This is challenging work you're taking on, Mrs. Devlin. If"—she paused delicately—"you are taking it on."

Brooke returned her look levelly. She could well understand Alma's doubts. Located on Stanton Street, not far from the Bowery, the Voter Education League was not in the safest of neighborhoods, nor did it deal with a fashionable clientele. While most ladies in society claimed to help such worthy concerns, their contributions were usually of the monetary sort. To give of their time was another matter altogether. "I'm quite up to it," Brooke said. "If you'll show me where to start?"

A short time later Brooke sat at an old, scarred desk, carefully studying the material Mrs. Cartwright had given her. She needed to educate herself before she could educate voters. And what she read was fascinating. She learned that the Society of St. Tammany had been founded a century before, by, of all people, Aaron Burr. By lending a helping hand to the waves of Irish arriving during the potato famine, Tammany had won loyalty and power. She learned that the police, who ran the city's elections, had, in the past, allowed many abuses, including repeat voting, in order to get Tammany's men in. And she learned that though reform was popular among the higher classes and the rest of the state, TR's campaign to enforce the Sunday closing laws on saloons had made him unpopular with both Dick Croker, boss of Tammany, and Boss Platt, a powerful Republican leader. Until recently Brooke had had little interest in politics, but her marriage had made her aware of certain realities. She was at last beginning to have a grasp of what Matt faced in his job, and not just in enforcing the law. She couldn't wait to get home, to discuss her newfound knowledge with him.

A figure loomed up before her, blocking the light from the window. Startled, Brooke looked up. The man she saw standing at her desk was only of medium height, and yet he seemed to fill the room. His shoulders were broad, his chest wide, and his suit of charcoal-gray worsted had obviously been tailored for him. In one hand he held a gray felt derby; in the other, a rosewood walking stick topped with a brass horse's head. Belying his fashionable image, however, was his face; his eyes were small and close-set, and his nose had obviously been broken more than once. "You're new here," he said, his smile displaying slightly crooked white teeth, and in his voice Brooke caught just a hint of a brogue. "A pleasant sight on such a dark day."

"May I help you?" Brooke asked, standing, in hopes of feeling less at a disadvantage. If this were an example of the League's usual client, Brooke's job was formidable indeed.

"That you may. May I introduce myself? Frank Horgan, at your service."

Frank Horgan. Now, where had she heard that name? "Mrs. Devlin." Brooke held out her hand, and was startled when Mr. Horgan bent to kiss it. Disconcerted, she drew away. "Yes, I— I just started today."

"Good. Good. I've been telling Alma that she needs more help. She does too much herself, the poor woman."

"Poor woman?" Alma bustled out from the back office. "And what nonsense are you saying now, Mr. Horgan?"

"Ah. Good morning, Mrs. Cartwright." His eyes, Brooke noticed, were dark and still. "A wee contribution for the cause."

Alma stared at the thick envelope Horgan held out to her. "Thank you, Mr. Horgan," she said, making no move to take it. "Of course, this in no way obligates us to advise people to vote for Tammany."

"Of course not, ma'am." His eyes gleamed with an emotion Brooke couldn't quite identify. Mockery, perhaps, and beneath that, anger. She suddenly felt chilled. "Do use it as you see fit. Of course, if the Tammany men happen to be the best for the job—"

"In that unlikely event, Mr. Horgan, I will still advise the voters to make up their own minds."

"Ah, you're a hard woman, Alma Cartwright." He raised his hat and strode to the door. "Mrs. Devlin. A pleasure to meet you. And I'll win you over someday, Alma," he said, and went out.

"Over my dead body," Alma muttered, glaring at the door.

"Good heavens." Brooke sank into her chair, her legs shaking slightly. Now that Horgan was gone, light and air and space had returned to the room. "Who in the world was that?"

"Better for you if you don't know, my dear." Alma sighed. "But since you'll be working here and he's likely to come around from time to time, I suppose you must. That was Frank Horgan."

Brooke waited. "Yes, so I gathered," she said, when no more information was forthcoming.

"Mr. Horgan is involved in some, shall we say, unsavory activities, the least of which is that saloon he runs. He is also a Tammany enforcer."

"Enforcer?"

"He gets the vote out for Tammany by whatever means necessary. At least, his gang does."

"His gang—he's that Frank Horgan? But, good heavens.

The man's a criminal." And what Matt would think when he heard about this, she didn't dare imagine. "How can he still be walking the streets?"

Alma's glance was pitying. "Really, Mrs. Devlin, and you married to a policeman. Don't you imagine Mr. Horgan has powerful protectors?"

"Good heavens. Of course he would," Brooke murmured. "Mrs. Cartwright, is he the kind of client we'll be dealing with? Because if we are, my husband won't approve—"

"And here I thought you were for women's equality."

"I am learning to pick and choose my fights, ma'am." Brooke pressed her lips together as she gazed about the room. She'd been so excited about the prospect of actually doing some good. In light of her partnership with Matt, however, this was not worth it. "And my husband will not want me dealing with known criminals."

"You disappoint me, my dear. I'd thought you were more independent than that. But you needn't worry," Alma went on before Brooke could protest. "We see very few like Mr. Horgan. Our people are generally just poor and uneducated. Unless that would bother your husband too?"

Brooke stared back at her. "In that case, ma'am, it's worth standing up for."

"Is it? Good." Alma smiled in a lightning-swift change of mood. "I do apologize for being so cross, Brooke—I may call you Brooke?—but Mr. Horgan has that effect on me. One can only be grateful Miss Warren wasn't here."

"Miss Warren? Linda Warren?"

"Why, yes. Oh, of course, you must be acquainted with her. She's not at all fond of Mr. Horgan, not after what happened with her mother—but there, I do not gossip! In any event, it's past history. How are you getting along?"

"What? Oh, well enough," Brooke said, her mind spinning. What did Frank Horgan have to do with Sylvia Warren?

"Good. If you have any questions, please feel free to ask," Alma said, and whirled back into her office, leaving Brooke to wonder just what that had been all about.

When informed that one of his captains had forbidden any more work on a case in progress, TR reacted as Matt had expected him to. Andrew Parker, his enemy on the board of commissioners and the commissioner in charge of the detective bureau, was behind this, he fumed, and, roaring with indignation, summoned O'Neill to his office. He then proceeded to give O'Neill a good dressing-down, albeit without Matt or Tony present. When it was over, O'Neill left TR's office, redfaced and considerably chastened, and Matt and Tony were back on the case. They had also just made themselves a powerful enemy. O'Neill was not likely to forget what they had done.

"So, tell me what you've got on Horgan," Matt said after the dust had settled. He and Tony were sitting on opposite sides of the desk, reports and other papers spread about them, drinking coffee and eating sandwiches.

"Damn all. Not enough to link him with Warren's death— at least not yet." Tony leaned forward. "I have a source who can make the connection between Warren and Horgan, but that's about all."

"What's the connection?"

"She was Warren's mistress. Before that, she was Horgan's." Tony took a bite of his corned beef sandwich, and Matt let out a low whistle. "Got the feeling she knows more than she's telling, but I haven't got it out of her yet," he said around a mouthful of food.

"Where is she now?"

"Working in Ma Meecham's cathouse. Which, as you know, is owned by—"

"Horgan," Matt said grimly. "How did she come to be Warren's mistress?"

"Apparently Warren saw her at the Golden Harp."

Matt leaned forward, surprised. "Warren frequented the Golden Harp?"

"A lot of society types frequent low dives and bars," Tony said, imitating Matt's tone, but without any malice. Something had grown between them in the last few hours, a bond that was unacknowledged, but nonetheless real. Both were stubborn cops who hated to be told to drop a case for political reasons; both were now in danger of being outcasts, because their need to work on the case had brought them to TR. "It's called slumming."

"Huh." Matt ran a finger across his mustache. "I have heard of it, believe it or not."

Tony flashed him a quick grin. "Yeah, well, it was something Warren liked to do, and if you knew his wife . . ."

"Haven't had the pleasure, though Brooke knows her."

Tony picked up the other half of the sandwich, frowning a little. "How much does she know about the case? Your wife, I mean."

"Everything I do. Hell, how do you think I found out about Earle and the forgeries?" Matt allowed himself a tight smile. "I have my sources too."

"Yeah," Tony said after a moment, grudgingly. "Looks like we're going to need all our sources on this."

"So." Matt leaned back in his chair, hands linked behind his head. "We have a victim who bought paintings that he may or may not have known were forged. We know he needed money, because his widow had to sell her house and is living in a rented flat. We have those same forged paintings being stolen. Why?"

"To hide the fact they were forged."

"Probably," Matt said, though his question had been rhetorical. "Now. Who wouldn't want that fact to get out? Warren, of course—"

"But he's dead, so he wasn't the one who wanted to keep the forgeries secret."

"Unless he was going to reveal them. We have a museum director who disavows any knowledge of the forger, and his secretary, who claims Earle has done work for the museum."

"Owen knows about the forgeries."

"That'd be my guess, yes. So." Matt rose and began to pace, the remnants of his sandwich lying forgotten in its butcher paper. "Owen arranges for the museum to buy forgeries—"

"Why Owen? Why not Warren?"

"Why Warren?"

"Because he needed money." Tony leaned forward. "Get the museum to put up the money for forged paintings, more than they're worth, and split the profits with the forger."

"Of course," Matt said softly, dropping back into his chair. "He was the curator of paintings. Who'd doubt his word? And since most of the paintings have since been stolen, there's no proof they were forged. They could be genuine."

Tony snorted. "Doubt it. I'll tell you something else." He balled up the butcher paper his sandwich had come in and tossed it, overhand, into a wastebasket across the room. "Warren owed Horgan money."

Matt stopped pacing and turned to look at him. "So you've said. How?"

"From gambling."

"Did he pay him back?"

"Not all of it. Look, this could be just coincidence, Warren and Maisie—"

"Maisie?"

"The mistress. Could be coincidence."

"Too many coincidences. I don't like it."

"Yeah," Tony said after a moment. "Horgan could have handled fencing the stolen paintings."

"Huh." Matt nodded. "Good point, and no way to find out. None of the art dealers knows what happened to the paintings, or if they do, they're not saying."

"I'd say we have a few things to look at. Warren's finances, for one." Tony ticked each item off on his fingers. "Did he get any unexpected payments, and if so, when? And where did it go? The same for Earle."

"Who six months ago was struggling to make a living in Greenwich Village."

"And now is a society painter on Washington Square. Finally, Horgan." He grimaced. "Tracing Horgan's money is next to impossible."

"Then let's not touch him yet. He's a pro. He'll have covered himself. It's the amateurs who probably messed up somewhere."

"So we find what we can on Warren and Earle?"

"Chandler Owen too. And Charles Seaton."

"Who?"

"Owen's secretary. There's something off about him."

"Okay." Tony leaned back. "Plenty to keep us busy."

"Yeah." Matt rose. "Look. Why don't we split it up? We've been working fine that way, as long as we keep each other informed."

"I go downtown, and you go uptown, you mean?"

"Something like that. A way uptown." Matt retrieved his

hat from the stand. "Morningside Heights, as a matter of fact."

"What's up there?"

"Warren's widow. I want to go back to the beginning on this and find out all I can about Warren."

"And I'll talk with Maisie." Tony stood, pulling on his jacket. "Looks like we'll have to raid Ma Meecham's again."

Matt grinned. "My sympathies," he said, and went out of the office.

Sylvia Warren herself opened the door to Matt sometime later. Though she was conventionally dressed in a black gown, her cheeks were flushed. On seeing him she looked startled, but quickly smiled and held out her hands. "Mr. Devlin," she said. "Why, how good of you to call. Have you come to tell me about the progress being made to catch my Joseph's killer?"

Matt gently pulled his hands away, startled by this greeting. "Among other things, ma'am. I wasn't certain you'd remember me."

"I remember just everythin' about that terrible day. But, there, I know you were just doin' your job, telling me of my Joseph's death."

"Yes. And I'm sorry for it, ma'am." Matt stood, hat in hand, ill at ease in the overstuffed, overly warm room. Brooke had described the apartment to him, with its heavy furniture and profusion of knickknacks, but it hadn't prepared him for the reality of it. He feared that if he so much as turned around, he would knock down a Dresden shepherdess here, or a crystal picture frame, there.

"There, now, the worst of it is past. Do please sit down. I was about to take tea, but I imagine a gentleman like you would like something stronger?"

Matt sat gingerly on a spindly chair of red velvet and gilt, out of place among the massive oak and mahogany pieces, and yet somehow very much a part of it. "Thank you, ma'am, tea would be fine." His gaze sharpened as his eyes lit on a glass on the marble-topped table next to him. It was half filled with an amber fluid. "I am sorry. Did I interrupt something?"

"What?" Sylvia glanced at the glass, and some of her color faded. "Oh, dear me, no. I had a caller earlier and my maid didn't clear away. Nancy!" she called, her voice sharp. "Where is our tea? And do take that glass away."

"Yes, ma'am." Nancy came in, carrying a tray. Her face was expressionless, though she frowned a little when she picked up the glass. So. Mrs. Warren was apparently receiving other visitors, male, to judge by both the contents of the glass and the maid's reaction. But then, Sylvia didn't strike him as the kind of woman who would be long without male companionship.

"We've made some progress in the investigation," Matt began when Nancy had left the room, "and we have some questions as well. I assume Mr. Owen's kept you informed?"

"Chandler Owen?" Sylvia paused, her teacup halfway to her mouth. "Why, I haven't seen him in weeks. Should I have?"

"Not necessarily." For politeness's sake, Matt sipped his tea, and then placed cup and saucer on the table. "Mrs. Warren, the questions I have to ask are difficult, but bear with me. There is a reason for them."

"I'll be happy to answer, Mr. Devlin, if it will bring Joseph's killer to justice."

He nodded, taking out his notebook. "When someone is murdered, we usually have to look at the victim to find out why." He looked up at her, his gaze level. "Was Mr. Warren having financial difficulties?"

"Now, how would I know a thing like that? Really, Mr. Devlin, it's hardly your concern—"

"Forgive me, ma'am," Matt broke in. "But it seems to me you

would not have given up your home and moved so far uptown unless you had to. There are other ways I could get this information." Matt's voice lowered. "From your husband's friends and business associates, or from his bankers. I think, however, it would be better coming from you, ma'am. Unless you want to be the center of gossip."

Sylvia took a sip of tea, and then slowly and quite deliberately set the cup in her saucer. "My compliments, sir. A very neat threat."

"Is it? My apologies. I didn't mean to imply one."

She cast him a quick look, her eyes unreadable, no longer the coquettish woman who had met him at the door. "You have deduced that Joseph had financial trouble."

"Yes."

"Oh, very well." She raised her cup and set it down again. "Now, it isn't really a secret. Ask anyone, they can tell you." She grimaced. "Most likely they will. But, yes,Mr. Devlin. I was stunned when Joseph died and there was hardly enough money to bury him, let alone keep up the Fifth Avenue house. It's why Linda and I moved here. And why Linda took a job." Her voice grew bitter. "We are not accustomed to such things."

"You had no idea of this?"

"None."

"Do you have any idea where the money went? I'm assuming there was a considerable bit of it."

Sylvia glanced away, toward the bedroom, and then looked back at him. "There was, from both our families. Gone, now, all gone." She rose and went to a window. "At least I have a fine view of the Hudson from here."

Matt waited for more. "Yes, ma'am."

"Joseph had other women," she said abruptly. "That was no secret, either."

"I'm sorry, ma'am."

"Oh, don't be." She waved a hand in negligent dismissal. "It wasn't surprisin'. Well, maybe at first, but I've grown up."

It was a different attitude than the one that Matt had grown up with. "Are you saying his money went to these other women?"

"A good bit of it, I'm sure." She turned to face him. "How much, I don't know."

"Mmm-hmm." Matt noted that down. A mistress could be expensive, and yet Matt doubted that Warren's women had taken all his fortune. "Did Mr. Warren have investments?"

"Now, gracious, how would I know that? He never discussed business with me. We had some fine paintings, of course. Gone, now."

"Then you don't know where the money went."

Sylvia faced him steadily. "No, sir, I don't. That's a secret Joseph took to his grave."

"No one knows?" Matt said sharply. "Not even his bankers?"

"Why does this matter, sir?" She paced toward him, hands on hips. "You are asking some very personal questions, and I don't like it."

"No, ma'am." He looked up at her imperturbably. "However, we need to know about anything unusual that happened in your husband's life, anything that could point to why he was killed."

"He interrupted a robbery."

"So it appears." Matt rose. Sylvia's shoulders were set, and her face was severe. If she knew anything, she wasn't about to tell him, not when her reputation was at stake. That much was clear. And that meant he'd done all he could here. For now. "Thank you, ma'am. I hope I won't have to bother you again."

"Find my husband's killer, Mr. Devlin," she said crisply, holding the door to the apartment open for him. "Then I need not be bothered by any police again."

Matt hesitated, and then put on his hat. An odd, and hostile, thing to say. "Good day, ma'am," he said, and went out. He would be back. Until he learned everything there was to know about Joseph Warren's life, he would have to keep coming back.

Located on Fifth Avenue, its high stone walls steeply slanted, the Croton Reservoir was a popular place to stroll on a warm summer's evening. The stone paths that circled the man-made lake were crowded tonight, but in the way of city dwellers, most pretended they were alone. "So that's how things stand," Matt concluded, stopping and standing at the railing. The sun was low on the horizon, and its light reflected on the dark, still surface of the broad expanse of water.

"Everything still seems so confused." Brooke stopped as well, taking a deep breath. "I never cease to be amazed by this place. I feel almost as if I'm in the country."

Matt's smile was wry. "Hardly," he said, twisting his head to look, far, far down, to the street, and the traffic that continued unabated. "Not with all the traffic and noise. And"—he gestured toward the other people who crowded the paths—"all these people."

"I suppose." She turned and they began walking again, the rectangular stretch of water to their left, the railing to the right. The promenade offered spectacular views across the city. Looking north, Brooke could see the tops of the trees in Central Park; south, the tops of the new concrete skyscrapers that towered over everything. Built in the Egyptian style, the reservoir was a familiar landmark in the city. It was also scheduled to be replaced in a few years. New York was changing. She would miss this respite from the noise and the traffic and the dirt when it was gone.

"So what do you do next?" she asked, forcing her mind back to the topic that had dominated their conversation all evening.

"Look into Earle's finances. We're still holding him on suspicion of fraud, but unless we get proof, we'll have to let him go."

"I wish we had some way of proving he's a forger."

Matt looked at her sharply as they turned a corner on the promenade, now walking west. Far ahead in the evening light, the Hudson glimmered. "What are you thinking about?"

She looked up at him. "Me? Nothing."

"Huh."

"I'm not. Matt, you sound as if you suspect me of something."

"I don't trust that innocent look on your face."

"Matt," she protested, and then let out a laugh. "Oh, very well. If you must know, Uncle Augie and I were planning a visit to Mr. Earle's studio tomorrow—"

"Augustus can go if he wants," Matt interrupted. "Not you."

"Matt—"

"Earle will know who you are. It could be dangerous."

"He wouldn't hurt me. At least, not there."

"And would you be able to spot a forgery?"

"Well . . . no," she admitted.

"Let Augustus do it."

"Fine." Brooke walked along beside him in silence for a few moments. Fine, except what was she supposed to do now? She could hardly help in investigating anyone's finances; nor was she capable of going up against a gangster like Horgan. "Matt, something strange happened at the Voter Education League today—"

"Detective!" a voice called behind them, and they turned, to see a uniformed patrolman hurrying toward them. "Detective Devlin?"

"Yes." Matt pulled his arm free. "What is it?"

"Detective Flynn sent me to find you, sir. If I could have a word?"

Matt looked back at Brooke, who shrugged. Police business, and she had no part of it. Arms crossed, she waited as Matt walked a few paces away, as if what they were discussing were too important for her to overhear, and pretended to study the view below, of Reservoir Square. She was foolish to feel this way, she chided herself. Matt was involving her more fully in this case than he had in any other. And yet, what could she actually do? She was his wife, not a policeman.

"What?" Matt exclaimed, his voice suddenly loud as he glanced back at her. She stiffened, aware of a new attitude in him. He had taken charge, was giving orders, and the patrolman was nodding. Something had happened.

"What is it?" she asked as the patrolman at last left and Matt strode back to her.

He shook his head. "I'll find a cab for you, and then I have to go. God knows what time I'll get home tonight."

"But what is it, Matt?"

His voice lowered. "There's been another murder."

Brooke's hand crept to her throat. "Who?"

"A woman who's been helping Flynn with the case."

"Oh, no. Is there anything I can do?" she asked, hurrying along beside him to the narrow stairs that led down to 42nd Street.

"Go home. I want to know that you're safe."

"I will be. Matt, does this have anything to do with your case?"

"Damn right, it does." He held her hand as they ran down the stone stairs. "She was Joseph Warren's mistress."

9

Tony stood by the battered dresser and stared down at the even more battered body lying on the narrow bed. "Damn," he said softly. "I didn't think things would come to this. What did you know, Maisie?"

"You don't know what got her killed," Matt said in a low voice. He stood next to Tony, taking in everything. Besides the bed and the dresser, the room, papered with cabbage roses, contained a washstand with a chipped brim, and a wardrobe from which the veneer was peeling. There was a popping noise and the smell of flash powder as the police photographer, bent over a camera set on a tripod, took pictures of the crime scene, the glare of his flash like lightning. In the hall outside, women in various stages of undress clustered, clutching stained and shabby wrappers about them and talking in excited whispers. Ma Meecham's was a well-known whorehouse, though not one of the fashionable ones. Maisie, no matter what she might have been to Horgan before this, had obviously been on her way down. "It could have been a customer—"

"No. This is Horgan's doing." Tony's voice was equally low. "And it was because of what she knew."

"What did she know?"

Tony shook his head. "Later. This is Horgan's place. Not a good idea to talk about him."

Matt nodded, moving away from the dresser as the medical examiner straightened up from the body. "Any idea how she died?"

The medical examiner shrugged, pulling on his black frock coat. "Hard to tell right now. Could have been the beating, could be strangulation. There are marks around her neck and contusions on her scalp. I won't know for certain until the autopsy."

"Could a woman have done it?" Tony asked.

The doctor looked down at the body. "Doubt it. Well, it's yours. Though I don't know why it matters," he said, and, clapping on his top hat, went out of the room. The hum outside increased and then abruptly lowered as the door closed, leaving Tony and Matt alone with the remains of Maisie Duncan.

Matt was the first to move. He'd seen bodies before, the bodies of people violently killed, but it was something he'd never get used to. Maisie sprawled on her back in the indignity of death, one knee crooked, one arm flung above her head. Her camisole was torn at the shoulders, and what was left of her face was bruised and battered beyond all recognition. She had been quite thoroughly beaten. "You're sure it's Maisie?"

"I'm sure." Tony at last ambled over to look down at the body, hands thrust into his trouser pockets. "Damn."

"Not much sign of a struggle." Matt had managed to detach himself emotionally and was leaning over the bed, studying both it and the corpse dispassionately. "Bedclothes are disturbed, but then, they would be. Hmm."

"What?"

"These marks on her wrists. Looks like she was tied up."

"Hell, that doesn't have to mean anything. Some men like that kind of thing."

Matt nodded, but his mind involuntarily focused on the earlier peace of the evening, walking along the reservoir with Brooke. Why the hell was he in this job? "Think it was someone she knew?"

"Maybe. Maybe not. In her occupation, would it matter?"

"Would she let a stranger tie her up?"

Tony glanced up, his face devoid of expression. "I don't know. I wasn't that close to her." He straightened. "I think we've seen enough here. We'll need to talk to Ma Meecham."

"In a moment." Matt continued his unhurried examination of the body. No bruising or scraping on Maisie's knuckles; no broken fingernails or blood from scratches on her hands, which meant she probably hadn't fought her attacker. Dark marks on her wrists, indicating that she'd been bound and couldn't fight. There might be similar dark marks around her mouth, evidence of a gag, but with the state her face was in it was hard to tell. With the state of her face, it seemed as if the beating had gone beyond any punishment she had merited. "Huh. Anything strike you about this?"

"Strike me? Poor choice of words."

Matt waved his hand in frustration. If he were detached, Tony had somehow managed to remove himself completely. "You know what I mean. The number of blows and the force used. It seems excessive."

"So?"

"So would a stranger go so far?"

"You know as well as I do that anyone who kills will do anything."

"And you also know damned well that killers are usually more violent with people they know."

"Of course he knew her. If they both worked for . . ." He tilted his head, leaving the sentence unfinished.

"Which means other people will know him too." Matt straightened. "We'll have that talk with Ma Meecham now."

"No, I don't know who was with Maisie last," Ma Meecham said in a frank tone of voice, adding more gin to her glass from the bottle that stood on the table next to her. "Sure you gents don't want a drink? You look like you could use one."

"No, thank you." Tony's voice was glacially polite. "So you didn't see her last customer, then?"

"I didn't say that."

"Then you did see him."

"Oh, yeah, I saw him. But did I know him? No." She took a hearty sip, and then set her glass down, gazing at Matt. "You're new."

Matt nodded. "More or less."

"Yeah. Thought I hadn't seen you before." Ma Meecham's eyes traveled leisurely over Matt, from head to foot, and it was all he could do not to squirm under her scrutiny. She was a fleshy woman somewhere in her forties, though she looked older, with henna-tinted hair and a hard-featured face that might once have been pretty. Her legs, propped up on a chair opposite her, were still shapely where her tea gown fell away; her figure still had a certain blowsy attractiveness. Matt felt as if he were being stalked for prey. "Anytime you want to come around, I can find someone to accommodate you." She gave a broad, exaggerated wink. "Maybe I'll even come out of retirement."

"I'm complimented," Matt said dryly, and noted the quick,

sardonic smile that flashed across her face. Ma Meecham was no fool. It would be well to remember that.

"What did he look like?" Tony asked, leaning forward, his dark eyes intent. "Can you describe him?"

"Well, I don't know." Ma Meecham ran a finger around the rim of her glass. "What's in it for me?"

Tony's gaze was steady. "We don't take you in for a suspect, for one."

Ma Meecham made a face. "You boys play rough, don't you? But then"—she splashed more gin into her glass—"I never minded it rough."

"What did he look like?" Matt put in quickly. Tony's hands, knotted on his knees, were white at the knuckles. "Tall, short, young, old—what?"

She tilted her head to the side. "Now, let's see. Things were busy. Was he the blond gent, or—"

Tony made a low noise, like a growl. "Was he a gent?" Matt asked.

"No." Ma Meecham was staring at Tony, all teasing gone from her face. "I can't swear to this, because we were busy, but I think he was sort of young. At least, I wouldn't call him old. But not a kid, you get me?"

"Mmm-hmm. Was he blond?"

"Nah. Brown hair, brown eyes, from what I could see. Could have been hazel, for all I know. Eyes aren't usually what I look at in a man." Her gaze flicked over Matt again, and he forced himself to stay still. "Not tall—not as tall as you."

"Medium height?"

"Yeah. Say. Either of you gents have a cigarette?"

Matt and Tony glanced at each other, and then Matt reached into his inside coat pocket for the silver case Brooke had given him last Christmas. "Here."

"Thanks. Say, that's a fine case. You're sure you're not interested in—"

"No," Matt said firmly. "So far we have someone fairly young, brown and brown or hazel, medium height. Build?"

"Build?" Ma Meecham's face screwed up. "Now, that I do remember. I remember thinking he must have been a boxer."

Tony straightened. "Why?"

"He was big, and he had that look. You know. Big hands, cauliflower ears, and a broken nose." Her face was serious. "But he was going to fat, so if he boxed, it wasn't recent."

"How was he dressed?" Matt asked.

Ma Meecham shrugged, and her tea gown slipped off one plump shoulder. She made no move to replace it. "Not bad, but not real stylish, either, like you." Her gaze sharpened. "That suit from England?"

"Yes. What was he wearing?"

"Dunno. I remember houndstooth, but that could be anyone. Ah!" She let out a stream of smoke. "His vest. Of course."

"What about it?"

"It was fancy. Bright and shiny, like satin, and red. And embroidered. But I guess he could get away with it." She wheezed with laughter. "Way he was built, no one was gonna call him a sissy."

"And what time was this?" Tony broke in.

"Dunno. 'Round about eleven."

Tony looked up. "This morning?"

"No. Last night."

"What!" Tony and Matt both stared at her. "You're telling us Maisie had her last customer last night and you're just now reporting her dead?"

Ma Meecham shrugged. "He paid for all night. Doesn't happen often, but it does happen."

"But what about this morning? Didn't you notice Maisie wasn't up?"

She shrugged again. "Maisie's got her own place, doesn't usually stay here. Thinks—thought—she was better'n us. Well, I guess she learned. It wasn't till it was comin' on evening and she wasn't back I got concerned. Thought she wasn't coming, and, I tell you, that got me. So I told Sally she could have Maisie's room for the night and to make sure it was neat, and that's when she set up that screaming and hollering." Ma Meecham swallowed, the first sign of genuine emotion she'd shown. "That's when I saw that Maisie was dead."

"Last night." Tony looked stunned. "My God."

"And at two A.M. Earle was leaving the city," Matt said softly.

Tony looked at him. "You think—"

"I don't know. But it's a coincidence, isn't it?" He rose. "We'll want to see the girls who were in the room next to Maisie's."

"They didn't hear anything. They would have said."

Huh. Women who worked in a cathouse were probably used to hearing sounds of a struggle that would alarm anyone else. "Still, we need to see them."

"Damn. Oh, all right." Ma Meecham swung her legs to the floor, displaying more of her thighs, and rose, straightening her gown at last. "That'd be Helen and Josie. I'll get 'em. But don't get 'em upset. I need them for tonight."

Tony had risen too. "You don't need anyone for tonight."

"What? You mean you're closing us down? Well, I never." She thrust her face forward, hands planted on her broad hips. "I got a business to run here, and I pay for it too."

"Who?" Tony's gaze sharpened. "Who do you pay?"

"Why, the landlord, of course." Her smile was falsely sweet.

"I'll get those two lazy girls. Helen!" she yelled, and went out of the room.

"Damn," Tony swore softly. "Who did she pay?"

"Someone's on the take?"

"Looks like it. Someone out of headquarters probably. Damn. And wouldn't the newspapers like to get hold of that."

"We know Horgan's involved." Matt's voice was equally soft. "He owns this place. He could bring pressure that Ma Meecham couldn't."

Tony looked up at him. "To close the case, you mean?"

"Maybe. I'd hate to think it, but maybe."

"Damn." Tony glanced away. "You know what this means."

"Yeah." Nearly a day later, and he still didn't know why Captain O'Neill had taken them off the case. It didn't look good, though. It looked as if he was covering for someone. "It means we have to talk to Horgan."

It was late when Matt at last returned to the apartment at the Dakota. Still, he wasn't surprised that Brooke was sitting in the parlor, waiting up for him. The odor of paint lingered and the furniture had yet to be restored to its usual place, but even at night he could see the improvement. The room wasn't nearly so gloomy as it had been. "It's late," he said, loosening his tie as he stood in the doorway. "I thought you'd be in bed."

Brooke swung her legs down from her curled-up position on the sofa. "You look like you could use a drink."

In spite of himself, Matt grinned. "You're the second person to say that tonight."

"Oh?" Brooke glanced over her shoulder at him as she stood at a trolley on which sat several decanters and cut-crystal tumblers. That was a new addition to the room, he noted, one he approved. "Who was the other one?"

"A witness." And never mind who. Brooke didn't need to know that he'd been propositioned by a notorious madam, something his cohorts in the detective bureau had found hilarious.

Brooke crossed the room, holding out a glass to him. "Was it bad?"

"Bad enough." He sprawled on the sofa, one arm flung across the back, and Brooke curled up next to him. "Lord, I'm tired."

"I'm not surprised, after the day you put in."

"Yeah. Well, it's over now. We can't do anything more until we find out exactly how she died, and when."

"Was she important?"

"Probably, yeah. Flynn thinks she knew something about Horgan."

Brooke opened her mouth, and then closed it again, glancing away. "Oh."

"We'll find out what, somehow. It just means we'll have to dig deeper."

"Horgan's dangerous, isn't he, Matt?"

"Yes. But I'll watch myself, don't worry about that." He stretched, yawning, and then rose. "It's late. I'm heading for bed."

"Yes. Matt, today I met—"

"You know, I never realized it before?"

Brooke gazed up at him as he stood in the middle of the room, looking around. "What?"

"How nice it is to have a place where I can get away from the job once in a while."

"Even if I talk about it?"

"Even then." He looked down at her. "Who did you say you met today?"

"It's not important." She slipped her arm around his waist. "Let's go to bed."

Much later, Matt lay drowsily in the big bed, thinking again of the contrasts between his job and his home. There were two sides to his life; two sides, he was discovering, to himself. Sort of like the Warren case. It had two sides too.

Something about that struck Matt as important, but before he could grasp it, it was gone. Tomorrow, he thought, letting himself surrender to this side of his life. He'd think of it tomorrow.

Matt rose abruptly, his chair rocking back. "You let Earle go? Without saying anything?"

O'Neill, sitting impassively at his desk, shrugged. "Where was the evidence to hold him? None I could see, to back up the charge."

"I have an eyewitness," Matt said through clenched teeth.

"Who you haven't produced. No, Devlin—"

"We're building the case against Earle. The eyewitness will be part of it."

"Regardless, Devlin, there wasn't anything to hold him on." O'Neill sat back, his broad face smug. "I tell you, you'll get nowhere on this lookin' in that direction."

"Are you so certain Earle didn't kill Warren, sir?" Tony asked quietly before Matt could erupt. He had been sitting back, watching the interplay between Matt and the captain.

"There's no proof he did. I told you, we're not going to find Warren's killer. The trail's gone cold."

"Mr. Roosevelt doesn't seem to think so."

O'Neill clenched his teeth. "TR's got nothing to do with this. The detective bureau isn't even his department. It's Mr. Parker I answer to on the commissioners."

"Is he the one who wants the case dropped?" Matt asked.

"No. That was my decision." O'Neill stood up, his bulk fill-

ing his office. "If you find evidence on Earle, then bring him
in again. But until you do, we don't go arrestin' law-abidin' citizens." He stalked to his office door and held it open. "Haven't
you got work to do, Detectives?"

Matt took a deep breath in an effort to control his temper.
"As it happens, yes. Maisie Duncan's murder."

O'Neill's head snapped up. "A prostitute?"

"Horgan's prostitute," he said, turning, and stalked out of the
office. Behind him he heard O'Neill's bellow and Tony's softer
reply, but he didn't care. Snatching his hat from the rack, he
strode out of the detective bureau, past the front desk, and out
onto the stoop.

"Well, that's done it." Tony caught up with Matt, running
down the stairs. "We won't get any help from the captain
now."

Matt's face was grim as he walked along. "I didn't think we
would."

"What is it with you?" Tony asked, sounding curious. "Do
you like making enemies?"

In spite of himself, Matt's mouth quirked back with amusement. "Not particularly, no."

"Well, you sure don't seem to know how to go around doing
things."

The two men stopped at Bowery Street to let a wagon loaded
with beer kegs rumble past, the horses' hooves stirring up dust
and straw, and then dashed across the street, turning south.
Scene of much of the vice of the city, the Bowery was lined
with bars and brothels, concert saloons and theaters. Since TR
had taken control, the area was better policed than it had
been. It was still a trouble spot, however, particularly with
gangsters like Monk Eastman and Horse-Face Horgan battling
for control of the East Side. "Actually, I've been told I'm better than I used to be."

"Hell. And they had to make you my partner."

"Your luck, I suppose."

"Yeah. So." Tony glanced over at him again. "No Brooks Brothers suit today?"

"No. Is that a problem?"

"Not with me." Tony sauntered along, hands tucked into trouser pockets. "Probably better you didn't, with going to see Horgan. Otherwise he might think you're on the take."

Matt swung around. "Listen, I never took—"

"Hey, I'm not saying that." Tony held his hands up in pretended innocence. "I'll tell you something else. I never did either."

Matt looked at him for a moment. "I believe you."

"Yeah. Well, let me warn you about Horgan. He'll find out what your weakness is, if he doesn't already know. If he thinks it's money, he'll go for that. So watch it with him."

"I intend to." They walked along in silence for a few minutes. Word of their progress apparently preceded them; men seemed to melt away from the fronts of saloons, while those who remained either glared or shifted their eyes away. No one appeared to doubt that Matt and Tony were cops. "Does he have any weak spots?"

"Not that anyone's found, no. Not with his gang to protect him."

"Yeah, and without his gang, what is he?"

"Trouble." Tony's voice was sober. "He knows too many cops, too many politicians. Too many of the upper crust. He's got power, believe me." He was quiet for a moment. "The one thing he doesn't have is family."

Matt glanced at him. "That matters?"

"I don't know. It might. He took good care of his mother. Word has it he went to pieces when she died. For sure he gave her quite a send-off. A grand procession, and a plot at Forest Lawn."

"Huh. Is he married?"

"No. No wife, no kids. He has a farm out on Long Island, keeps horses there. That's about it. That, and music. He tried to join the Metropolitan Opera House when it was organized."

Matt's lips tucked back in sardonic amusement. When they had been refused membership at the old Academy of Music, such society upstarts as the Vanderbilts and J. P. Morgan had opened, instead, the Metropolitan Opera House. "I take it they wouldn't let him?"

"Nope. Consorting with him in private is one thing. Public, another. Like slumming. They might go to the Golden Harp or Eastman's, but they don't tell everyone about it."

"Which is probably why Warren could keep things so quiet." He frowned. "Doesn't Horgan have any enemies?"

"Other than just about everyone in the city? Yeah. Monk Eastman, for one. The two of them fight every now and then over who's going to control the East Side. So far Eastman's stayed on the lower side, but it won't last. He's got a big gang too. We turn here." They headed east, along a narrow unpaved street. To either side rose grimy, dark brick buildings, tenements that, as on Mulberry Street, held the city's poor. Barefoot children played on the street, while women, some toothless, some gaunt, none very clean, leaned over fences or sat on stoops, talking to one another. Peddlers, their trays hanging about their necks on thick leather straps, ambled along the street, crying their wares and occasionally stopping to make a sale. No one appeared to pay the two detectives any mind, and yet Matt felt their gazes like blows.

"Things have been quiet between him and Eastman lately though, haven't they?"

"Yeah." Tony shook his head. "Honestly, these guys."

"What?"

"Horgan with his music, and Eastman. He loves animals, cats and birds especially. He walks around with a bird on his shoulder, and he's been known to shoot anyone who hurts a cat."

"Probably no loss."

"Nah. But he'd love to know who started the fire at the pet store down the street from his saloon last spring."

Matt looked at him sharply. "Did he own it?"

"Yeah. Mostly birds, some dogs, some cats. It looked like a lantern fell over. Funny thing though."

"What?"

"The building had gaslight. No need for lanterns. And the manager swears he didn't leave one lit."

"So someone set the fire."

"Yeah. Rumor was it was Horgan."

"Huh."

"But Eastman blamed the manager." Tony's face was grim. "We found him in an alley with his throat cut."

They walked in silence for a few minutes. "Was it Horgan?" Matt asked finally.

Tony's shoulders hunched. "Yeah. Or so my sources tell me."

"Then it's true."

"It's true."

"Hmm." Matt rubbed at his mustache. "What would happen if Eastman found out?"

"He'd go after Horgan. Last thing we need is a gang war. Though it would get rid of some of the nasties for us."

Matt surprised himself by laughing. The sound drew the attention of several loutish-looking young men lounging on the stoop of a run-down brick building just ahead. "Horgan's men,"

Tony said in a low voice, and Matt's amusement abruptly died. "We're in his territory. The Golden Harp's about a block ahead." One of the young men rose from the stoop and walked away, apparently at ease, but quickly enough to widen the distance between him and the two detectives. "He's going to warn Horgan cops are coming."

"Horgan probably already knows."

"Yeah." Tony glanced at him. "You ever face anything like this in that hick town you come from?"

"Yeah. My in-laws," Matt said, and this time it was Tony who laughed.

"Well, be on your guard. There's the Harp." He pointed to a building at the next corner. Though it was still early, the Golden Harp was already doing a fine business, judging by the number of men going in and out. Except for the gilded harp hanging over the door, the building itself was ordinary, brick with a few small windows shaded by awnings. It didn't look much like the seat of a criminal empire, but Matt had learned long ago not to judge by appearances. With over one thousand men at his command, Frank Horgan was a powerful man.

They had reached the door of the saloon. "This is it," Tony muttered, and turned the knob. Matt walked in behind him, blinking for a moment to adjust from the bright sun to the dim, dusty darkness. What he finally saw looked like any other saloon: a good-sized room with a U-shaped bar of highly polished wood in the center, and a stage at the far end. Men of various ages and sizes leaned against the brass rail, some staring at the newcomers, others studiously avoiding their gazes. Behind the bar a big, beefy man polished a glass, over and over, seeming not to see Matt or Tony. A hush had fallen over the room; Matt felt rather like a sheriff walking into a Wild West saloon at high noon.

"This way," Tony muttered, stepping forward, and at that moment they were seized from behind. "Hey!"

"We're police," Matt said, struggling, but the pair of hands that held him were strong and hard.

"Save it," a voice growled behind him. Matt twisted his head to see a man well over six feet in height, and nearly as broad. "We know who youse are. Skinner, search 'em for weapons."

"Don't fight it," Tony called over to Matt. He, too, was held by a ruffian, though not as big as Matt's captor. "I expected this."

"Yeah, well, I sure as hell didn't," Matt growled as Skinner, a tall, thin man who lived up to his name, patted Matt expertly down, finding his Colt service revolver. Tony received similar treatment, and then they were abruptly pushed forward. "Hey!"

"Save it," the giant growled again. "The boss don't like cops, and he don't like cops with guns. Maybe he'll let you have 'em back when you leave. If you leave."

Matt glanced at Tony, whose face was oddly calm. His own heart was beating erratically, though not with fear alone. They were getting somewhere, at last.

The giant pushed them both up a staircase at the back of the room, where they made stumbling, halting progress. At the top of the stairs another man waited, this one smaller, dapper except for the bulge in his jacket that betrayed a shoulder holster. Matt had a quick glimpse of a long, narrow hall leading deep into the building, quiet at this time of day, and an even quicker glance at a room across the hall, furnished in what looked like red plush. One of the private parlors for Horgan's wealthy customers? He'd have to find out.

The small man opened a door, and they were shoved inside. It was no utilitarian office, but an opulent room with a thick

Oriental carpet and a desk that Matt recognized with some surprise as an antique mahogany partners desk. Bookshelves lined the wall, holding volumes bound in leather and gilt, most looking well thumbed. Behind the desk was a large leather chair, its back turned to them; the cord of a telephone stretched across the desk, the telephone itself apparently held by the man who sat in the chair. Taking pride of place was a gramophone in a fine mahogany cabinet; the music that spilled from its horn was, to Matt's surprise, a Viennese waltz.

The receiver was abruptly banged down. The small man stepped forward to retrieve the telephone and place it on the desk. Only then did the leather chair swivel around so that its occupant faced Tony and Matt at last.

"Welcome, gentlemen," Frank Horgan said, gazing at them over the tips of his manicured fingers. "I've been expecting you."

10

"That's out," Iris Gardner shouted, and galloped toward the net of the red clay tennis court in the Dakota's private garden, her hand extended. "Good game, Brooke."

"Whew!" Brooke approached the other side of the net more slowly. "I should have known better than to get into a game with you."

"I like to win," Iris said matter-of-factly, putting her racquet in its press and then leaving the court, ceding it to a mixed doubles group attired in natty flannel blazers and straw toppers. "Why don't we sit in the rose garden? My mother thinks living in an apartment is déclassé, but I must say it's nice to have a private tennis court for your own use," she went on, falling onto a bench. "I wish I could convince Father to build one at our house, but he doesn't think it's necessary."

"Most people wouldn't, Iris." Brooke patted at her forehead with a lace-edged handkerchief, dabbing away the sweat that had collected there. She was hot and cranky, dressed as she was in an ensemble supposedly designed for exercise, but which included a full blue-and-white striped skirt, white blouse, and corset and petticoats beneath. Brooke shifted on the bench, wishing it was proper to take off her straw boater hat and her high-buttoned shoes, which seemed to have caused a blister on her heel. How one was supposed to move in such an outfit, she didn't know, Brooke thought, gazing ruefully at the hem of her skirt, now edged with red dust. Not that it seemed to hamper Iris.

"Well, I would." Iris smiled, a toothy grin that made her look a little bit like a horse. "I wonder you don't use it more often."

"I'm not as fond of tennis as you are, Iris. Especially not in this heat." She rose. "Shall we go inside? We could have lemonade, or something else to cool us down."

"But it's heavenly out here, Brooke." Iris stayed sprawled on the bench. There was nothing dainty or elegant about Iris, with her large frame and easy manners, and yet somehow no one minded. She was a good friend, Brooke thought, with not a bit of harm in her. "I hate being confined."

"The garden is lovely," Brooke said, sitting down again and resigning herself to being out in the warmth. At least they were shaded here, on the west side of the apartment building. On the tennis court the new game was already in full stride, though the grass croquet court was quiet. Iris was right. It was rather nice to have such amenities in an apartment house, even if the side of the Dakota that overlooked the garden was curiously unadorned. "Whatever are you doing in New York? You still haven't said."

Iris glanced away. "Newport's boring this year."

"With Tennis Week coming up at the Casino? I don't believe it."

"True. Of course, it would be better if they let me play." She grinned again. "Since that's not likely, I came to do some shopping. And to talk to you."

Brooke shifted on the bench. Iris's voice had turned serious. "About what?"

"About something that just happened." She glanced away. "I want to be certain it won't ruin our friendship," she said gruffly.

"Silly. Nothing will do that. What's happened, Iris?"

"Well." Iris took a deep breath. "Eliot Payson asked me to marry him, and I accepted."

"Well! He worked fast," Brooke said, feeling an odd, unexpected pang go through her. A year ago, her own engagement to Eliot had been a certainty, to everyone but Brooke. Though she had broken it off and was now happily married, she felt an irrational spurt of annoyance.

"Does it bother you?" Iris's eyes looked huge and wounded. "Do you wish you'd married him instead of Matt?"

"Good heavens, no!" Brooke exclaimed, blowing out her breath. What her life would have been like had she married Eliot didn't bear imagining. "I'm being silly, Iris. Of course it doesn't bother me." She grasped Iris's hands. "I'm so happy for you. You deserve someone nice."

"Yes, Eliot is nice. He plays tennis well."

"Oh, of course. A most important requirement in a husband." Brooke smiled. "So that's why you came to New York."

"Yes." Iris's gaze was steady. "I wanted to be certain it was all right with you. And to ask you to be my matron of honor."

"Of course it's all right with me. I have no claim on Eliot, and you know I want to see you happy." She paused. "But, I'm sorry. I can't stand up for you, Iris, and I don't think you'd really want me to."

Iris's chin thrust forward. "I would."

"With all the talk it would likely cause? No." She laid her hand on Iris's. "I'm honored, and I wish I could accept. I truly do. But you don't want people to talk about old history on your wedding day."

"I suppose not." Iris's eyes suddenly gleamed. "It would annoy your aunt Winifred no end."

Brooke sat back against the bench and let out her breath again. "Aunt Winifred is already quite annoyed with me. I had a letter from her just yesterday, scolding me."

"About what?"

Brooke grimaced. "I'm afraid I've gotten myself involved in another investigation."

"No!" Iris shifted, sitting with a knee up on the bench, careless of the petticoats and stockinged legs thus exposed. "How exciting! What is it about this time?"

"Do you remember Linda Warren?" Brooke said, and quickly sketched in the circumstances surrounding Joseph Warren's death.

"You do run into the most amazing things," Iris said when Brooke had finished. "I almost envy you."

Brooke laughed. "Then you have very little company. I'll admit it's interesting, but Matt's doing most of the work."

"Oh, nonsense. Look what you found out about Mr. Warren all on your own. And encountering a real gangster like Mr. Horgan." Iris shivered with delighted fear. "I'm sure my life won't be half so exciting."

"Please don't say anything about this, Iris." Brooke turned to face her, her expression serious. "No one's been accused of anything, and no one knows a lot of what we've found, besides the police. And," she added, making a little face, "I haven't told Matt about meeting Mr. Horgan yet."

"Whyever not?"

"Partly because I haven't had the chance. But also . . ."

"What?"

"I'm afraid he'll try to make me stop working at the Voter Education League."

"Well, I can understand that, if you're actually going to meet up with gangsters."

"I'm safe enough, and I like the work. At least, the little I've done." She frowned. "And there's something else," she added, more to herself than to Iris.

"What?"

"Oh, nothing, really. Something Mrs. Cartwright said yesterday when Mr. Horgan came in. That she was glad Linda wasn't there."

"Gracious, why?"

"I've no idea. I'd ask, but Mrs. Cartwright is rather intimidating."

"I've never met her." Iris gnawed at a cuticle. "I wonder."

"What?"

"Something I remember hearing my mother say. I didn't really listen at the time, you know I don't care for gossip."

"No, neither do I, but sometimes it's the only way I can get any information."

"It might not mean anything." Iris glanced at her slantwise, unusual in someone so direct. "But Mother said that Mrs. Warren liked to go slumming."

"Slumming?" Brooke drew back in surprise. "You can't mean that she'd go to low taverns, do you?"

"I'm sure that's what she meant. That Mrs. Warren and a few other ladies like to go into bad neighborhoods. Like the Bowery and Mulberry Bend."

"Good heavens. Why?"

"I suppose they thought it exciting. Mother knows several people who have done it. One of them had a long conversation with Frank Kelly at his saloon and pronounced him charming."

"And if they went to Kelly's, then they could very well have gone to Horgan's," Brooke said slowly.

"It's just gossip, Brooke."

"I know, but if it's true—good heavens." Brooke rose. "Let's go in and have something cool to drink. I have to think about this."

"All right." Iris bounded to her feet and strode along beside Brooke. "What are you going to do now?"

"I've no idea. Tell Matt, I suppose, though I don't know what it all means." Her brow knotted. "And I might just have to pay another call on Mrs. Warren."

"Please sit down," Frank Horgan said, gesturing to the two straight-backed wooden chairs that faced his desk. "Morley." He snapped his fingers. "Crank up the gramophone."

The small man who had escorted Matt and Tony into Horgan's office jumped forward. "Yes, boss."

"That's better." Horgan leaned back as the music filled the room. "What can I do for you gentlemen this morning?"

Matt settled himself in the chair, crossing his legs and reaching into his jacket. The motion made Morley step forward, hands flexed, and Matt instantly went still. "Am I allowed to get a cigarette? Or do you always treat visitors in this way?"

A small smile touched Horgan's lips, and he nodded at Morley, who backed off. "Perhaps you would prefer a cigar instead. I import them myself from Cuba."

"No, thank you." Matt withdrew his cigarette case, and with slow, deliberate movements went about the business of choosing, tapping, and lighting a cigarette. Only when it was well alight did he glance up at his reluctant host. Though he'd been forewarned, Horgan still wasn't what he'd expected. He'd gained the nickname Horse-Face because of the cane he habitually carried, though no one dared use it to his face. Nor did he look it. In his well-cut conservative suit he looked more like a clerk than a gangster, until one looked at his cold, impenetrable eyes. "So this is the famous Golden Harp," Matt murmured.

That faint, wintry smile flitted across Horgan's face again. "So it is. Would you care for a tour?"

"I've had one already, thank you," Tony said, and Matt could feel his puzzled glance. "Look, you know why we're here, so let's just get on with it—"

"A few questions, that's all." Matt's voice was mild. "By the way, that was an interesting greeting your men gave us."

Horgan pursed his lips. "I do apologize for that. But I can't very well have people coming in with guns, can I? They tend to fire at inopportune times, and I did just have this office redecorated. Morley." He snapped his fingers again, and Morley leaped to the gramophone, this time to change the record, and a baritone began singing, of all things, "Come Back to Erin."

"Of course we wouldn't want to do any damage," Matt agreed, and saw Horgan's eyes briefly flash. He had no idea if he was handling this right. Horgan was not a man to be underestimated, not with his power both in the underworld and with the city's elite. "We have a few questions regarding Maisie."

"Maisie?" Horgan frowned. "I seem to recall the name, but . . ."

"Maisie Duncan," Tony put in in a growl. "And if you don't remember her, you should. She was found dead at Ma Meecham's yesterday."

"Ah, yes. Maisie. What a shame. But then, it's a dangerous business she was engaged in."

"One you got her started in."

Horgan's eyes widened. "I assure you, I am not in the business of ruining young women."

"Not directly, no. We're trying to track down her killer," Tony went on before Horgan could protest.

"And you think I know something about it? I assure you, gentlemen, that I do not. A regrettable incident, but it can't be helped."

"When did you last see Maisie?" Matt asked.

"I have no idea. She meant nothing in particular to me."

"She was your mistress," Tony said.

Horgan toyed with the silver pen on his desk. "A long time ago, and it doesn't mean I had any special fondness for her. Truth to tell, I found her quite tiresome."

"Yet you introduced her to Joseph Warren, here in a private parlor," Matt said.

Horgan's eyes narrowed, the first true sign of wariness he'd shown. "I introduced many people to each other here. Why does that matter?"

"They've both been murdered, Mr. Horgan." Matt let the words hang there. "And they're both connected to you."

"Are they?" Horgan's fingers steepled. "How is Warren—who, I believe, was killed by a burglar—connected to me?"

"He gambled here."

Horgan let out a laugh. "So do most of the city's leaders. Come, gentlemen, you'll have to do better than that."

"How about that he owed you money?" Tony said softly.

Horgan stared at him. "Did he? I wasn't aware of it."

"But he did, didn't he? He made some unwise choices gambling, and lost. And we know you don't like to lose money, Horgan."

"Who told you this?" Horgan demanded.

"Can't tell you."

"Did he owe you money?" Matt asked, watching Horgan. His question about their source had seemed perfunctory at best. Horgan knew Maisie had been talking. Matt could feel it to his fingertips, could tell from the way the man reacted to the questions, with very little surprise or anger. He was clever, but instinct and experience told Matt he was lying.

"At one time, he did," Horgan said, surprising Matt. "I assure you, gentlemen, that he paid me back." Again he smiled, coolly. "Anyone who owes me pays me back, or he gets paid back."

"Where did he get the money?"

"I've no idea. That wasn't my concern. In fact, gentlemen, none of this is my concern." He rose, and though he had seemed imposing when sitting behind his desk, on his feet his height was only average. "I'm afraid I'll have to ask you to leave. I have business to attend to."

Both detectives stayed seated. "But Maisie was your concern," Tony said, his eyes sharp. "Very much so."

"Maisie was on her way down, and I have already told you I know nothing about her death. Now. Will you gentlemen leave peacefully, or will I need to have Tiny show you out?"

Tony slowly rose, and after a moment Matt did too. He wasn't satisfied with the little they'd learned, but what could they do? On Horgan's own territory they couldn't coerce him to talk. "We'll see ourselves out," Matt said, shrugging off the giant's hand as it clamped on his shoulder. Tiny, indeed. Horgan was not without a sense of humor. "I assume our revolvers will be returned to us."

"When you reach the door." Horgan's eyes were flinty. "Oh, and Mr. Devlin."

Matt turned in the doorway. "What?"

"I had the pleasure of meeting your wife yesterday. Charming woman," he went on as Matt suddenly surged forward and was grabbed again by Tiny. "I look forward to seeing her again."

Matt tugged himself free. "If you so much as go near her, I'll—"

"Now, now, Detective. Threats? I thought better of you." Horgan smiled, that wintry smile. "I will keep our dealings between us, if you will."

Matt stared at him. The thought of Brooke in this gangster's hands was terrifying, and yet he had a job to do. "Touch my family, and you'll suffer," he said flatly.

Horgan's eyes darkened. "If that is the way you want it, so be it. And, gentlemen. Do not come here again. I may not be so hospitable next time."

"Come on, youse," Tiny said, and Matt found himself being dragged out of the office, fuming with impotent anger. The sound of a soprano singing an aria followed them as Tiny gave Matt another push, making him and Tony clatter back down the stairs to the main saloon. There they retrieved their revolvers and at last stepped out onto the street. Horgan had won that round, Matt thought grimly, holstering his revolver. And why hadn't Brooke told him about the meeting?

"I told you he'd find your weak spot," Tony said.

Matt grunted. Brooke was his concern, not Tony's. "Didn't do much, did we?"

"Nah. Not much. Except let him know we suspect him." Tony's eyes flicked over the tenements that ranged to either side as they hurried along. "And that he'll be watching us."

"He was lying."

"Of course he was. But you got any proof? Christ, Devlin!" Tony rounded on him. "The way you spoke to him, I thought we'd be in the suds for sure."

"He let us go."

"Not before threatening your wife." Tony glanced at him. "Where'd he meet her anyway?"

"I don't know." Matt's teeth were clenched. "But I'm going to make sure it doesn't happen again."

"You'd better. He meant what he said. Damn." Tony kicked at a stone. "I have a family to think of too."

Matt glanced at him. "Your weak spot?"

"Yeah. My wife and son."

"Yeah." Matt frowned. "Yeah, well, as you said, there's no proof." *But we'll find some*, he vowed to himself as they trudged back to headquarters. *We'll find some*.

Horgan had found his weak spot. The thought was very much on Matt's mind as he pedaled his bicycle toward the Dakota, unusual for him in the middle of the afternoon. A quick telephone call had reassured him that Brooke was there, but after the events of the morning he needed to see for himself that she was safe. And, dammit, he needed her help, even if she had somehow managed to attract Horgan's attention. He scowled as he swung onto Central Park West, ignoring the leafy greenery to his right. James Carter Earle was still going about his business. He needed Brooke to check on the painter. It would also keep her out of Horgan's clutches for now.

"Matt," Brooke said in surprise when he walked into the apartment. She was standing in front of the huge umbrella stand, gazing in the mirror as she straightened her hat. For the first time, he noticed that the cushions and draperies that had made the entrance hall so fussy and dark were gone. "Whatever are you doing home at this time?"

"I need to talk with you." He took her elbow, steering her toward the parlor. "When did you meet Frank Horgan?"

Brooke opened her mouth in surprise. "How do you know about that?"

"Never mind how I know. Answer my question, dammit."

"I'm not one of your suspects, Matt." Brooke closed the parlor door with a quiet but definite click. "Would you care to ask me again?"

Matt glared at her, and then turned away, running a hand through his hair. "Sorry. I—dammit, I saw Horgan this morning, and—"

"Oh." Brooke sat down, carefully spreading her skirts about her. Some of her anger had faded, but she was still wary. "I tried to tell you about it, Matt, but things kept happening."

"That's no excuse—"

"No? I tried last night, and you had to go off to see a dead body. Then later you talked about being able to get away from the job. Anyway, nothing really happened."

"Nothing?" He rounded on her. "The man's a gangster, Brooke. A dangerous one. He'll use anything he can to protect himself. If that means going after you to stop me, he'll do it."

"It wasn't much," Brooke said after a moment, her voice small. She hadn't forgotten Horgan's presence, or its effect on her. "Just that he came into the Voter Education League yesterday."

"So he knows where you'll be."

"Yes. No! It was chance. He works for Tammany. You know that."

"Yeah. But he happened to come in while you were there."

"What am I supposed to do about it, Matt?" she asked stiffly. "I can't help where he goes."

"No, but you can be careful yourself. I don't want you going there anymore." He paused. "Where is it anyway?"

"Stanton Street."

"Stanton Street!"

"I knew you'd react this way."

"Yeah? I think I have a right to. That area's dangerous. Horgan is dangerous. This isn't a game, Brooke."

"I never said it was!" She rose, pulling on her gloves. "I haven't time for this. But I'll do what you want, for now. I won't go to the League anymore. At least until you catch him."

"We might never catch him, Brooke."

"Well, then, we'll have to see. I'm sorry, Matt, but I'm late for an appointment. I have to—"

"Where are you going?" he said sharply.

"Why, nowhere special. I'm to meet Iris in a few minutes for tea."

Matt followed her out into the hall. Through the doorway into the library he could see the furniture covered by sturdy dropcloths, and a man in spattered overalls standing on a ladder, slapping some pale color on the walls. "Iris?"

"Iris Gardner. She was my maid of honor, remember? I told you this morning she was in town, and—"

"Yeah, you did. Listen. I didn't come home just to scold you."

"Oh?" Brooke focused on buttoning her glove. "Why did you come home?"

He leaned toward her. "O'Neill let Earle go this morning," he said in a low voice.

"What!" Brooke's head snapped up. "Why?"

"Claims there's no evidence to hold him."

"But then he could just go anywhere."

"We're watching him. So far he's going about his business. Which is the other thing I wanted to talk to you about." He took her elbow, leading her back over to the umbrella stand and away from the open library door. "I'd like you to go to the Manhattan Museum and take a look at the paintings again, see if you can spot more forgeries."

"I can't, Matt. Besides." She frowned. "I thought we'd decided to let Augustus do some prying."

"And he will. But the more I know, the better. I wish there were some way for you to keep the appointment we made to have Earle start your portrait."

"I already canceled that."

"What?"

"He was in jail. How was I to know he'd be released? He wouldn't talk to me anyway."

"Yeah." Matt rubbed at his mustache. "I suppose not. But if you go to the museum—"

Brooke shook her head. "I told you, I have to meet Iris."

"Dammit, Brooke. Why is it you interfere when I don't want you to, and now when I ask for help, you refuse?"

"Because I don't think this will do any good. Besides, this is important, too. Iris told me—"

"I don't give a damn about Iris."

"Matt!"

"Well, I don't," he said in a more moderate tone. "This is a case we're working on. Nothing's as important as that."

"I've made plans to meet her," Brooke said quietly. "It wouldn't be polite to break them so close to the time."

"Polite." Matt scowled, slashing with his hand to his forehead. "I'm fed up to here with politeness."

"Matt—"

"You wanted to help investigate, fine. I'm letting you help. But you can't have things both ways. Make up your mind what you want to do."

Brooke held out her hand to him. "Matt—"

"Will you go to the museum?"

Brooke stared at him for a moment, annoyed. Once again he wasn't giving her the chance to tell him something important. Well, so be it. "No."

"Dammit. All right." He turned on his heel and stalked toward the door. "But don't expect me to let you dabble in police work whenever you feel like it," he said, and slammed out of the apartment.

"Dabble!" Brooke exclaimed, staring at the door. As if her contributions to the case weren't just as important as his. As if she didn't take it just as seriously.

"Madam?" a tentative voice said, and she turned to see Fuller. "The carriage is downstairs."

Brooke took a deep breath, belatedly aware of the painters watching this drama with interest. "Thank you, Fuller," she said, and headed for the door, her nerves singing with anger and tension. If Matt had been patient, if he had just listened, he would have learned that she was working on the case, no matter how it appeared. Iris had arranged for her to talk with a friend who had gone slumming with Sylvia Warren. But if he didn't want to listen, fine.

Straightening her hat again, she went out to the lobby, where the elevator waited. Maybe she'd tell him about it tonight, she thought as the cage descended. Maybe not. Maybe she'd find out enough information today to lead to Mr. Warren's killer. And wouldn't that show him, she thought, smiling grimly and ignoring the startled look the elevator operator gave her. Dabble, indeed. She'd show him.

Matt was just rising from the breakfast table the next morning, when the telephone jangled. "Who on earth could that be at this time of the morning?" Brooke said.

"Maybe your friend Iris," Matt said, going out into the hall.

Brooke made a face at his back. Usually Matt didn't hold a grudge, his anger disappearing as quickly as it flared, but this time was different. There was a cool politeness between them that had started the evening before, and had yet to let up. Because of that, Brooke still hadn't told him what she'd learned. Childish, she knew, but his words of yesterday still stung, implying as they did that investigating was somehow a game to her. That it wasn't to him was obvious. After seven months of marriage she and Matt had had many quarrels, and come to terms with many of the differences between them. Oddly enough, none of those more personal arguments had had the effect of this one. Only his work seemed capable of doing that.

Sighing, she placed her napkin on the table and rose, to get ready for the day. The sight of Matt, still in shirtsleeves, in the kitchen hall, standing with the telephone receiver to one ear and his hand to the other, stopped her. His face was grim, and the set of his shoulders tense. For a moment Brooke forgot her own lingering anger. Something had happened.

"What is it?" she whispered, drawing closer, and Matt gestured her to silence.

"What? No, sorry, the connection's bad." His glance flickered to Brooke, evidently trying to communicate something. "Is he dead? No? Well, thank God for that . . . unconscious? Damn." They stood together in silence for a moment; faintly Brooke could hear the crackle of a voice, mixed with static. "Yeah, this might crack things open."

"What things?" Brooke asked, and again Matt gestured.

"What? No, I was just getting ready to come in. But I'll meet you at the museum instead."

"The museum!"

"All right. Yeah. It's just across the park for me, so it won't take long. Yeah. I'll see you there." Matt replaced the receiver on the hook and let out a whistle. "Holy God."

Brooke looked up anxiously, the tension between them forgotten for the moment. "What is it, Matt? Did something happen at the Manhattan?"

"Damn right it did," Matt said, and, very much to her surprise, grinned. "Someone broke in last night and stole a lot of paintings."

11

"Upon my soul," Chandler Owen said as Matt and Tony sat facing him across his desk at the Manhattan. Late morning, and this was their first chance to interview him. Detective Kramer, who had investigated the earlier thefts, was still very much on the scene, but currently was interviewing other staff members. "That there could be such goings-on in our museum. I thought our troubles had ceased, but apparently they have not. The telephone has been ringing all morning," he went on as Matt opened his mouth to speak. "I believe every trustee has called me, demanding explanations. They plan to call a meeting soon, and I very much fear"—he dabbed at his forehead with his handkerchief—"that I shall be asked to resign."

"What happened last night was unfortunate," Matt said carefully. Especially since a security guard had apparently come across the thieves in the act, and had suffered a severe blow to his head as a reward for his vigilance. Whether he would live was still in doubt. "I didn't expect there to be any more thefts."

"Nor did I," Owen said absently, and then looked sharply at

Matt. "You surely don't believe this is connected with Joseph's death, do you? That happened months ago."

"What was taken, sir?" Tony asked, as careful and deferential as Matt, and as alert.

"I've already told that other detective. He has a list of what's missing."

Matt looked up from his notebook. "The lost masterpieces?"

"Truly lost now. All gone, gentlemen. The thieves knew what they really wanted." He stared into space. "Some drawings as well, though those are only copies. Not only the museum, but the world, has lost a true treasure."

"And the chance to find out if they were forgeries," Tony said.

Owen shot him a look. "I told you before, we don't traffic in such things."

"Hard to prove now, isn't it? The paintings are gone, the man who acquired them is gone, and no one seems to know where they came from. Convenient, isn't it?"

Owen frowned. "What are you implying?"

"It's to your benefit, isn't it, if it's never proven those paintings were forged."

"It most certainly is not!" Owen's face was red. "I've already told you, I'll likely lose my position over this, and—"

"Better that than being arrested for fraud," Matt said softly.

Owen stared at them, and then pressed a buzzer on his desk. The door to his office opened. "Yes, sir?" Seaton said.

"Seaton, these gentlemen are leaving. Please see them out of the building."

Seaton glanced from Owen to the two detectives, who were still seated. "But, sir—"

"Now, Seaton!"

"We're not leaving the building." Matt rose leisurely from his chair. "Not while this phase of the investigation is in progress. But we will leave you to cope with your telephone, sir." Matt bared his teeth in a fierce smile. "And we will be back."

Owen muttered something, but otherwise made no protest as Tony and Matt left the office. "He's in it up to his neck," Tony said in a low voice.

"No proof," Matt said just as quietly, and turned to look at Seaton. "Unless we found someone who knew something. And"—he smiled that fierce smile again—"we stir something up."

The rumor that paintings acquired by the Manhattan may have been forged took the art world, and New York City, by storm. It had been an easy rumor to create; all that was necessary was to leave an anonymously written report about the paintings in a cubbyhole where one of the police reporters would be sure to find it. Now all the New York papers were carrying the news, and both Detective Kramer and the Manhattan were besieged. No one yet suspected that Matt and Tony, engaged in investigating other crimes, might be at all involved.

Matt folded back the wide pages of the New York *World* and smiled grimly. "This should stir something up," he said across the breakfast table to Brooke the following morning.

"Yes." She set down her teacup. "Are you sure it's stirred up the right people?"

Matt looked at her over the top of the paper. "What do you mean?"

"I mean that you believe Horgan's connected to this. Matt, there's something about him I found out I think you should know."

The look he gave her was sharp. "I told you to keep away from him, Brooke."

"And so I have." Calmly, she folded her napkin. "Would you please listen to me for a moment?"

"I always listen to you."

Brooke's lips tightened, but otherwise she didn't comment "The other day, when you wanted me to go to the Manhat- tan—"

"You went to have tea with Iris instead."

"Iris and Mrs. Sawyer," she said, somehow holding on to her temper. What had gotten into Matt? It was rare he held a grudge about anything. "Mrs. Sawyer went with Sylvia War- ren to the Golden Harp."

It took a moment for that to penetrate, but then Matt's gaze came up sharp, searching. "When?"

"About a year ago. They decided to be daring and go slum- ming . . ."

". . . and so we decided we would go to a saloon," Jennifer Sawyer had said, pouring out tea for Iris and Brooke in her par- lor. Her home on Madison Avenue was comfortable, a bit too cluttered for Brooke's taste, but at least bright from the sun streaming through the open draperies. "A foolish thing to do, I see now."

"Why?" Brooke asked. "Why did you do it, and why do you think it was foolish?"

Jennifer shrugged. A tall woman with smooth auburn hair, she gave the impression of being constantly in motion, even when sitting still. Her foot tapped; her fingers danced as she talked; her head tilted. Brooke could not imagine anyone less likely to have visited Frank Horgan's saloon. "Boredom," she said. "I hadn't had my son yet, and I'd quarreled with my hus- band—though that's beside the point. What I find amazing"— she set her fine Limoges teacup carefully in its saucer—"is that I went with Sylvia Warren, of all people."

Iris shifted in her seat, porcelain clinking loudly. "I thought you and she were friends."

"Not really." Jennifer shook her head. "I knew her, of course, but we aren't of an age. We were never more than acquaintances. It was just"—she shrugged—"when she suggested it, it sounded as though it might be interesting."

"And was it?" Brooke asked quietly.

"Oh, very." Jennifer sipped her tea. "Is Sylvia in some kind of trouble?"

"No. Why?"

"You're gaining a reputation, Mrs. Devlin."

Brooke smiled a little. "I suppose I am. But, you see"—she set her cup down on the tea table—"I've met Mr. Horgan, just briefly, and I find him impressive."

"You wouldn't think of visiting his saloon!"

"No, Matt would have my head." Brooke's voice was wry.

"Most husbands would. That is the point, isn't it?"

Brooke looked up in surprise. "Is it?"

"Perhaps. More tea?" They sat in silence while Jennifer poured. "Sylvia made all the arrangements," she said abruptly. "She hired a detective to escort us, for safety. We didn't get terribly dressed for it—no Worth gowns, no jewels. I think we had this idea of trying to fit in." She laughed softly. "As if we did."

"What happened?"

Jennifer shrugged again and took up her cup. "Nothing so very much. Sylvia provided the carriage, and, as I said, the escort. I had second thoughts about going, which Sylvia seemed to think was silly—"

"So you'd feel foolish if you didn't go," Brooke concluded.

"Yes. And frightened if I did, even if there were five of us. It was late night, dark. I won't venture into that part of the city even in daylight. But I must say, the Golden Harp was a surprise. Not at all the rough place I expected, though the people there were." She paused to take a sip. "There was a musicale of some kind on the stage, with dancing girls and such, and the music was very loud. Many more men than women, and those that were there—well, you can imagine. The detective found us a table. I was glad he stayed close by."

"Who was he?" Brooke interrupted.

Jennifer shook her head. "I'd better not say. Actually, things were pretty tame. No one accosted us, and the one man who did speak to us was quite the gentleman. Very nice suit, very soft-spoken."

"Mr. Horgan."

"Yes, though I didn't know it at the time. He sat with us for oh, close to an hour, and I must say he was very charming." Her lips curved in a rueful smile. "After we left, Sylvia said what a pity it was we hadn't met a gangster, to make the evening complete, and that was when the detective told us we had. We were shocked. Some were thrilled." She set her cup and saucer down. "I came home, and that was all."

Iris stirred again. "I thought you went back."

"No. Oh, no. Everett—well, my husband wasn't pleased. Besides, I didn't enjoy it so very much." She frowned. "We went there for a thrill, and what we saw were just people. In worse circumstances than ours, of course, but still, just people, and we stared at them as if we were at the zoo. None of us was terribly proud of that."

"You were lucky," Brooke said. "Mr. Horgan is a dangerous man."

"Yes." Jennifer's gaze was direct. "I hope you're not thinking of tangling with him."

"Oh, no, of course I wouldn't—"

"Wouldn't you?" Matt interrupted.

Brooke blinked, brought back to reality. She was in her own dining room, safe, protected. Odd, but for a few moments she'd felt she could almost see the Golden Harp. She could, on some level, understand its draw. "No, why would I?"

"I know you, Brooke."

"I wouldn't—oh, very well." She blew out her breath. "I won't."

He nodded. "Good. It's a dangerous place."

"Give me credit for some sense, Matt! I wouldn't go alone. No, I'm not going to go," she said as he opened his mouth to speak. "Not when I've given my word. But I think I understand why someone would."

"Why?"

She frowned, trying to articulate the reasons for herself. "It's fascinating, Matt. Someone who looks so much like everyone else. He even has a taste for music."

"Don't romanticize him, Brooke," he said, voice sharp. "Horgan's nothing more than a common thug, no matter his other tastes."

"I know. That's what fascinating, that he has such a dark side."

"Dark as hell, and the love of a good woman won't reform him," he retorted.

"Well, no," Brooke said after a moment. "I suppose that happens only in stories. But, Matt—"

"Excuse me, Mr. Devlin, Mrs. Devlin," Fuller said apologetically from the doorway.

Matt gave Brooke a last searching look, and then turned to Fuller, crisply folding the paper. "What is it, Fuller?"

"There's a call from the reception desk, sir. A man wishes to see you, but won't give his name."

"Damn." Matt frowned. "A reporter probably. I don't want him sent up here."

"Very good, sir."

"Damn," Matt said again, turning back to Brooke. "It's bad enough when they go after us at the station, but here at home is different."

"You said yourself you stirred something up."

"Yes." His eyes sharpened. "With what you just told me about Mrs. Warren—"

"Excuse me again, sir, ma'am," Fuller said.

Matt held up his hand, his eyes on Brooke. "Not now, Fuller."

"But, sir, the man won't go away."

"The man can go to the devil, for all I care."

"He said, sir," Fuller persisted, "to tell you that he's only a secretary, but he does notice things."

"I don't give a—a secretary?" Matt looked back at Fuller. "Ask who his employer is."

"Yes, sir."

Fuller went out again, and Matt turned back to Brooke. "Let me get rid of whoever this is, Brooke. Then I'll be able to listen to you without being interrupted."

"I will say one thing," Brooke said, refilling her teacup. "Life is rarely dull around here."

"Sir." Fuller was back. "He wouldn't give the name, only the initials."

Matt turned to look at him. "Well?"

" 'C. O.,' sir."

"Chandler Owen?" Brooke said in surprise.

"It's Seaton," Matt said, and rose, his smile wolfish. "I thought he knew something. Tell the desk to send him up, Fuller. And if it's a reporter, I'll send him packing," he added to himself.

"Matt," Brooke said, her voice tentative. "How do you think the forgeries fit in with Mr. Warren's murder? Or do they?"

"I think so." Matt pulled on his suit coat. "Too coincidental if they don't. What I know is that Warren was in debt to Horgan. He needed money. If he conspired to bring in forgeries, he could split the money the museum used to acquire what appeared to be genuine works of art with the forger."

"And Horgan? Do you think he's involved with the thefts?"

"No, I'd say that's someone else altogether. And we'll soon see," he said as the doorbell rang. "If this is Seaton, then it is someone else."

Brooke followed him into the hall. "Who?"

"Owen," Matt said, and stepped forward to greet the slight young man who stood in the entrance hall, hat in hand. "Mr. Seaton? You want to see me?"

Seaton's mouth opened and closed as he spotted Brooke, with Fuller behind her. "I—this wasn't a good idea," he said, turning to the door.

"Oh, but you mustn't go," Brooke said, bustling forward before Matt could say anything. "You look tired, Mr. Seaton. Have you had breakfast yet?"

"No, ma'am, but—"

"Then come with me. Come on." She took his arm, urging him toward the dining room. "Matt and I were just finishing, but I'm sure Mrs. Fuller wouldn't mind making a plate for you."

"No, but—"

"Fuller, will you see to it? And then leave us to talk to our guest."

"Of course, ma'am," Fuller said, eyes gleaming, and strode down the hall to the kitchen.

Matt followed Brooke, his own eyes gleaming. Seaton looked bemused, as well he might, and his expression only intensified when he was seated at the table and a plate of ham and eggs had been placed in front of him, along with a steaming mug of coffee. "Eat," Brooke urged. "Whatever you came for can wait."

The dining-room door had closed behind Fuller, and now Seaton glanced from Brooke to Matt. "Mr. Devlin, if I could see you alone—"

"Whatever you have to say you can say before my wife," Matt said. "She helped to discover the forgeries."

Seaton's face paled, and he set down his fork. "Oh."

"Please don't let it upset you," Brooke said. "Were they forgeries?"

"Oh, Lord." Seaton leaned back in his chair, so pale he looked ill. "Yes. They were." He looked at Matt. "Am I in trouble?"

"Not necessarily." Matt leaned forward. "Did you know they were forgeries when the museum acquired them?"

"No."

"And did you have anything to do with their acquisition?"

"No!" Seaton pulled out his handkerchief and mopped at his face, much as Owen had. "Lord, I didn't think this would be so hard. After what Mr. Owen did—"

"What did he do?"

Seaton shook his head. "It doesn't matter." He stared blankly at his plate, and then looked up. "All right. I'll tell you. It's why I came. Mr. Owen doesn't think I know anything, but he's wrong. He's wrong. I hear things. I make it my business to."

Matt held out his cup for Brooke to pour him more coffee. "Why?"

"Knowledge is power, Mr. Devlin." The color had returned to Seaton's face. "If it's used properly."

"What knowledge?"

"About the forgeries. About the thefts."

"About Warren's death?"

"I don't know. Maybe."

"Did Owen—"

"Excuse me." Seaton held up a hand. "Let me tell this my way."

Matt stared at him for a moment, and then nodded. "Go ahead."

"I want you to know, first of all, why I'm doing this, so you'll know I'm telling the truth. Last spring, 1895, that is, there was an opening in the statuary department. I didn't train to be a secretary, you know," he said, glancing at Brooke and holding out his hands. They were large, broad, surprisingly strong-looking for a man who worked as a secretary. "I wanted to be a sculptor."

"Why didn't you stay with it?" Brooke asked.

"I wasn't good enough, if you want the truth. I liked the work, but all I seemed to be able to do was turn out third-rate copies of second-rate Powers groupings." He grimaced. "Even I realized I didn't have the talent, so I decided to do the next best thing."

"Work in a museum."

"Yes. Starting as a secretary was just a way to get myself in. When the opening came in the statuary department, I applied for the job. I should have gotten it." He glowered at his plate. "I would have, if Owen hadn't interfered."

"What did he do?"

"He said he needed me. I knew the museum, his staff. Still, he wished me well. And still, I didn't get the position."

"Why not?"

Seaton stared at his plate. "I found out, quite by accident, that Owen told the head of the statuary department that I was wrong for the job." He took a deep breath. "Among other things."

"You're here for revenge, Seaton," Matt said, his voice hard.

"Yes." Seaton faced Matt directly. "But that doesn't make what I have to say any less true. And"—he raised his coffee cup—"I don't want to be implicated in the mess at the museum, and I'm afraid I will be."

"Why?"

"Because when I went to the office this morning I found one of the drawings that had been stolen in my desk."

"You didn't put it there?"

"No, I did not," Seaton said quietly but forcefully. "Nor was it there when I locked up last night. And if you're asking who has keys to that office—"

"The security guard, you, and Owen."

"And I don't think it was the guard who put that drawing there. I took one look at it, and got out of there fast as I could and came to you."

Matt nodded. "Good idea. Though you realize we'll be checking on your story."

"You may." Seaton's color was high. "The only thing you'll find out about me is that I sometimes frequent the Golden Rule Club."

Matt's eyebrows rose. "Oh?"

"Yes."

"Where is that?" Brooke asked.

"It doesn't matter," Matt said with such quiet conviction that, after studying him for a moment, Seaton relaxed.

"No, it doesn't matter," he said. "You want to know about the forgeries."

"Yes."

"Very well. One evening last summer I was getting ready to

go home. Dismal day, dark and rainy. We'd had thunderstorms all afternoon. I got downstairs before I realized I'd forgotten my umbrella. When I went back in the office I could hear voices in Owen's office, and that surprised me."

"Why?"

"Because he'd left before I did. Well. I wasn't going to stay, but it was obvious that he and whoever he was with were fighting. Quarreling. And after being passed over for the job, I wanted to learn whatever I could about Owen."

"So you listened."

"Yes." Unexpectedly, Seaton smiled. "Wouldn't you?"

"Probably."

"I realized pretty quickly it was Warren in with Owen. They didn't get along too well, so I wasn't surprised by the argument, but what I heard Owen say stunned me."

"Which was?"

Seaton tipped his head back. "I remember the exact words, they shocked me so. 'What the hell are we going to do when someone discovers those so-called masterpieces are forged?' "

Matt let out a whistle. "Owen knew?"

"Yes. He'd found out, I don't know how, and he was giving Warren hell. Warren said no one would find out, he'd covered himself, and the forger was someone beyond suspicion. It was Earle, of course. I saw him leaving Warren's office one day."

Matt let out his breath. "Hot damn."

Seaton grinned again. "Yes. Owen and Warren went on quarreling, and then it got quiet. I was just thinking I'd better leave before they heard me, when Owen spoke again. He said they'd have to find a way to get the forgeries out of the museum, or he'd be finished, and so would Warren. And then Warren said there was a way to do it, and they could make a little money too."

"How?"

"By stealing the paintings and selling them to a private collector."

"Holy—" Matt looked startled. "There really is a collector in all this mess?"

"Yes. I don't know his name, but it's no secret a lot of people wanted those paintings. You might even hear from him."

"Doubt it. Whoever he is, he'd realize he's an accessory to a crime. Guilty of receiving stolen goods, if nothing else. What might happen is that those paintings will appear on the market, or they'll be destroyed, and no one will ever know."

Seaton considered that, and nodded. "Probably. In any event, once I heard what Warren had said, I knew I had to hear more. Owen was reluctant, called Warren insane and other things. But in the end he agreed. And by then I decided to get out of there, before they realized I'd overheard." He paused to take a sip of coffee. "The first theft took place the next week."

"And you didn't say anything."

"No proof."

"And now?"

"I'm willing to testify. I am telling the truth."

Matt nodded. "Good. That will help. But it would be better if you had something concrete."

"Well." Seaton let the word drag out. "Am I going to be charged with anything?"

Matt looked startled. "Did you have knowledge of the thefts before or after they occurred?"

"No. I can't prove that, but I can prove where I was those nights."

Matt nodded. "You did know about the forgeries, but that's minor, and the fact that you've come forward will help. Do you know anything about Warren's death?"

It was Seaton's turn to look startled. "Good Lord, no. And

if I thought Mr. Owen had done it, I'd have gone to the police immediately."

Matt's head jerked up. "You don't think Owen killed Warren?"

"No. He was very upset when Mr. Warren was killed." He paused. "But he could have, couldn't he? He would know how to make it look like it happened during a theft, because he knew how the thefts were done."

And, Matt thought, remembering the discrepancies between the major thefts and the one that had occurred when Warren was killed, he would know what to do differently. "But you don't really know anything about Warren's death?"

"No." His face had paled again. "Good Lord, have I been working for a murderer all this time?"

"As if the thought never occurred to you," Matt said dryly, and rose. "Thank you for coming, Mr. Seaton. If there's anything else—"

"There is, actually." Seaton stood, putting his hand inside his coat pocket. "You asked if I had any proof."

Matt leaned forward as Seaton withdrew a sheet of paper, folded, from his pocket. "You have it?"

"Maybe." He unfolded the paper. "Would a letter from Earle to Mr. Owen do?"

The letter from Earle, dated the previous May, was indeed a prime piece of evidence. In it Earle hinted that he was willing to do more work for the museum, in return for the same remuneration as before. Since Owen had denied ever hiring Earle, the letter was a weapon. Added to that were other documents Seaton had managed to smuggle out from the museum: authorization for payments for the paintings, a staggering sum; and a short note directing that Earle be paid for his work, signed by Joseph Warren. There was also a recent letter from a man well known in New York both for his position in society and his extensive collection of art, thanking Owen for helping with his collection, and enclosing a substantial donation. Seaton had carefully and quietly collected the documents after Warren's death, wanting revenge against Owen, and also to protect himself. Individually the documents were innocuous; collectively they pointed to Owen's involvement in the thefts, if not in Warren's murder. Since that had happened during a theft, however, Owen seemed involved in that as well.

"What we've got is good, but not good enough," Tony said as he and Matt climbed the stairs to the second floor offices in the Manhattan Museum. "Some letters that don't mean anything and a witness you know will be seen as unreliable, given who he is. It's circumstantial. Owen can still claim he didn't know anything about anything."

"I know. But he struck me this morning like a man ready to break. If he thinks we have more than we do . . ."

"And that he'll be put in a cell? He'd hate that."

Matt's smile was fierce. So Tony had noticed Owen's aversion to small, enclosed places too. "Yes. He would, wouldn't he."

They reached the top of the stairs and began walking through the galleries that led to the offices. Here and there gaps on the walls attested to the museum's recent losses. "O'Neill isn't happy about this."

"I know." Matt frowned. "Owen could be the one who put pressure on him to stop us. If he went as far as thefts to cover up forgeries, he wouldn't want us coming any closer."

"Makes sense," Tony agreed. "He's got a lot of power."

"Unfortunately," Matt said, and opened the door to Owen's office. The outer office, Seaton's domain, was empty, and his usually neat desktop was scattered with papers. The inner door stood ajar, though there was no sound from within. Matt glanced at Tony and then rapped on the doorframe. "Mr. Owen?"

"Who is it? Oh, it's you. Come in, gentlemen, come in." Owen, standing behind his desk, gestured them to come in. He had lost the distracted air he'd worn yesterday, and instead appeared calm, in control of himself and his world. "You are the very people I wanted to see."

Matt and Tony glanced at each other again. "Really?" Matt said mildly. "Why is that?"

"I've found something important. No, don't sit down. I want to show you something." Owen bustled around his desk, leading them back into the outer office. "Seaton never showed up today. I found out why."

"Oh?"

"Yes. The top drawer of his desk, gentlemen."

"What about it?"

"Look inside."

"Perhaps you should open it, sir," Tony said.

Owen stared at them for a moment, and then turned away. "Oh, very well," he said, stepping toward the desk. "I was looking for copies of correspondence I'd sent and I came across— this." He opened the drawer with a flourish and stepped back. "One of the drawings that was stolen the other night. A copy of a drawing by Michelangelo."

"Really." Face expressionless, Matt peered down at the drawing. "Was this here yesterday?"

"I've no idea. I usually don't rummage through my secretary's desk. But don't you see what this means?" He rose up on the balls of his feet, his face eager. "I hate to say it, gentlemen, but Seaton must be involved in the thefts."

Matt took another glance at the drawing, and then closed the drawer. "Not too smart of him to hide it here, then."

"Perhaps not. But he always did get above himself."

"And where are the other objects that were stolen?"

"I don't know, gentlemen." Owen spread his hands in an apparent gesture of openness. "Now that you know Seaton's involved, you can make him tell you."

"Mmm. Let's go back into your office, Mr. Owen."

"But why? I've told you who our thief is—"

"There are a few things we have to tie up." Tony smiled. "For our reports. They like us to have full reports."

"Oh, very well," Owen muttered after a moment, and turned on his heel, heading back into the office. Matt and Tony exchanged looks again. This was not going to be easy. "Now." Owen sat down, hands flat on the smooth leather surface of his desk. "I suppose you have to ask questions, but shouldn't you be out looking for Seaton?"

Matt took his time opening his notebook. "In good time."

"I suppose you want to know everything about him. Well, gentlemen—"

"No."

Owen blinked. "No?"

"Actually, the questions we have are about you. When did you learn the paintings Warren acquired were forgeries?"

"The other day, when you told me."

"No." Matt shook his head. "You knew a long time ago. Last year, to be precise. And we have documents that link you, not only with James Carter Earle, but with the thefts as well."

"You're mad," Owen said, but perspiration started to bead on his forehead. "I had nothing to do with them."

"Oh, but you did." Matt's voice was all the more menacing for its softness. "You not only knew about the forgeries, but you helped engineer the thefts, and you made a profit from them as well."

"That's not true—"

"But we can prove it," Matt interrupted. "And if we can prove you're connected to the thefts, then we can also connect you to Warren's murder."

"I didn't kill Joseph. That theft wasn't one of—"

"One of what, sir?" Tony said when Owen didn't go on. "One of yours, is that what you were going to say?"

Owen was sweating profusely now. "Yes. No. It wasn't one of mine. I mean, I had nothing to do with the thefts."

"But we know you did, Owen," Matt said, "and we know that you quarreled with Warren. We have enough evidence to get a search warrant for both your office and your home, and I'm betting we'll find the knife you used. Aren't you, Flynn?"

Tony lounged in his chair, one arm carelessly thrown over the back. "One way or another."

"One way or—" Owen stared at them, his eyes narrowing. "You mean you'd put it there, don't you? Oh, I know about the methods you use—"

"Maybe." Matt leaned forward. "Maybe we will. Maybe we won't have to. Maybe you'll tell us what we need to know."

Owen's face was stony. "I know nothing, gentlemen."

"No?" Matt stared at him and then rose. "Then, Mr. Owen, we'll have to take you in for the murder of Joseph Warren."

"Fine. But you'll have to let me go."

"Not before you spend some time in a cell," Matt said very softly. "A small, cramped cell. Dark. Isolated. Not enough room to pace in. Maybe not even enough room for a man of your height to stand upright. And—"

"No!" Owen exclaimed, and, just like that, broke down. "No. I swear to you, I didn't kill Joseph. I helped him with the thefts, I didn't know what else to do, but before God, I didn't kill him."

The tension in Matt's shoulders eased. *Hot damn.* "And the forgeries?"

Owen's shoulders slumped. "I knew about them."

"From the beginning?"

"No." He looked up, his eyes resigned. "I found out last year, after we acquired them. We were so proud to have such great pieces of art," he said bitterly. "I used to like to go look at them before I left for the evening."

"How did you find out?"

"It was an accident. A little thing, really." He shrugged. "Since I was a little boy, I've been fascinated by sailing ships. Once I wanted to be a sailor, but . . . In any event, I believe I can claim, gentlemen, to know a great deal about ships and their rigging. And in the Rembrandt landscape, there was a boat with a rigging that was not developed until the early years of this century. Long after Rembrandt's death." Owen took out his handkerchief and mopped at his forehead. "It was only a little detail, but if I saw it, others would too. I called Warren in here, thinking he could explain, that perhaps Rembrandt had made a mistake and it was already known. Instead, he thought I was accusing him, and he admitted the truth."

"Which was?" Tony said quietly.

"That the painting was forged. Upon my soul, gentlemen, I knew nothing about it before then! The stain on my reputation—"

"So you planned the thefts to hide the fact that you'd helped acquire forged paintings, and made some money for yourself in the process," Matt accused.

"I gave the money to charity."

"Admirable. And when Warren threatened to expose what you were doing, you killed him."

"No! You must believe me, gentlemen." He stared at them earnestly, pleadingly. "I knew about the forgeries. I planned and helped carry out the thefts, and the disposal of the paintings. But, upon my word, I did not kill Joseph Warren."

12

Brooke stared unseeingly at the gold velvet sofa in the parlor. "Partners, indeed," she muttered.

"Madam?" Fuller said. He stood in shirtsleeves, holding one end of the sofa up, his face dabbed with sweat.

"What? Oh. Sorry, Fuller." She made herself focus on the present. With the parlor repainted and lace curtains at the windows, the furniture no longer looked quite so massive or dark. The important thing now was to place it properly. The only important thing in her life, apparently. "I'm sorry, Fuller, Katie, I know it's heavy, but I think it should go back where it was."

"The center of the room, madam?"

"Yes." Brooke leaned down and grasped the other end of the sofa, along with Katie. "Ready when you are."

"No, madam!" Fuller appeared shocked. "This isn't work for you."

"The sooner we start, the sooner we'll be done," she said, and lifted her end, grunting with the effort and giving Fuller no choice but to pick up his end. Together, sweating and straining, they heaved the heavy, solid piece around, until it was at last in its original position. "There." Brooke straightened, hands on her hips. "We'll leave it there whether it should be there or not."

"Yes, madam. Madam, let me do the rest—"

"Since redecorating seems to be my lot in life, I want to get on with it." Brooke moved to one of the chairs, nudging it into place with her knees. It was late morning, and she had yet to hear from Matt about his confrontation with Chandler Owen. She doubted she would, until that evening. "I ask you, Fuller, what good is it being partners?"

"Ma'am?" he said, startled.

"Nothing," she muttered, turning away and blowing out her breath. It wasn't Fuller's fault that she couldn't be more involved in figuring out the goings-on at the Manhattan Museum. Nor was it his fault that her partnership with Matt seemed to be falling apart. "Let's just move that chair, and I think that will be it. . . ."

"The doorbell, madam," he said, and fled the room with what appeared to be relief. Katie followed. Brooke stared after them, a little line between her brows, and then let out her breath again. And it wasn't Matt's fault either. Not really. He'd acknowledged her role in the investigation more than once. That she couldn't follow up as he could was unfair, but something neither could do anything about. Women simply did not become police officers.

The sound of a familiar voice in the hallway made her turn, her forehead smoothing. Fuller walked in, carrying the silver card tray, but she didn't have to read the card to know who her visitor was. "Uncle Henry!" she exclaimed, slipping by Fuller into the hall, her hands outstretched. "How wonderful to see you!"

"Hello, darlin'." Henry bent to kiss her cheek, smelling, as always, of bay rum and leather and, just faintly, whiskey. "I had to come to New York on business—this business with the Manhattan, you know—and I thought I'd stop in to see you before going on to the trustees' meeting."

Brooke slipped her arm through his. "A good thing too. I can fill you in on recent events."

"Recent events? Brookie, have you been up to—oh, my." He stopped in the middle of the floor, staring around the parlor. "Winifred will have a fit."

"She will, won't she?" Brooke's grin was unrepentant. The parlor was so much lighter, so much more appealing with the new paint and draperies. She hoped the other rooms would be as successful. "It was just that it was so dark in here. Once we hang the paintings again, the walls won't look so stark. And at least we kept the furniture."

Henry was shaking his head as he lowered himself into a chair. "I'm not going to be the one to tell her, Brookie."

"It's my job. Fuller, we'd like—a whiskey and soda, Uncle? And lemonade for me."

"Make mine a lemonade too. I have to keep a clear head for this afternoon," he explained to Brooke.

She nodded. "You'll stay for lunch, won't you? I know the smell of paint isn't appetizing, but except for breakfast, Matt and I have been eating in the dining room downstairs."

"I'd like that, darlin'. So." He studied her, slouching in the chair, hands tucked carelessly into his pockets. Henry's habit of drinking too much and his sometimes vague mannerisms had fooled many a person. Not Brooke. She knew he was much sharper than he appeared, and that she was in for an inquisition. "What have you been up to, Brooke?"

"What could I be up to, Uncle?" she said with pretended innocence as Fuller came in with tall, frosted glasses of lemonade.

"I know you too well. Are you involved in this mess at the Manhattan?"

"Well—yes." She curled her legs under her and sipped from her glass. "You do know about the forgeries?"

"The forgeries—what?"

"Oh, dear. I see I've let that out. Uncle Augie and I discovered that the paintings Mr. Warren acquired were forged. And—"

"Lord, Brooke," Henry groaned. "What have you been getting yourself into? And you've involved Augustus too?"

"He's enjoying it. And this morning, Uncle, Mr. Owen's secretary came here and confirmed that the paintings were forged. And"—she took a deep breath—"that Mr. Owen planned the thefts to cover up the forgeries."

"My God. I should have had the whiskey after all." He looked stunned. "You might as well tell me all."

"I'd love to," Brooke said, and launched into a recital of all that had happened since she and Matt had returned to New York. "And so when Matt left this morning, he was planning to confront Mr. Owen," she finished.

"My God," Henry said again, shaking his head. "What is Matthew about, letting you get involved like this?"

"I'm not doing any actual police work, Uncle, so you don't have to worry about that. As for letting me—I don't think he could stop me."

"My God. If your mother were here to see this—"

"If my mother were still alive, I would probably have married Matt sooner." She paused. "And I probably never would have gotten involved in crime solving. I wouldn't have been living with you when the body was found on the Cliff Walk near us, and I wouldn't have known who she was, and—"

"You wouldn't have asked the wrong people questions and almost been thrown off the Cliff Walk."

"I'm safe enough, Uncle. Really." She made a face. "Lately all I seem to do is redecorate."

"This Seaton fellow," he said abruptly, sitting forward. "Do you believe him?"

"Yes, I think I do. It's true he had reason to dislike Mr. Owen, but he struck me as the type who would listen at keyholes. A snoop, in other words."

"Brookie, if he's involved in the thefts—"

"He's not. He was at the Golden Rule Club when at least one of them occurred, and his friends will back him up."

Henry looked at her sharply. "Brooke, don't you know what the Golden Rule Club is?"

"No."

"It's a—well, it's exclusively for men."

"So? Every club in the city is. You belong to several yourself."

Henry shifted in his chair, his face red. "Not of this type, darlin'. In this type of club, men actually like—well, they prefer men to women."

"Oh? Oh!" She felt her cheeks burn. "You mean—"

"I'm afraid so, darlin', and that means Mr. Seaton is not a reliable witness."

"But that's silly! He's worked at the museum for years, and he was telling the truth today. I'm sure of it."

"Regardless, darlin', no prosecutor will want to use his testimony, and no jury will believe it."

"It's not right. It's not fair."

"It's the way things are, darlin'." He paused. "You'd be better off if you just accept it."

Brooke rose, placing the empty lemonade glasses on the tray. "People should be judged by what they do, not who they are," she said, not looking at him.

"But you can't get away from who you are, darlin'."

"I'm Big Mike Cassidy's daughter."

"And granddaughter of Cornelius Low. I think you forget that sometimes."

"How can I?" Brooke spun around. "When everyone reminds me? When everyone expects me to act a certain way, be a certain thing—"

"Brookie, darlin', I understand."

"Do you. Oh, do you, really."

"Yes. Do you think I haven't had any disappointments?"

Brooke opened her mouth to protest, and then shut it again. "I suppose you have."

Henry got up and went to her, taking her hands as she had earlier taken his. "We all do, darlin', and sooner or later we learn it's easier to accept what is." He looked down at her, his eyes grave. "Sooner or later we grow up."

"I'm not playing at what I do, Uncle."

"You'll never be able to investigate seriously, Brooke. No, it's not me stopping you, but society." He paused, searching her face. "Aren't there some parts of the rest of your life that you like?"

Brooke bit her lip, remembering the argument with Matt when she'd had tea planned with Iris; remembering, too, how fulfilling she'd found the work at the Voter Education League. "Yes."

"You're going to have to decide what you want, darlin'. Whether to be a detective, or a wife."

"Why can't I be both?"

"You can." His gaze was intent. "But can you do both well?"

"Men can."

"What about when you have children?"

"I don't know. I suppose—I don't know."

"I know it's difficult." He patted her shoulder and stepped away. "But you'll have to think about what you really want."

"Uncle, I want—"

"Shh." He laid a finger on her lips. "Give it some thought Now." He straightened. "You promised me lunch."

"Yes," she said distractedly. "Let me just change my clothes I won't be long." She smiled and left the room, and only when she was in the privacy of her bedroom did she let the smile drop. Uncle Henry had asked her some hard questions, questions she couldn't answer. Because, when it came down to it what did she want in her life?

She let out her breath and began pulling pins at random from her hair. "Well, Brooke," she muttered to her reflection, "he's right. It's time to grow up." And in doing so, what would she have to give up?

If the earlier hints of forgeries at the Manhattan had stirred interest, the latest news caused a sensation. Even the normally discreet *New York Times* blared in its headlines that the museum's director had been a party to forgery, theft, and, possibly, murder. From the very top of society down to the lowest workingman, everyone avidly discussed the story. The Devlins' telephone rang almost unceasingly, with calls from acquaintances in Newport or Bar Harbor pretending to be shocked, but wanting to know all the details. Matt let Fuller and a harassed-looking Brooke handle them. He was more interested in what was being said in the cells in the headquarters basement, where the crimes were discussed with an odd kind of relish. Even the rich got caught, the common criminals assured one another gleefully, and it served them right. If they knew anything about the crimes, however, that information was not forthcoming.

"No one's talking." Tony, shirtsleeves pushed back, straddled a chair facing Matt's desk. Though it was Sunday, the air rests of both Owen and Earle meant that Matt and Tony were putting in more time. "Not Owen and Earle with their fancy lawyers, and not anyone else either. No one knows nothin' about nothin'. Or so they say."

Matt picked up a pencil and let it drop to the desk, idly watching it roll away from him. "That's because they don't. Not the ordinary criminal, anyway."

Tony's gaze was steady. "Horgan's involved in this somehow."

"How? Do you think Owen used him to fence the paintings? I don't. You'd have heard about it before now, and so would I."

"I don't care. He's involved."

Matt let the pencil drop again, and then nodded. "Probably," he said, and remembered again the gangster's implied threat against Brooke. In spite of the day's heavy heat, he felt chilled. "But where's the link?"

"I don't know. Will you stop playing with that damn pencil?"

Matt paused as he picked up the pencil again. "Sorry. Look, I'd like to get Horgan as much as you would, but we've got to do it right." If they didn't, without the evidence to prove Horgan's involvement, they'd be in trouble. They'd been told so by no less than Roosevelt himself. The law applied to everyone, he'd said, and wasn't that what he'd been trying to prove? If Horgan was involved, find the proof. If Owen and Earle had something to do with Warren's death, they'd have to find out by investigating. No more of this third-degree stuff that had forced confessions in the past. For, if the law's penalties applied to all, so did its rights.

"Yeah," Tony said after a minute, and then rose, yawning. "Think Earle's had enough time to stew?"

Matt checked his watch. "Probably. All right, let's go talk to him. And his lawyer." He shrugged into his suit jacket as he got up. Savile Row's best for today, a lightweight pearl-gray wool Brooke had persuaded him to buy last spring. He was beginning to realize that even in this job there was some value to dressing well. Especially when he had to deal with well-to-do criminals and their lawyers.

In the basement, Matt and Tony waited in a corridor near the cells while a uniformed officer unlocked a heavy metal door set with bars in a small window. The door swung open, and they stepped inside, into a small, whitewashed room containing only a scarred wooden table and several old chairs. James Earle Carter, standing near the barred window set high in the wall, spun around at their entrance, while the man seated at the table, papers spread before him, looked up calmly. "Why am I still being held?" Earle demanded.

"We explained it to you, Mr. Earle." Matt pulled one of the chairs away from the wall and sat down, one leg casually crossed over the other. "As it's Sunday, there won't be a bail hearing for you until tomorrow."

"Bull crap. Owen's going to get out."

"Where did you hear that?" Tony asked, straddling a chair as he had upstairs.

"It's all over the place. Look, if you don't let me out, I'll—"

"James." The man at the table rose, walking to Earle and placing a hand on his shoulder. "I suggest you not say any more."

Earle shook off his hand. "I'll speak my mind, damn you. What kind of lawyer are you anyway? Can't you get me out?"

"I'm afraid we don't have Mr. Owen's, ah, resources." The lawyer sat down again. Tall and portly, he exuded an air of calm confidence in his well-tailored suit. "My client does, however, have a point." He looked directly at Matt. "He is being held on the flimsiest of evidence and should be released immediately."

Matt shrugged. "As you said, Mr. Latham, he doesn't have Owen's resources," he said, and had the satisfaction of seeing the lawyer's face tighten. Owen apparently had enough power to get a judge to hold a special bail hearing. Interesting, that. "Of course, you realize that Owen's been cooperative."

"What?" Earle spun around again. He had been arrested upon his return home from an evening out, and had obviously not had a chance to change his clothes. His black pants sagged at the knees, and his white dress shirt was wrinkled. "What has Owen been telling you?"

"James, I really suggest you let me handle this," Mr. Latham put in. "If Mr. Owen has said anything of interest, gentlemen, I'd appreciate knowing what it is."

Tony crossed his arms on the back of the chair. "Depends on what you think is interesting."

"He told us quite a tale," Matt said. "About the forgeries and the thefts—"

"And your part in them," Tony put in smoothly.

"I never had anything to do with stealing my—those paintings!" Earle exclaimed, and Latham winced.

"Then you admit you forged?" Matt said, relentless.

"Which means you conspired with Warren. You must have," Tony said. "And quarreled with him too. Was that when you decided to kill him?"

"I didn't! Hell, is that what Owen's saying about me?"

"Mr. Earle." Latham's voice was like a whip. "Let me handle this."

"I'm not going to be stuck with something I didn't do."

"James, please." Latham briefly closed his eyes, as if in pain, and then rose. "Gentlemen. Will you allow me a few minutes alone with my client?"

Matt and Tony looked at each other, and then Matt, shrugging, got up. "All right. Five minutes. We've got a lot to discuss," he said, staring hard at Earle, and went out of the room.

Somewhat more than five minutes passed before Latham came to the door of the interview room, signaling to Matt and Tony to come back in. Neither minded the wait, not with what had been implied in their conversation with Earle.

Inside the room, Earle paced quickly back and forth, chewing on a thumbnail. Latham, sitting again, had a resigned air, his shoulders slumped. "I have advised my client not to talk. He, however, has different ideas." He raised his hands palms-up to indicate his helplessness. "I will, however, counsel him not to answer any question I consider to be incriminating."

"Fair enough." Matt sat down, pulling out his notebook. "Well?"

Earle turned, staring directly at Matt. "I didn't kill Warren."

"What did you do, Mr. Earle?"

"Don't answer that, James," Latham said swiftly.

"Shut up."

"What?"

"I said, shut up." Earle braced his hands on the table. "Look, you want to know what happened?"

"We have a fair idea of it," Matt said.

"Yeah? Not all of it, you don't. I painted those paintings. They know, so I'm going to admit it," he said to Latham, who had let out a groan. "Besides, I'm proud of them. Yes, I am." Earle actually grinned. "My paintings fooling all the experts and hanging at the Manhattan. It was priceless."

"Was it?" Matt scribbled in his notebook. "Were all the so-called lost masterpieces yours?"

"Yes." His face darkened. "But they're all gone now."

"Do you know where?"

"No."

Matt simply nodded; he had a fair idea where the paintings were. "How did you come to paint them?"

"It wasn't my idea. No, really, it wasn't," he protested, though no one had said anything. "I went to the Manhattan one day, about two years ago, and I ran into Warren. We went for a drink, and he mentioned my talent."

Tony looked up. "What talent would that be, Mr. Earle?"

Earle drew himself up. "I can copy any painter, living or dead, and make you believe it's the real thing. My own work wouldn't sell. But if I did a copy, I'd get paid."

"Yet you're doing well as a portrait painter," Matt said.

The look Earle shot Matt was full of resentment. "I am. Did you ever intend to have your wife's portrait painted?"

"Maybe. By someone else. Now—"

"Tell her not to wear pink." Earle's tone was derisive. "When she said that I nearly laughed out loud. What are you, on the take?"

Tony tensed; Matt remained calm. "Not quite. My wife's uncle is Augustus Low," he said, and had the satisfaction of seeing Earle's eyes flicker. "Let's get back to your conversation with Warren. Did he suggest you put this talent, as you call it, to use?"

"Not then. Later though." He glanced at Matt over his shoulder. "It's no secret I wasn't doing well. As I mentioned, my own works weren't selling. Too advanced for most people."

"Mmm-hmm."

"To put it bluntly, I needed money. When Joseph suggested I do painting in the styles of the old masters for someone he knew, I saw no harm in it."

"No harm in committing forgery?" Tony said.

"It isn't forgery if the client knew who really painted them."

"But the client didn't, am I right?" Matt said. "When did you find out it was the Manhattan buying your paintings?"

"Don't answer that," Latham put in.

"I have nothing to hide. I found out when everyone else did, that the museum had acquired some lost masterpieces."

"Come on, Earle," Tony said. "You expect us to believe that?"

"It's the truth."

"But then you saw you had something profitable going," Matt said. "That's when you went to Warren again. You were overheard quarreling with him."

He glowered at Matt. "Why shouldn't I? He cheated me."

"James," Latham groaned.

"Shut up. So I suggested a better arrangement. I would continue to supply paintings for an increased payment."

"And was Warren getting paid as well?"

"The museum was putting out the money. Warren got some of it. I'd ship the paintings to a friend in England, and then Warren would have them sent back here. It caused a sensation." He grinned. "All those experts, fooled by my work."

"But then it ended. Owen found out they were forgeries."

"Yes." Earle's smile faded. "In a way, that was even better because I got paid again—"

"You did?" Matt said in surprise.

"Sure. You didn't know that? Whoever bought the paintings paid well. We all shared in it."

"Did you."

"Yeah. Don't know everything, do you?"

"But how did you feel, having your paintings stolen? You works, that you were so proud of, in a museum."

"It didn't bother me."

"No? I think it did." Matt leaned forward. "I think it made you angry. Furious. And when you found out Warren was planning to have more of them removed, you decided to stop him—"

"Gentlemen, I must insist you stop now," Latham said, rising.

"I didn't kill him," Earle said as if Latham hadn't spoken. "Why should I? We had a good thing going."

"Revenge, Mr. Earle. And you have a reputation to protect now, as much as either Warren or Owen."

"I didn't kill Warren!"

"Then who did?"

"I don't know." Earle's frown was sullen. "Ask Owen."

"Are you saying Owen did it?"

"Really, gentlemen, this is enough." Latham took Earle's arm. "This interview is over."

Earle looked at his lawyer as if seeing him for the first time, and then nodded. "I've told all I know. But take my advice," he said as Matt and Tony went to the door. "Ask Owen what happened to Joseph Warren."

As Matt walked back into the detective bureau a few minutes later, he caught a glimpse of Captain O'Neill, just coming out of his office. Matt turned, but it was too late. "Devlin," O'Neill called. "Get in here."

Matt shrugged, and turned, Tony behind him. Owen's arrest had everyone talking, except O'Neill. Who, Matt wondered again, was he protecting? "Yes?" he said, standing at the door to O'Neill's office.

"Come in and close the door, both of you." O'Neill gestured toward the straight wooden chairs that faced his desk. "We need to have a talk."

"Past time," another voice said, and for the first time Matt realized there was someone else in the office. It was Andrew Parker, a member of the police commissioners. He stood in the shadows, a vague and yet solid figure. "You've stirred everyone up, Devlin."

"Mr. Parker." Matt nodded easily though his muscles had

tightened. In the past months Parker's opposition to Roosevel
and his attempts to get TR off the board of commissioners had
rocked the department. He'd worked hard in the year past to
weed out corruption in the department, particularly in the de
tective bureau, his special responsibility. Some said he wa
motivated by jealousy of TR, who seemed to get the credit for
any improvements in the department; but now Matt won
dered if there was something more. Parker's face was calm
composed, but his eyes were alert. He was a man to be carefu
of.

"Mr. Parker has been asking about the progress of your case,'
O'Neill said, sitting behind his desk. "I'll be straight with you
We're getting a lot of heat about it."

Parker stepped into the light at last, and yet his face was stil
shadowed. "How good are the cases against Owen and Earle?

Matt and Tony exchanged glances. "We haven't spoken
with Owen yet, sir, since he isn't talking. But Earle did tell u
a lot," Tony said, and went on to relate all that Earle had said
Sitting back and watching Parker's eyes flicker as he listened
Matt had the strange feeling that Parker already knew every
thing.

"So you have no evidence Owen was involved in the mur
der," O'Neill said when Tony had finished.

"No, except that he admitted being in on the thefts."

"Are you saying, sir, that Owen wasn't involved?" Mat
asked.

"Why would he be, and he a fine, upstandin' citizen?"

"We wouldn't want to charge the wrong man with murder
now, would we?" Parker put in. "Remember what happened
Devlin, the last time you did that."

Matt's face tightened at the reminder, and the threat behin
it. Something was going on here, something else beside th

hunt for a murderer. Something he didn't want to be involved in. "No, sir, we don't, but what evidence we do have points to Owen."

"Why?" O'Neill said. "You still haven't told us why he'd do such a thing."

O'Neill was protecting Owen. That had to be it. What Parker's motives were, Matt wasn't so sure. "Sir, everyone we've talked to has said that Chandler Owen has been a good director of the museum, but not an outstanding one."

"So?"

"So if it came out that he'd participated in buying forgeries, Owen would probably lose his job. He has some family money, but not that much. Besides, the prestige of the position matters to him."

"All of which says he wouldn't steal from the museum."

"But he wouldn't want it known that he'd been involved in buying forgeries either," Tony argued, "whether he knew about them or not. So if the paintings were stolen, no one would know they were forged."

"And that's one thing we do know for certain," Matt said before O'Neill could protest further. "Earle's confessed to it."

"I don't like it." O'Neill was shaking his head. "It's not enough. Maybe Owen was involved with the thefts, but with murder? No. I don't believe it."

"And yet Roosevelt told you to keep investigating him," Parker said.

Matt stiffened, finally realizing why Parker was there. If they arrested the wrong man because they'd been told to by Roosevelt, Parker would have another weapon in his fight against his fellow commissioner. "I'm not satisfied with the case we have either," he said carefully. "Which is why we're still investigating—"

"I don't agree." O'Neill slapped his hand flat on the desk. "From what I've seen, you've got your thief and murderer already."

Matt frowned, puzzled. "Owen? But you said—"

"No. Not Owen. Earle. He had a motive for wanting Warren dead, didn't he?"

"Not much of one, but—"

"And no alibi for the night Warren was killed?"

"Not that he remembers, no."

"So there you have it." O'Neill sat back, smiling smugly. "I'm thinkin', gentlemen, that you'd better investigate this Earle feller a little further."

"Yes, sir, and then?"

"Why, then you arrest him for killin' Warren."

13

"Dammit, I still don't see it," Matt said, pacing across the parlor floor the following morning, coffee cup in hand. "I still don't see what O'Neill's up to."

"Matt, do please sit down and eat something." Brooke held a plate out to him. Mr. Eichhammer and his men were to begin painting the dining room today, which meant that breakfast had been served in the parlor. "You had such a long day yesterday, and—"

"Yeah. And probably longer today. Dammit, of course Earle doesn't have an alibi for the night Warren died. It was three months ago. Do you remember what you were doing on a specific evening three months ago?"

"Matt, sit down," Brooke said again. This time Matt stopped pacing and looked at her. Then, without further protest, and somewhat to her surprise, he dropped down into one of the gold velvet chairs facing her. The morning sun streamed into the room, making it pleasant and bright. "You didn't get in until late last night and then you didn't sleep well, and today's likely to be more of the same. At least have some breakfast."

Matt muttered something under his breath, but he at last pulled the small tea table toward him and began to eat, if distractedly. "Earle had something to do with it," he went on. "At least the forgeries and the thefts. But the murder? I don't think so. Warren was making him money. Why kill him?"

"Revenge?" Brooke refilled his coffee cup. "Because his works wouldn't be hanging in the museum anymore?"

"Maybe." Matt frowned. "Still, I think what he liked was the idea that he fooled everyone, and not just that he had pictures in the Manhattan. Maybe I'm wrong, but . . ."

"You need to investigate him more."

"Yeah. I suppose I do. And Owen too." Matt chewed thoughtfully on a piece of toast. "O'Neill has a point. I can see why Owen would plan the thefts, but why kill Warren?"

"Maybe Warren was going to tell what he did. Maybe—"

"What, and be arrested for fraud? I doubt it."

"Matt, wasn't the theft when he was killed different from the others?"

Matt stopped chewing and set the mangled piece of toast down. "Yeah. It was. This whole thing with O'Neill and Parker has gotten me so worked up, I forgot about that." He cast Brooke a look. "Parker's trying to use us to get at Roosevelt."

"I know. So you must be absolutely certain of your case, Matt, and you're not."

"Owen's motive—"

"Do you really think it was Owen?"

Matt picked up the piece of toast, and then set it down again. "I don't know," he said finally. "Something doesn't fit, Brooke. Maisie and what she knew, and her involvement with Warren—and how does Horgan fit in with this?"

"Maybe he doesn't. Maisie could have been killed for entirely different reasons." She frowned. "Maybe Sylvia—"

"Maisie was killed because she knew something. That's the only thing we could turn up on her."

"Maybe." Brooke set down her fork. "Poor Linda. And Mrs. Warren. This must really have hit them hard."

"Hmm." Matt slouched back. "I wonder if they knew about the forgeries."

"Oh, I doubt it, Matt. At least, I'm certain Linda didn't. Else why would she have come to me?"

"Mmm. She'd have wanted it kept quiet." Matt tossed his napkin onto the tea tray, pushed it away from him, and rose. "I've got to go. There'll be a lot to do today."

"I know. I'll be busy too." Brooke uncurled herself from the sofa. "I'll be glad when all the redecorating is done."

"So will I. No more smell of paint."

"No. Matt?" She followed him to the doorway of the parlor. "Do you think that, when your case is settled and the apartment is done we could go down to Newport?"

In the hallway, Matt stopped in the act of putting on his hat. "Do you mean for a weekend?"

"No. A week, perhaps two. You look as if you could use the break, and—"

"For God's sake, Brooke." Matt's tone was no less fierce for being so low. "I can't just take time off like that."

"But if you've solved a major case—"

"There'll be another, and another. For God's sake." He stared at her. "You know what my work is like. And don't forget, I haven't been back long from our honeymoon."

"You're not going to forgive me for that, are you?"

"Forgive you—hey, I wouldn't have gone if I didn't want to. But now it's time to face reality." He stared at her. "I don't have time for this, Brooke."

"I don't care." Her voice was as low as his, so as not to attract the servants' attention. "You never have time. You've been telling me that since we got back, and how hard it is for you, having to prove yourself, and—"

"It is hard, dammit."

"But you're proving yourself now. I'd think—oh, never mind." She turned away, all the annoyances and aggravations of the past week rising within her.

"No." Matt followed her back into the parlor. "You were going to say something. What was it?"

Brooke turned. If she spilled out all that was on her mind, they'd quarrel. She didn't want that, and heaven knew he didn't need it. Yet her mouth opened and she heard herself talking, as if against her will. "It's not how I thought it would be," she burst out. "We're supposed to be partners, Matt, but since we came back I've hardly seen you. I'm supposed to find other ways to fill my time. Yet when you need me to ask someone questions, I'm supposed to jump to it. What do you want of me?" She turned to face him, her hands gripping the back of a chair so hard her knuckles were white. "You don't seem to want me to live the way I did before I married you, but I can't live the way you do. What do you want of me?"

Matt gazed at her, eyes steady. "I think you're asking the wrong person, Brooke."

"What?" She blinked. "I don't understand."

"Do you want to go to Newport?"

"Yes, a little bit, but—"

"You can't have it both ways," he said almost gently. "If you're going to be my partner—and I do see you that way, Brooke, no matter what you think—then there are some things you'll have to give up." He clapped his derby hat on. "What do you want, Brooke?"

She stared at him. "I don't know," she said finally.

"I think you'd better decide, don't you?" He turned. "I don't know what time I'll be home tonight," he said, and went out, the apartment door closing firmly behind him. Brooke was alone, and confused. Because he was right. What did she want?

Faintly she heard the telephone ring. If the call was for Matt, then whoever it was was out of luck. "Mr. Devlin's just left," she told Fuller when he appeared in the doorway.

"Yes, madam. The telephone call is for you, madam."

"For me? But who could be calling at this hour of the morning?"

"Mrs. Olmstead, madam."

Brooke involuntarily made a face. If her aunt was calling from Newport so early, it didn't bode well. "All right, Fuller, I'll be right along." She went to the telephone and picked up the receiver with some trepidation. "Aunt Winifred?" she said, and sat back, resigned, as Winifred let out a spate of words. Little was required of Brooke in this conversation, except for an occasional murmur of agreement or acquiescence. Uncle Henry apparently had talked to Winifred yesterday, and, in spite of his promise, had mentioned the redecoration of the apartment. Winifred was not, as Brooke had expected, pleased. It took all Brooke's diplomacy and tact to calm her down, and to assure her that the redecoration was not meant as an insult.

By the time she hung up, Brooke felt bewildered and a little battered. So much was expected of her! She was supposed to be a model wife; supposed to decorate her home in keeping with current styles even if she didn't like it; supposed to keep up her social obligations. Not at all should she be a partner in crime, which Winifred gathered she was. New York was so uncomfortable this time of year. Was that really where Brooke wanted to be, and did she really want to dabble in such distasteful things as murder?

Yes, Brooke thought, staring at her reflection in the bedroom mirror, and set down the silver-backed hairbrush. Matt had asked her what she wanted; Aunt Winifred demanded to know; and though Brooke didn't have all the answers, she knew what she didn't want. She didn't want an empty life where socializing and gossip and fashion were the most important things. She wanted a life with meaning. If having that meant giving up some of the traditional social pursuits such as spending summers in a cooler climate, so be it. She'd known what she was getting into when she married Matt.

Brooke dressed quickly, filled with purpose at last. Like Matt, she was bothered by certain aspects of the case, if not the same ones as he. Why had Sylvia Warren gone, not once, but several times, to the Golden Harp? Setting her hat on her head, Brooke nodded firmly at her reflection. She'd made her choice. She was going to be Matt's partner, as best she could.

Earle's bail hearing would be held late that morning; it was likely he'd be out of jail by the afternoon. Owen, already free, was keeping to himself at his home and refusing, on his lawyer's advice, to answer any questions. Even Seaton had nothing more to add. The case had come to a standstill.

"So Earle's butler doesn't know where he was the night Warren died," Matt said from his desk in the detective bureau, glancing over a report compiled by another officer.

"Looks that way," Tony agreed. "According to Earle's diary, he had a dinner engagement, but he doesn't remember if he came home directly afterward or went someplace else. Neither does the butler."

Matt grunted, leaning back with his hands linked behind his head. "So where are we, Tony?"

"Stuck. Earle could possibly have done it, but there's no proof. And Owen."

"No, I don't think so." Matt straightened. "The painting

that was stolen when Warren was killed was cut from its frame."

"Yeah, so?"

"I don't think Earle would have treated a painting that way. I'm sure Owen wouldn't have."

"Then who did?"

"If we knew that, we'd have Warren's killer. Yeah, what is it?" he said, looking up at the officer who stood near his desk.

"Detective Schmidt thinks you should come to the cells, Detective," the officer said. "He said to tell you he's learned something interesting."

"Oh?" Matt glanced at Tony as he rose, pulling on his suit coat. It was another hot, sticky day, and he'd rather be anyplace than Mulberry Street, with its heavy humidity and fetid air, and a case that looked as impossible to solve now as it had three weeks ago. "Damn, I wish I'd agreed with Brooke to go to Newport," he muttered as they clattered down the stairs to the basement.

"With your in-laws? You're a better man than that," Tony said.

Matt let out a laugh. "Yeah. My rich in-laws."

"In-laws, all the same."

"Yeah," Matt said again, continuing down the stairs, his good humor restored. How it had happened he wasn't quite sure, but his wife's relatives weren't being held against him anymore. He had been accepted. "Wonder what Schmidt wants? We haven't been working with him on anything."

"Don't know," Tony said, stopping in front of the door leading to the room where yesterday they'd questioned Earle. "Schmidt in there?"

"Yeah," said the officer who stood at the door. "He said for you to go in."

"What's it about, do you know?"

"Naw. Schmidt was on a burglary last night, that's all I know."

Matt and Tony looked at each other as the door closed behind them. Schmidt came forward, a heavy, florid man in a suit of large houndstooth check, one meaty hand extended. "Devlin. Flynn. I've got something for you."

"What?" Tony asked, though he was already grinning at the sight of the man sitting at the table. He was small, his build shrunken, with gray hair thinning on top and large eyes deep-set in a long, hound-dog sad face. "Bert. So you're up to your old tricks?"

"Not me, Mr. Flynn, I swear," Bert said, and sneezed, rubbing a grimy handkerchief over his nose. "Bloody cold."

"My sympathies. What's he in for this time?" he asked Schmidt.

"Fencing." Schmidt leaned against the wall, looking amused. "We had word there was a burglary ring going on, so we've been watching Bert's place. And last night, who should go there but Smiley Malarkey and One-Eyed Jones. Caught 'em in the act."

"Can't a man have visitors?" Bert interrupted.

"Not when they've got sacks of silver and stuff that's been stolen from people's houses," Schmidt retorted.

"Bert runs a pawnshop," Tony explained to Matt, who had been standing back, observing, a little mystified. "Sometimes he pawns stuff for people who aren't the right owners."

Matt nodded. "A fence."

"No, sir, I ain't no fence!" Bert straightened, and promptly ruined his impression by sneezing again. "I don't deal in stolen goods—"

"Save it," Schmidt said wearily. "You told me you had something we'd be interested in."

Bert stared sulkily at his hands. "Maybe I do, and maybe I don't."

"What could he have that would be of any interest to us?" Tony said with contemptuous amusement. "A small-time fence like him."

"I ain't small-time!" A crafty look passed over his face. "If I tell you what I got, do I get something for it?"

"Such as?"

"Dunno. Let me go?"

"Can't do that, Bert." Tony sounded almost regretful. "But we can tell the judge you've been cooperative. Maybe he'll go easy on you."

"Yeah? Well." Bert sneezed again, making a great to-do out of wiping his nose. "Okay. I'll come clean. I hear you been looking for some pictures."

Matt and Tony both stiffened. "What kind of pictures, Bert?" Tony said mildly.

"Pictures. You know, paintings. The ones stolen from the Manhattan Museum."

"Do you have them, Bert?"

"Nah, and I don't know who does. Not the ones everyone's talking about anyway. But I do got this one picture—can I show 'em?" he appealed to Schmidt.

"Why not?" Schmidt shrugged and crossed to the door, talking to the officer outside. "It'll be here in a minute."

"Where'd this picture come from, Bert?" Tony asked.

"Dunno."

"Now, Bert." Tony leaned over him. "You know better than that."

"I swear, I dunno, Mr. Flynn."

"You don't know who brought it in?"

"Well, yeah, but—see, it was just an ordinary pawn. He needed money, said he'd lost some gambling, and his wife was mad but this was what he had to sell."

"Huh," Matt muttered, wondering what this had to do with them.

"Yeah. I didn't think nothing of it, but then there's been all this fuss about missing paintings, and I got to wondering. I looked at this picture again, even though it's got no frame—"

"What?"

"Cross my heart, Detective," Bert said, startling Matt by drawing a cross over his heart. "It doesn't have a frame. Anyways, I looked at it, and I thought it looked familiar. Like I'd seen it somewhere."

Matt looked blankly at Tony. "I don't know if it means anything," Schmidt's voice rumbled, "but I thought you should see it."

Tony shrugged. "We weren't doing anything more important," he said, and at that moment the key rattled in the door behind them. The officer handed in a small, rolled-up canvas. "Is that it?"

"Open it." Bert leaned forward, some life in his hang-dog eyes. "Yeah," he said as Schmidt unrolled the painting. "Yeah, that's it."

"William Morris Hunt," Matt said involuntarily, because he knew this particular work.

"Cut from the frame," Tony murmured, fingering the ragged edges of the painting, and his eyes met Matt's, serious now. There was little doubt: this was the painting stolen when Warren was killed. "Where did you get this?"

Bert straightened in unconscious response to the urgency in Tony's voice. "Told you, an old friend—"

"Who?" Tony was across the room before anyone could blink, his hands at Bert's collar. "Tell me, or by God I'll—"

"Flynn." Matt clamped his hand on Tony's shoulder. "Not that way."

Tony didn't move. "He deserves it, if he's had this all along."

"Please," Bert whispered, and sneezed. Tony released him so fast he fell back against his chair. "I told you, I don't know nothing more about it."

Tony had taken out his own pristine handkerchief and was rubbing at his hands, a look of revulsion on his face. "Who brought it in, Bert? And don't tell me you don't remember," he said as Bert opened his mouth to protest. "If you want us to help with the judge, you'd better tell us."

Bert looked at the three detectives ranged against him, and then shrugged. "All right, though I don't know why it matters, if it's not one of the stolen paintings. Lew Gilmore brought it in."

"Gilmore," Tony said, and breathed out, a satisfied sound. "Well, well."

"I won't get in trouble, will I? I mean, I told you what you wanted to know, and—"

"But you see, Bert, this painting was stolen," Tony said almost gently. "From the Manhattan, the night someone was killed there."

Bert's eyes opened wide. "I didn't have nothing to do with that. I—"

"I didn't say you did. You know who Gilmore works for, don't you?"

Bert stared at him, and his already pale face turned a sickly chalk-gray. "Horgan," he whispered.

"Yeah." Tony nodded. "You've just peached on Horgan, Bert."

"Jesus! I didn't mean to—"

"If I were you, I'd be more worried about him than the judge." Tony turned away, gesturing to Matt. "But we'll talk to the judge anyway," he said, and he and Matt left the room.

"Horgan," Matt said, stunned, as he and Tony walked along the corridor to the stairs.

"Yeah. You see it, don't you?"

"Oh, yes. I see it." Somehow Horgan had been involved with that fatal theft at the Manhattan, and thus perhaps with Warren's death. "Goddamn. We know who killed Warren." He stared blankly at Tony. "But why?"

The little house in Morningside Heights seemed a far more pleasant place this sunny morning than it had when Brooke had first seen it. Leaves rustled in the fresh breeze and the Hudson glinted in the sun; there was little noise or bustle from traffic or congestion. It was really a nice place to live, Brooke thought as the victoria drew to a stop, actually more appealing than the more fashionable areas of the city. Yet she knew that to someone as involved in society as Sylvia Warren had been, it must seem like exile.

A shiny black buggy was pulled up before the house, Brooke noticed as she stepped down to the sidewalk, and a man was just climbing in. A vaguely familiar man, she thought, and stood very still as he tipped his hat with the head of his walking stick, smiling very slightly, before climbing in. Frank Horgan. She couldn't be mistaken. She'd seen him only once, yet she would recognize him anywhere. What in the world was he doing here?

Dread coiled in a heavy lump in the pit of Brooke's stomach. Frank Horgan and Sylvia Warren. Before today she would not have connected the two, despite Sylvia's visits to the Golden Harp; in spite of the fact that she'd been seen talking with Horgan. Brooke climbed the stairs mechanically. That had been months ago, however. Since her husband's death Mrs. Warren had lived an apparently blameless life in a small flat far removed from her usual surroundings. So why, Brooke thought, standing at the top of the stoop and watching as the buggy drove away, was Horgan there?

"What is it now?" a distracted voice said a few moments later when Brooke knocked at the door of the Warrens' apartment. "I've told you I've nothin' more to say, and—oh!" Sylvia stood in the doorway, staring at Brooke. "It's you."

"Yes." Brooke stepped back, as startled as Sylvia appeared. "I'm sorry. You appear to be going out. I've come at a bad time."

"No, no, I'm not going anywhere." There was more than a trace of bitterness in her voice. "You might as well come in."

"Thank you. I shan't stay."

Sylvia shrugged. "It really makes no difference," she said, dropping down onto the maroon plush sofa, and, to Brooke's surprise, lighting a cigarette. "Would you please close the door? The latch doesn't always catch."

"Oh, of course." Brooke absently swung the door closed. "I'm sorry if I'm intruding—"

"Never mind that. Do sit down. Forgive me if I seem to have forgotten my manners, but then, manners don't seem to matter very much anymore. We had to let our maid go, you know."

"No, I didn't." Brooke perched on the edge of a spindly white-and-gilt chair. The surface of the table set between sofa and chairs was coated with a film of dust. Atop it sat a cut-glass ashtray littered with several cigarette butts, and two tumblers, one half filled with an amber fluid, the other containing only a residue. To Brooke's astonishment, Sylvia picked up the half-full glass and took a long swallow. "I am sorry."

"Sorry. Yes. Everyone seems to be sorry." Sylvia blew out a long stream of smoke. "Joseph left us with nothin', did you know that? Oh, I know, it's not done to talk about money. All very well when you have it." Another sip from the glass. "Quite different when you don't. I am actually supposed to cook and clean this place." Sylvia looked scornfully about the small, overcrowded flat. "You'd think Linda would help, wouldn't you, but she—"

"Isn't she working?"

"Typewritin'. Not very hard work. She could do more around here."

Brooke started to rise. "I think perhaps I'd best go—"

"No, no, stay." Sylvia gestured with the cigarette. "Don't mind me. It's the bourbon talking. Fine thing, bourbon. Would you like some?"

"Uh—no, thank you."

"Well, I think I'll have a wee bit more. If you'd be a dear and fetch me that bottle?"

Privately Brooke thought Sylvia had had enough, but if she got the bottle, perhaps she could find an excuse to leave. The floor creaked under her feet as she crossed to a cabinet, and she noted absently that the door to the flat had swung ajar. She gazed at it longingly, wishing she could escape. "Mrs. Warren, if you don't mind my saying so, it's early in the day for this."

"I do mind!" Sylvia glared up at her. "And what would you know about it? You fell into clover and you almost threw it away, marryin' as you did. Winifred is far more generous than I would have been." She splashed a generous measure of bourbon into her glass. "But then, she can afford to be. Oh, sit down. You make me nervous, standing there."

Brooke settled uneasily on the chair again, carefully spreading the skirts of her beige walking ensemble about her. "I can't stay long—"

"Of course not. I would have credited you with more tact, though, coming to gloat about all that Joseph did—"

"No, I'm not! I wouldn't." Brooke stared at Sylvia. "I was horrified to hear about him—"

"Oh, I'm sure."

"—and I realized you and Linda must be feeling this terribly. As I can see you are." Of course Sylvia had taken to drink and to bitterness, Brooke thought with a sudden stab of compassion. Her whole world had been shattered. Rising, she skirted the table and sat on the sofa, laying her hand on Sylvia's. "I came because I wanted to see if there is anything I can do."

"Do? Ha." Sylvia's gaze roamed aimlessly about the flat. "What can you do? Can you change the past?"

"No, I'm afraid not."

"Can you undo what Joseph did? Or what I did?"

"No. I'm sorry." Brooke's voice was soft. "But surely you know you're not alone. You have friends. I'm here, and"—she swallowed, wondering if she should bring this up—"I saw Mr. Horgan leaving—"

"Damn!" It came out as a hiss, startling Brooke. She pulled back, but Sylvia caught her hand in a tight, pitiless grip. "Is that what this is about?"

"Mrs. Warren, please. I don't know what you mean."

"Oh, so innocent, but you don't fool me. So you saw Frank?" Sylvia drained her glass, looking at Brooke over the rim of it. "I'm not surprised. It's just my luck. And so now you know."

"Mrs. Warren, I don't know what you're talking about."

"Don't try to fool me, dear. Your husband's a cop and you help him with his work. You know."

"Very well." Brooke sat still. She'd play along. Sylvia would have to let her go eventually. "I suppose I do. About you and Mr. Horgan—"

"Oh, him. No, not him. Just because we're friends—no. Me. You know about me, don't you?" She splashed more bourbon into her glass and took a long draft, her eyes never leaving Brooke's. "You know that I helped kill my husband."

14

"Where is Horgan?" Matt asked. He and Tony had just returned to the detective bureau from the interview with Bert, and were still trying to absorb what they had learned.

"Don't know." Tony shook his head as he turned from his desk. "I called the Eldridge Street station and they say he left the Golden Harp a while ago, but not where." He paused. "We don't have any evidence against him, you know."

Matt slammed his fist into his palm. "We don't have any evidence against anyone, dammit. Or a motive."

"I can guess that." Tony tilted his chair back on two legs. "Warren owed him money."

"So wouldn't he want Warren alive to pay him back?"

"Ordinarily, yeah. But if Warren had been warned—remember he was roughed up a few weeks before he died?"

"Yeah." Matt frowned slightly, remembering. "That was Horgan?"

"Probably. It's the way he works. Give a warning, and if the mark doesn't pay up . . ."

"Kill him." Matt nodded. He'd seen it happen before. Someone like Horgan couldn't afford to let anyone defy him if he wanted to keep his power. Yet, according to Horgan himself, Warren had paid him back.

"He probably ran up more debts," Tony said as if reading Matt's mind. "It sounds like he was the kind of gambler that couldn't keep away. And without the forgeries to bring in money?" Tony shrugged. "Reason enough for Horgan to have him killed."

"But Warren was getting money from the thefts too. Unless—hell." He stared at Tony. "He probably didn't share it. Horgan got rid of only the one painting. Warren didn't need him for the others."

"So he cut Horgan out? Mmm-hmm." Tony nodded. "It fits. All the more reason for Horgan to want to kill him, for revenge."

"But not in the museum." Matt's frown deepened. "Hell, Tony, I can't see it. Warren wouldn't have gone out to meet Horgan by himself. Not knowing that Horgan was angry. Dammit." Matt rose and began pacing. "There's something missing. Horgan's involved somehow, but so is Owen. And if he doesn't talk—"

"I have an idea that might make him talk," Tony said.

"What's that?"

"It worked with Earle." Tony's eyes gleamed. "Let's accuse him of the murder."

Matt turned and stared at him. The idea had possibilities. "O'Neill will never go along with it."

"So we'll go to TR."

"Yeah, but—" He paused. "This whole thing could blow up in our faces, Tony. There's something else." He resumed his pacing. "O'Neill's protecting Owen. We're agreed on that? Okay. So no matter what we do, Owen probably won't talk." He stopped. "We're stuck."

"Damn, there's got to be something we can do."

"No, dammit, we're stuck. We can go to TR and tell him what we think, but we don't have any evidence. Dammit." He pounded on the desk. "Two people who could've done it, and we don't have any proof."

"There's got to be a way," Tony said again. "If Byrnes was still chief of police, we'd—"

"What? Beat it out of them?"

"There's more to the third degree than that. I'll tell you, Devlin." The legs of Tony's chair banged down. "I've never seen anyone question someone the way Byrnes did. He always seemed to know just what to say to get people talking."

"But he wouldn't go against someone like Owen, would he? Not if he were being paid."

Tony glanced away, lips set. "No," he said finally.

"And TR won't go against him without proof. Dammit." Matt dropped into his chair. "We're stuck."

"Hell. I wish I knew what Maisie wanted to tell me. Hey." He straightened. "There was a raid on some of the cathouses last night."

"Yeah, so?"

"So maybe we're holding someone who knew Maisie. Or something."

"You're reaching, Flynn."

"Maybe." Tony bounced to his feet. "But I think I'll just check the cells to see who's there."

"Good luck," Matt said ironically, and turned back to the reports on his desk as Tony left the room, a bitter taste in his mouth. Stuck, and partly because his superior officer was on the take. Stuck, and a known gangster was going to get away with theft and extortion, if not murder. Stuck. They weren't going to solve this case. For the first time, Matt regretted taking this job; for the first time, he wished he and Brooke had indeed gone to Newport as she'd suggested.

He was involved in reading the report of a burglary that had happened overnight, when he heard a noise at the corner of his desk. Looking up, he saw Tony, his face pale and his eyes distant. "No luck?"

"Yeah. No. I don't know." He glanced toward O'Neill's office. "I could use a cigarette."

"So have one."

"Outside. Want to come?"

"No, I . . ." Matt frowned. Tony was staring at O'Neill's office again, that same strange look in his eyes. "You found out something," he said in a low voice.

"Not here," Flynn said equally low.

"Then I guess I will have that cigarette," Matt said, and rose, not bothering to reach for his jacket or his cigarette case.

No one in the room seemed to notice as he and Tony walked out; no one at the front desk appeared to see anything out of the ordinary. As they came out of the building, some of the reporters sitting on the stairs of the press building across the street yelled questions, but Tony put them off easily, smiling and waving his battered packet of cigarettes. "Take one," he said in a tone that brooked no argument.

Matt reached out for a cigarette, though it was the last thing he wanted. "What did you find out?"

Tony turned so that his back was to the fence that edged the building, the hand that held the cigarette shielding his mouth. "Maybe some of what Maisie knew."

"Holy—you mean there was someone in the cells?"

"Not exactly. And for God's sake, turn around. You don't want anyone to see you talking like this."

"Aren't you being overcautious?" Matt asked, but he, too, turned, leaning against the iron fence.

"I don't think so." Tony waited until a wagon had clattered by, and he could be heard again. "Her name's Eileen. Never mind her last name, it doesn't matter. What does is that she's talked to me in the past, and her information's always been good."

"So?"

"So she's madam at one of the cathouses and she was here to get her girls out. And when she saw me, she started raising holy hell."

"Why?"

"Because"—Tony glanced around to make sure no one could overhear—"she said she's paid enough in protection—"

"What!"

"—to keep her house from being raided."

"Holy God."

"She was damned mad. I played along like I knew what she was talking about. Said we have to raid places now and then so the public thinks we're being tough on vice. But she didn't buy it. She said she's put too much out."

"To who?"

"Well, that's the thing. I didn't ask her right away, because I figured maybe she knew some other stuff and I could find it out. So I mentioned Maisie, and that started her off again. She and Maisie started together."

Matt leaned forward, sensing something in Tony's voice. "And?"

"And guess whose mistress Maisie was last April."

"Warren's?"

"No, after he died." Tony puffed at his cigarette again. "Did you know she owed Horgan money, too? Yeah. From when she was with Warren. You'd think Horgan's men would have known better, but they let her place bets."

"So Horgan made her pay him back by working it off," Matt said slowly.

"Yeah. And then when he was done he sent her to Ma

Meecham's. No wonder Maisie wanted to talk. She was scared of Horgan, but mad too."

"I can see that." Matt frowned. Something more had happened to Tony than an encounter with a prostitute. "So are you saying she knew what Maisie would've told you? Because it still doesn't do us any good."

"Maisie overheard an argument," Tony went on, as if Matt hadn't spoken. "Horgan, on the telephone with someone. Horgan was just talking and she wasn't paying attention, and then he started yelling. Something about not knowing how to take a painting without cutting it out of its frame."

"Holy—"

"Then he looked at Maisie and made her leave the room. Guess when this was?"

"Last April."

"Got it. Right after that Horgan sent Maisie to Ma Meecham's, and she started putting things together."

"Holy God," Matt said softly. "Then he could have killed Warren."

"Yeah. And we'll never prove it."

Matt glanced at him. There was a note of bitterness in Tony's voice that hadn't been there before. "Why not?"

"When Eileen was talking about payoffs I said I didn't realize she owned a house, and that's when she let it slip. Who the real owner is."

"Holy God. Horgan?"

"Yeah." Tony tossed his cigarette butt into the street. "Horgan's been paying off O'Neill."

"Come now, Mrs. Devlin," Sylvia said as Brooke stared at her openmouthed. "You knew about this."

"I—no, I didn't."

"Of course you did." Sylvia leaned back against the sofa, the tumbler of bourbon in her hand. "I suspected it the first time you came here. Your reputation has preceded you, my dear."

Brooke opened her mouth and then closed it again. Of all the possible outcomes she had envisioned for this meeting, she had not foreseen this. Sylvia wouldn't believe her, however. "I'm surprised you admit it," she finally said, amazed that her voice sounded close to normal.

Sylvia laughed an odd, lighthearted sound. "But, my dear, why shouldn't I? Oh, I know you'll go home and tell your husband, I quite expect that, but what else can you do?" She tilted her head to the side. "It will be your word against mine, and why should anyone believe I wanted my Joseph dead? Certainly I've suffered since his death. And all for nothin'."

"That is what I don't understand, Mrs. Warren," Brooke said carefully. "Why would you want him dead?"

"Why? Oh, my foolish girl, don't you see? But no, you wouldn't, you're too newly married. Well, wait a few years, my dear. Wait until your husband's eye strays."

Brooke forced herself to remain calm. "Other men have mistresses, ma'am, and they're not killed because of it."

"She was a prostitute!" Sylvia spat out. "Do you know what people would have said if they'd known that? A common whore. Oh, I should have known better, my daddy warned me about him. Common, that's what the Warrens were. Just because they made some money in coal they thought they were good enough to enter society. Well, they weren't, not until Joseph married me. I gave him entree to that life, and how did he repay me? By consorting with gangsters and prostitutes!"

"Mrs. Warren," Brooke said, feeling her way, "you were seen with a gangster yourself."

"Mr. Horgan. I wanted to see what the enemy looked like. But then, I must admit, I began to find Frank quite charmin'.

Oh, I knew Joseph owed him money. I also knew what he did to get that money."

"You know about the forgeries?"

"Shameful, isn't it? Oh, the scandal if that had gotten out. Well, it did, and look how everyone is talkin'. Why, I can't hold my head up in society anymore. I couldn't. So I had to do somethin' about it."

"I appreciate that, ma'am," Brooke said, though she didn't. "But surely murder wasn't the answer."

"Oh, but I didn't kill him. Is that what you thought? It is, isn't it?" Sylvia said, peering at Brooke's face and giving that odd, girlish laugh again. "A lady doesn't kill people."

"No. But there are other ways, ma'am. Divorce—"

"Bah. And be ostracized?"

"You are now."

"Not by my choice! How was I to know Joseph had gone through all the money? His, and mine. There was always enough. Always plenty. But when he died, we found bills, and more bills, and tradesmen actually dared come to our door to dun us! Shameful. And now I am reduced to living here, with no help. Oh, yes, Mrs. Devlin, I have paid for what I did."

"But you didn't kill him yourself?"

"Of course not. I merely made it possible for someone else to."

"Who?"

"Oh, no, no, no, no, no." Sylvia waggled a finger at her. "That would be tellin'. This bourbon really is excellent, Mrs. Devlin. Are you sure you wouldn't like some?"

"No." Brooke shook her head. "How did you, as you said, make it possible?"

"Why, didn't I say? Well, it was quite easy. I called Joseph and told him I would meet him at the museum. I knew he was goin' to see *her* that night. But I told him it was important, and so he agreed. But it wasn't me he met. Oh, no, no." She twinkled at Brooke. "There are many people who can say that I was at home when he died."

"But you set it up." Brooke spoke slowly. "You arranged it so he would meet his killer."

"But of course, my dear." Sylvia drained her glass. "Oh, dear, this appears to be empty. I had to. I had to do something, you see. And so now you know."

Brooke closed her eyes. This was madness. "I'm not sure I do, Mrs. Warren," she said carefully. "I'm not sure why you went to Frank Horgan's saloon so often. Or why he was here."

"Oh, as to that." Sylvia waved her hand in dismissal. "He did me a very great favor."

"You mean—"

"No, no, you won't get me to say any more. Now, do run along, dear." Sylvia let the glass drop onto the marble-topped table with a thud, and reclined on the sofa, one arm over her eyes. "I am rather tired."

"You mean—you're just going to let me go?"

"Of course." Sylvia lowered her arm and peered up at Brooke. "Oh, my dear, you thought I would try to keep you here? How darlin' of you. Why would I?"

Brooke stumbled to her feet. "Because I—you—because you said—"

"Now, dear, there's no proof, is there? No evidence against me. And as I said earlier, it's only your word against mine."

"No, Mother," a voice came from behind Brooke, and the apartment door swung open to reveal Linda, standing in the doorway. She was very pale, and her eyes were huge. "My word too."

"Linda!" Sylvia shot up. "My heavens, what are you doin' home?"

"I'm not feeling well. Oh, Mother. The door was ajar and I heard—"

"You were eavesdroppin'!" Sylvia accused. "How dare you, Linda? Didn't I raise you better than that?"

"Eavesdropping." Linda pressed the back of her hand to her forehead. "Eavesdropping."

"Well, it isn't done, dear."

"Oh, my good Lord." Linda turned to Brooke. "You'd better go."

"Are you sure?" Brooke looked up at her. "You'll need help."

"I'm sure." Linda's eyes were stony as she pulled off her gloves. "I've been taking care of my mother for quite some time now. Do please go, Brooke."

"Yes." Brooke started for the door, and then stopped. "Linda, you know I have to—"

"Do what you must," Linda said, and gently but quite firmly closed the door behind Brooke.

Brooke paused on the landing for a moment, her mind whirling. Good heavens! When she had set out from home this morning she certainly hadn't expected this, to find out that Sylvia Warren was involved in her husband's murder. Most likely Horgan was too, though Sylvia hadn't said so. But with Linda having overheard, perhaps she'd admit to that too, Brooke thought, and at last headed down the stairs. Poor Linda. All she had wanted was to have her father's name cleared, and instead her world had been destroyed.

Brooke emerged onto the stoop into surprisingly bright sunlight. Odd, because it had felt so very dark in the Warrens' apartment; it still felt dark inside her. Shaking off the feeling, she walked down the stairs and headed toward the victoria, wondering absently where John, the coachman, was. Ordinarily he'd be on the box, and would jump down when he saw her, to open the carriage door. But today . . .

A hand grabbed her arm, hard and unexpected, and she whirled around. "Good morning, Mrs. Devlin." Frank Horgan smiled down at her. "I think it's time you and I took a ride together."

15

Brooke gazed at Horgan across the victoria as it rode along. He had pulled down the shades, and the interior was dim. "Where is John?" she asked steadily, though her heart was racing and her hands were clasped together to hide their shaking.

"John? Oh, your driver. He's quite well." Horgan's smile flashed in the shadows. "He'll have a headache for a time when he comes to, but that is all."

Brooke clasped her hands more tightly together. "Was it necessary to hit him?"

"I'm afraid so. I doubt he would have driven us where I want to go. No, my dear, I did what I had to. I usually do."

"Terrorizing helpless women is something you have to do?"

"I'd hardly call you helpless, Mrs. Devlin." The smile flashed again as Horgan reached down to rub his shin. "You landed a good kick."

"My sympathies."

Horgan let out a laugh. "I like you, Brooke—I may call you Brooke?"

"No."

"You've got spirit," he went on, as if she hadn't spoken. "And beauty. Pity you work on the wrong side."

"Pity you do, sir," Brooke retorted, wondering where she found the courage. "With your intelligence and resources you could make a fortune at business."

"Ah, but, my dear"—he looked at her over his steepled fingers—"that is precisely what I am, a businessman. And before you protest, may I point out that my methods aren't so very different than, say, a Rockefeller's or a Vanderbilt's."

"Except for murder."

Horgan smiled. "Yes, except for that."

"You admit it, then?"

"Why not? There's nothing you can do about it. I make very certain that nothing can ever be traced to me."

Brooke was silent for a moment. "Then why are you doing this? What good does abducting me do you?"

"More than you might think. You've become a bit of a nuisance, you and your husband." His face subtly hardened, the planes of his cheeks standing out in a chiaroscuro sketch of shadows and light. "I warned him once. I also told him that if I had to warn him again, I would not be so polite. Actually, I think I've restrained myself rather well."

"If this is meant to be a warning to Matt, it won't work," she said, her voice surprisingly steady. "If anything, it'll make him want to go against you more."

"I doubt that, Brooke. I doubt it very much." He shifted on the seat. "Do you not even wish to know where I am taking you?"

"You talk very well, sir. For a gangster."

He inclined his head. "Thank you. I try. I understand you like the arts. Shall we discuss, oh, poetry, or the theater—"

"No. Where are you taking me?"

"All in good time, my dear." His gaze on her was steady. "Do you know, I didn't think I'd enjoy this, but I am."

"I am so glad that I'm so entertaining."

Horgan laughed again. "Ah, but you do have spirit. You should come work with me. You're wasted in your world."

"Am I?" Brooke's gaze was as steady as his. "I helped discover that the paintings at the Manhattan Museum were forged, and who did the forging. And I know, sir, who killed Joseph Warren."

"Do you? Satisfy my curiosity, then. Who did?"

"You did."

There was silence. "Quite a remarkable observation, Mrs. Devlin. And how did you come to this conclusion?"

"Joseph Warren owed you money. That, I know. He paid you with the proceeds from the forgeries, but it wasn't enough, was it?"

"I don't know. Was it?"

"Then he made more money by stealing and selling the very paintings he had earlier acquired for the museum. But he didn't sell them through you, did he? If he had, people would have known, and so would the police. So. He owed you money, yet he cut you out of a chance to make some. Is that reason enough?"

"Fascinating tale, Mrs. Devlin. There's just one problem. If it's true, he would have taken care not to let me near him, and yet he did. So I'm afraid your theory falls apart right there."

"Oh, no, Mr. Horgan. Because his wife called to say she would meet him. He went to the gallery, not suspecting that it would be you he'd meet, am I right?" She lifted her chin. "And it was you, wasn't it?"

"You'll believe the word of a drunken woman?"

"Over that of a gangster? Yes, Mr. Horgan, I believe I will."

"Mrs. Devlin." His voice had gone quiet. "It isn't wise to insult me when I have you in my power."

"Then perhaps I'd best stop talking." She turned her head, trying in vain to see past the lowered shade, wondering if there was some way she could attract attention from outside. By the increased sounds of traffic, of wagons and horses' hooves and the clanging of trolleys, they were farther downtown. Where Horgan was taking her, she could only guess.

"You're an unusual woman." Horgan leaned back in his corner, his arms crossed on his chest. "Does Devlin know what he has in you?"

"Yes." She turned to stare at him. "And I warn you, sir, that if anything happens to me, he won't rest. He'll keep coming after you until—"

"Bah." Horgan flicked his fingers. "I've taken care of that."

"I beg your pardon?"

"I've taken care of Devlin."

Brooke leaned forward, panic shooting through her. "What have you done to him?"

"You disappoint me, Mrs. Devlin. Where is your courage?"

"What have you done to Matt?"

"Nothing. Yet." He let the silence stretch out. "But I doubt very much he'll come after me. I've seen to it that he can't. And if he does." He shrugged. "Then so be it."

Brooke sank back against the seat, chilled in spite of the day's warmth. "Then please let me go."

"Oh, no." His gaze flicked over her, cold, impersonal, and yet oddly tactile, making her shiver. "I find this conversation tedious. We will not talk anymore," he said, and with that turned away, contemplating the window opposite. Brooke opened her mouth, and then closed it again. He was a dangerous man. Not because of the gun he carried, but because he wouldn't hesitate to use that gun if he felt he had to. He would use other methods, too, to gain his ends. What did the life of one New York policeman mean to him?

She hugged herself, trying to still the shivers, knowing she had to hold up. What Horgan had in mind for her she didn't know, but she could not give in. Not yet. She had to find some way out. Her life, and Matt's, depended on it.

The carriage jolted as it rolled from the smooth paving of the street they had been traveling onto rough cobblestones. The sounds of traffic and of people hadn't lessened, but Brooke, listening hard, noticed a change in the voices. She heard Italian accents, which gradually gave way to what she recognized as Yiddish. They were on the East Side, then, not so very far from Mulberry Street, and yet far enough. She was in Horgan's territory, and no police could help her.

The carriage stopped. "Ah, here we are." Horgan rose, opening the door and holding out his hand. "Mrs. Devlin?"

Brooke pressed her lips together, but gave him her hand and let him help her down from the carriage, blinking against the bright sunlight. About them swirled clouds of dust from the unpaved street, stirred up by people going about their business and apparently paying little heed to the fine carriage stopped on the street. She was on a flagstone-paved sidewalk, the bulk of a building rising to her side; above her hung a gilded harp. "My empire, Mrs. Devlin," Horgan said, taking her arm and leading her to the doorway. "Let me show you around."

From somewhere Brooke found courage. So this was the Golden Harp, his saloon. Fleetingly she remembered her conversation with Jennifer Sawyer, and her own guilty desire to visit here. How foolish of her. "As you did with Mrs. Warren?"

He smiled. "She's a silly woman. But you, Brooke." Again his eyes raked her over. "You'd be a worthy adversary. Or ally."

"Over my dead body."

He merely smiled at that, opening the door and leading her inside. "Hello, Patrick."

The big man behind the polished mahogany bar inclined his head. "Mr. Horgan. Not many customers yet."

"It's early. I have a guest, Patrick. I am not to be disturbed." Patrick nodded. "No, sir."

"This way, Mrs. Devlin. Have you been in a saloon before?"

"Slumming, you mean? No, not very often."

"Come, come, my dear, this is hardly a slum." The wave of his arm encompassed the entire room: the shining, U-shaped bar, the dazzling rows of glasses, the bright brasswork, the Tiffany stained-glass lamps wired for electricity, the gilt-framed paintings. "My establishment is as fine as any you'll find on Fifth Avenue."

"Except for your customers." And there were, in spite of the early hour, more than a few men at the bar, or sitting in booths. Most were dressed poorly, shabbily; most avoided her gaze as she looked around. "Hardly the fashionable set."

"You would be surprised. But come, you haven't seen all of it, have you? This way. Yes, up those stairs. My saloon is open to every man, working or not," he went on as she reluctantly preceded him up the narrow staircase. "I offer a fine free lunch, and if they wish to have a beer along with that, why, I see no harm in it. Up here, however, is different." He stopped in the corridor that stretched away from them and opened a door. "Do you call this slumming, Mrs. Devlin?"

Brooke stepped into the room, and in spite of herself her mouth opened in a surprised gasp. The room was spacious and well proportioned, with tall windows draped with red velvet curtains and flocked red-patterned paper on the walls. The carpet underneath was as thick and plush as any in her own apartment, and the two crystal chandeliers as fine. Several tables with green baize tops were set up in the room, obviously for playing cards. Again, as downstairs, this room already had customers; a few men sat at one of the tables, the tailoring of their clothing far superior to any worn by the men downstairs. A woman wearing a gown that Brooke recognized as coming from Worth stood beside one of the men, her hand on his shoulder. "The rugs are from Persia, Mrs. Devlin," Horgan said, "and the chandeliers are Baccarat."

Still slumming, Brooke thought, but held back the words. How much more could she insult him before he grew angry? "They're quite fine, Mr. Horgan."

"I'm glad you think so. But, come. I haven't shown you everything." Taking her arm again, he led her back into the corridor, to another room. It was as sumptuously furnished as the first, except that the center of attraction was a large wheel for *rouge et noir*. "We have other games of chance in here. And here." He opened yet another door, disclosing a room as conventionally furnished as any parlor, except for the painting of a nude over the marble mantel. "We provide private parlors for patrons who wish to hold their own parties."

"I see," Brooke said, her stomach flipping. There was only one role that she could see for women in this place, and it sickened her. If that was the fate Horgan had in mind for her, she would fight him with everything she possessed.

"Then we have the rooms where business is transacted." Another door was opened; she saw two orderly rows of desks, at which sat men who looked like nothing so much as clerks. "Here is where my bookmakers work, and where the runners report."

"I—see."

"The liquor is stored in the basement," he said, turning back into the hall. "Of course I do a good business in that as well. Never underestimate a man's vices, Mrs. Devlin."

"No."

"One of which is taken care of there." He pointed to a door at the end of the corridor, ordinary in every respect, except for its impressive array of locks. "Shall we go in?"

"What is in there?"

"It opens into the building next door, which is, you might say, a place where, ah, women are employed. Ah, yes, I see you understand."

"I don't need to see it, thank you," she said faintly.

"No? Perhaps later. Let us go to my office, then, and talk."

"Talk?" Brooke was escorted into an office as workaday, and as luxurious, as any she'd seen on Wall Street. Horgan seated her courteously on a wooden chair with a deep, burgundy leather padded seat, and sat himself behind his desk. "Coffee, Tiny," he said, and Brooke turned to see a giant of a man filling the doorway. "Mrs. Devlin?"

Her stomach clenched. "No. No, thank you."

He clicked his tongue. "Come, now, that is hardly polite. Two cups, Tiny. Morley!"

Another man, smaller, neat in dinner clothes, jumped forward. "Yes, boss?"

"You know what to do."

"Yes, boss," Morley said, and to Brooke's astonishment scurried to open the lid on a console of inlaid mahogany, which apparently contained a gramophone. "I'm changing the needle, boss." He lifted the arm of the gramophone and slipped in a wooden needle. "Should sound real good."

Horgan smiled, seeming genuinely amused. "Thoughtful of you, Morley. Ah, that is better." He sat back, eyes closed, listening to the rich music of a Strauss waltz. " 'Tales from the Vienna Woods.' Do you like music, Mrs. Devlin?"

"Very much so," Brooke answered.

"I thought you might. I'd ask you to dance, but unfortunately there's not enough room."

"Thank you," she said inanely. Tiny had returned, carrying a tray. He set down fine porcelain cups—Meissen, she noted—and poured in a dark, steaming liquid that smelled delicious and yet nauseated her. Mechanically she stirred cream and sugar into her cup, though she knew she wouldn't be able to drink it.

"So, Mrs. Devlin." Horgan sipped at his coffee and then set the cup down. "What do you think of my empire?"

"Impressive." She raised her cup to hide her face, and then set it down again; her hands were shaking too much for her to hold it steady. "I don't quite understand, though, why you wanted me to see it."

"Don't you?" He leaned back, studying her. "Then let me make it clear to you. I am a powerful man, Mrs. Devlin. What you see here—the gambling, liquor, women—is just the start of it. And I have my fine, upstanding customers, who have reason to be grateful to me. You may be assured of that."

"Never underestimate a man's vices."

"Exactly. You learn quickly. Is the coffee not to your liking?"

"I'm not thirsty."

"You see, Mrs. Devlin," he went on as if the polite social interchange hadn't happened, "you can't win. You can fight me all you want, but you'll never win."

Once again Brooke gathered her courage. "You killed a man."

Horgan laughed. "I have killed many men, my dear. And where is your proof, hmm? There is none, is there?" He set his cup down again. "I thought so."

"I'm tired of this," Brooke said suddenly, no longer caring how Horgan might react. She was in his power; nothing she said or did could change that, even if she groveled. "What do you want of me?"

Horgan regarded her over his steepled fingers, and then rose. "What do I want? Dangerous question, my dear. But I think— yes, perhaps that should come later. You are very attractive, you know." He perched on the edge of his desk, forcing her chin upward with his fingers. "I could find many uses for you. But not yet." Abruptly he turned away, returning to his chair, and Brooke sagged in relief. For only a minute though. "Consider this a warning of what could happen if you or your husband continue to cross me."

Was he possibly going to let her go? "What do you mean?"

"Haven't I made that clear?" He leaned forward. "All this is mine," he said, the wave of his hand encompassing the Golden Harp and the brothel attached to it. "So are the thousand men who owe their loyalty to me. And more. The Olympia Theatre? Mine." He held up a finger. "Judge Bradshaw. Mine." Another finger. "Senator Hart, Mr. Taylor of the brokerage firm—shall I go on?"

"No," she said through bloodless lips.

"I own them all. So you see, my dear, opposing me is quite fruitless."

Brooke looked down at her hands. If she were to have a chance of getting out of there, she would have to be very careful. "I can't speak for my husband."

"But you had better, Mrs. Devlin. Because if he doesn't comply, he'll know what will happen to you."

She shuddered. It was only by a great effort that she kept her head held high. "I can't speak for him," she said again, aware of the tremor in her voice.

Horgan considered that. "That's honest," he said finally. "I shall send him a message, then, and he will comply, I assure you." He paused. "And you, Brooke?"

Brooke took a deep breath. "Yes," she whispered. "I will comply too. I won't interfere in your affairs."

"Very good." He beamed at her. "I knew you were an intelligent woman. Would you like more coffee?"

"No. If you don't mind, I'd rather go home."

"Of course. How thoughtless of me." Horgan rose and crossed to the door. "Tiny, please see Mrs. Devlin to her carriage."

"Yes, boss."

"Mrs. Devlin." Horgan stopped before her. "It's been a pleasure." Brooke nodded, not trusting her voice. "And remember. If you ever tire of the straight life, I'll be here."

Brooke's shoulders stiffened, but she forced herself only to nod at that outrageous statement. The stairs were before her, and she was going down them, no one was stopping her. No one stopped her as she walked through the saloon; nobody stopped her when she at last stepped outside. Bowing, Tiny held the door of her carriage open for her, and she climbed in. Only when the victoria was driving off did she give into the shaking that had threatened her for the past hour.

The victoria pulled up at last on West 71st Street, in front of the Dakota. Brooke, lips stiff, face pale, passed under the arched gateway into the courtyard, ignoring the doorman's greeting; passed the man at the desk without so much as a word; barely glanced at the woman operating the elevator. Safe. She was safe, and yet she didn't feel truly secure. Not until, inside her apartment, with all the doors closed and locked, she picked up the telephone and spoke a few numbers into it. A moment later a voice came through the receiver, and she made her request with admirable calm. Then Matt's voice came over the line, and she crumpled. "M-M-Matt?"

16

"Dammit," Matt said again, striding back and forth across the parlor, the whiskey in his glass breaking against the sides like waves. "If I'd been there—"

"What could you have done, Matt?" Brooke sat on the sofa, her legs curled under her, and, unusual for her, a glass of sherry in her hands. She had stopped shaking, but her color had yet to return. She wondered if she would ever feel truly safe again. "He had all the power. If you'd tried anything—"

"I know. Dammit, I know." He took a long gulp from his glass and then wheeled sharply around, splashing in more whiskey. "He had you in his territory, with his men around him, and you couldn't fight. But, dammit, Brooke!" He glowered at her. "Didn't I tell you this could be dangerous? Didn't I?"

"Yes." Brooke stared into the depths of her goblet, understanding his anger, and then raised her head. "But for heaven's sake, Matt, all I did was pay a social call. I had no idea of what was going to happen."

"You knew Mrs. Warren was involved—"

"No, I didn't. Did you?"

Matt glanced away. "No," he said finally, and threw himself into a chair. "I knew there was a piece missing, but I never thought she was it. What did she have to gain?"

"Respectability."

"Hah."

"Well, she didn't know what it would lead to. She thought Mr. Warren's death would end everything."

"She associated with a gangster and thought she could get away with it? Huh. Almost as naive as you."

"I am not naive! I've never thought Horgan was anything but dangerous."

"But you've never really thought investigating is."

"Yes, I have." She faced him stubbornly. "Don't baby me, Matt. I've known the risks all the time."

"Yeah? Well, would you like to go through it all again?"

Involuntarily, she shuddered. "No. I don't think I'll ever be able to listen to a Strauss waltz again."

"Dammit." He got up and began to pace again. "She confessed?"

"Yes. Everything except that Horgan was involved, and he filled that part in."

Matt shook his head. "I would never have suspected her."

"I told you she went to the Golden Harp."

"So? She wasn't the only one. Regardless." He sipped from his glass. "She confessed, but there's no evidence against her. Only your word."

"And Linda's," she said softly, remembering the moment when the door had opened to reveal Linda Warren's stricken face.

"Huh. Will she testify against her mother? I doubt it. No, Sylvia's gotten away with it, dammit. And Horgan . . ."

"You have some proof, Matt."

"Yeah? What?"

"The painting stolen when Mr. Warren was killed is linked to him."

"Maybe."

"And does he have an alibi?"

"He can get someone to give him one. But where is the weapon, Brooke? Where is someone who can place him at the scene of the crime."

Brooke was silent a moment. "Then he gets away with it too."

"Yeah." Matt gulped the rest of his drink down. "For now."

"Matt." She straightened. "You're not going after him, are you?"

"On this? No. There's nothing to go on. But sooner or later he'll slip up. He's not as powerful as he thinks." Matt sat down again, legs stretched before him and hands linked behind his head. "I didn't get a chance to tell you our excitement. Tony found out today who Captain O'Neill was protecting, and why."

"Who?

"Horgan."

"Good heavens!"

"Yeah." Matt's lips stretched in a humorless smile. "Not anymore, though."

"Good heavens," Brooke said again. "No wonder he didn't want you investigating."

"No. Horgan apparently paid him enough for protection." He raised his glass, saw that it was empty, and lowered it again. "TR hit the roof."

"Good."

"Yeah. As of this morning, O'Neill's been suspended until there can be a hearing before the commissioners."

"And then?"

"If our witness will testify, he's out. I don't think even Andrew Parker would vote to keep him on, even to spite TR. It would make him look like he's not tough on corruption."

"So you'll have a new captain."

"Yeah. All in all, that's worked out all right. But, dammit." He slammed the glass down on the marble-topped table next to him. "It kills me that Horgan's going to get away with this. And Sylvia."

"She'll pay, Matt," Brooke said softly. "Maybe not in court, but she'll pay somehow. I think she already is."

"It's not enough."

"No, but it's all we'll get." She ran a finger around the rim of her glass. "Matt?"

He turned his head to look at her. "What?"

"I've been doing a lot of thinking lately. You've told me more than once I'd have to decide what I wanted—no, please don't interrupt—and the other day Uncle Henry said much the same thing."

"Yes, and so?" he said when she didn't go on.

"I thought a lot about it. At first I was angry that everyone was telling me what to do." She looked up at him. "Part of the reason I investigated was to prove I could."

"I know that, Brooke."

She lowered her head. "It's rather shameful to admit, but there it is. It makes me sound spoiled."

"I don't know about that," he said after a moment. "Stubborn, maybe."

"And foolish. I didn't take your warnings seriously enough."

"Brooke—"

"I realized today all that you've been trying to tell me. Even if I got into that situation by accident, I still got into it, and on my own. At least you'd have police to back you up. No, please hear me out," she said as he opened his mouth. "I've thought about this, Matt, and you're right. This is no kind of work for me."

He rose and crossed the room, pouring more sherry into her goblet. "So you're going to stop."

"Yes."

"Think you can?"

"I'll have to, won't I?" she said, watching him as he sat again.

"Mmm. Scared?"

"After today? Of course I am. I'd be stupid not to be."

"Good."

It took a moment for that to penetrate. "Good?"

"Yeah. Good. Maybe you'll be more careful next time."

"Next time—Matt, there won't be a next time."

"Oh, yes, there will." He grinned at her. "It's in your blood, Brooke. The next time something comes along that involves someone you know, you'll be in it up to your neck."

"But—"

"At least now you'll know enough to be cautious."

She lowered her glass. "Are you saying you want me to continue investigating?"

"I don't think I could stop you. And I could use your help, Brooke. On some cases," he added quickly. "I wouldn't have solved this one without you."

"You wouldn't have been involved without me."

"No. True. But I was, and there's no changing it. And I'll be involved in things in the future too." He sat down again. "You said you gave the matter a lot of thought. If you hadn't had that scare today, which way would you have decided? For detecting, or for society?"

She put her chin up. "Detecting."

"I knew it." He grinned again. "I didn't think you'd quit."

"Quit!" She straightened. "Then you do want me to keep on investigating?"

Matt gazed into the depths of his glass. "Yeah, I guess I do," he admitted. "I've just been fighting the inevitable."

"I'll be more careful now, Matt. I promise." She hesitated. "You have to promise too."

"I'll be as careful as the job will let me be, Brooke." His face was serious. "That's as much as I can promise."

"It's enough." She sat back again, cradling her glass in her hand. It was more than enough. Within her marriage Brooke had found a freedom she hadn't known existed, and a lasting partnership. "Now, if we could just think of some way to prove what Horgan did."

"Brooke," Matt said warningly.

"And Sylvia, too. Maybe Linda will testify. And if she does, maybe Mrs. Warren will testify against Horgan."

"Huh. Don't get your hopes up."

"But we can't just leave things like this, Matt."

"We probably have to." His face, as he stared down at the floor, was somber. Then he jerked his head up, stared at her for a moment, and, surprisingly, grinned. "On the other hand . . ."

"What?"

"I think I know how to bring Horgan down."

Epilogue

From *The New York Times*, August 15, 1896, Obituaries.

MRS. JOSEPH WARREN, FORTY-SIX.

Mrs. Joseph Warren, *née* Sylvia Marsden, died unexpectedly yesterday at her home in Morningside Heights. Mrs. Warren was born in Atlanta, Georgia, where she was married. She was the daughter of the late Cory Marsden and Mrs. Marsden, and the widow of Joseph Warren, late of this city. She is survived by a daughter, Linda. . . .

From *The New York Evening Sun*, September 11, 1896

GANG WAR CONTINUES ON EAST SIDE

ONE FATALITY IN LATEST BATTLE

by Max Fischel

The war between Monk Eastman, a gangster, and Charles Francis "Frank" Horgan, a rival gang leader, erupted into further violence last night on the East Side. Men belonging to the Eastmans set upon the Golden

Harp, Horgan's saloon, breaking windows, glasses, and bottles of liquor. A wild melee broke out when the patrons of the saloon rushed to its defense. One man, apparently an Eastman, was killed when he was hit on the head with a beer bottle. His name is being withheld pending further investigation.

Acting Captain O'Brien of the New York Police Department's detective bureau said that this latest war between Eastman and Horgan began in early August, when Eastman learned that Horgan was responsible for the fire that destroyed a pet store owned by Eastman. How he learned this is unknown at this time. . . .

From *The New York Herald,* October 18, 1896

LOST MASTERPIECES FOUND!

FAMOUS ART DEALER TRIED TO SELL THEM

The so-called lost masterpieces stolen from the Manhattan Museum have been found in the shop owned by Jacob Wallace on East 45th Street. Mr. Wallace was charged by Detective Paul Kramer with receiving stolen goods. The paintings, by Rembrandt, Hals, etc., were stolen from the Manhattan Museum by Joseph Warren and Chandler Owen to disguise the fact that they were forgeries. Mr. Warren was killed thwarting an apparent theft last April. Mr. Owen is currently serving a term for fraud and larceny at Sing Sing Prison, along with James Carter Earle, who actually painted the works.

Though the lost masterpieces have no apparent value, Mr. Wallace planned to sell them, until his arrest. At this time he has refused to name his source for the paintings. . . .

From *The New York World*, October 27, 1896
GANGSTER KILLED!
SPECTACULAR FIRE LEVELS EAST SIDE SALOON!
by Arthur B. Brisbane
Frank Horgan, the notorious gangster, was killed yesterday evening during the latest battle in the war between him and Monk Eastman, at Horgan's East Side saloon, the Golden Harp. The East Side has been the scene of frequent battles lately between Eastman and Horgan, with many casualties on both sides. A gang of toughs carrying torches marched to the Golden Harp last night, and a fight ensued. During the fight one of the torches set the building aflame, resulting in a spectacular fire that lit up the East Side and could be seen as far away as Brooklyn. In trying to save his saloon, Horgan was struck by a bullet and was killed instantly. Police at this time have no suspects in the killing. . . .

And so, justice was served.

Author's Note

This book is a work of fiction, though I have tried to be as accurate in my detail as possible. Discerning readers have probably already guessed that the Manhattan Museum is actually the Metropolitan Museum. Though I ordinarily dislike fictional settings, I made the change because of the intense involvement of museum staff members in this novel. Had I used a real location and real names, I would be slandering some fine reputations. Nor have I found that any of the events at the Manhattan ever happened at the Metropolitan, or that any of the other events depicted in this book occurred. My intent is to entertain, not offend.

The characters are fictional as well, with a few exceptions. Theodore Roosevelt was president of the board of commissioners of the New York police from 1895 to 1897, when he left to take a post as Assistant Secretary of the Navy; from 1896 on he was involved in a struggle with fellow commissioner Andrew Parker. The various reporters mentioned, Jacob Riis, Max Fischel, and Arthur Brisbane, were on the police beat at the time. Monk Eastman was a gangster who controlled the Lower

East Side; Frank Horgan is fictional. So is police captain O'Neill, though Captain O'Brien, mentioned in the epilogue, was the actual head of the detective division at this time. The Devlins' apartment is fictional, especially since there weren't any vacancies in the Dakota from 1884 to 1929. The Dakota itself, however, is gloriously real.

As always, I had help in writing this book. My thanks first and foremost to Meredith Bernstein for her unswerving support; Jennifer Sawyer for comments, friendship, and the use of her name; the terrific members of RW-L who helped with research; John R. Podracky, curator of the New York City Police Museum, for his invaluable help; and, not least, John Sconamiglio, whose input helped enormously. My thanks also, and always, to the fine staff of the New Bedford Free Public Library, who were able to find me any research books I needed, in spite of the upheaval of major reconstruction. Any mistakes in this book are mine, not theirs (darn it). Thanks also to my mother, Madelyn Kruger, for her support, and to Rona Zable, Jeanne Goldrick, and Kathy Shannon, for listening to me kvetch. What would I do without writing buddies?

I enjoy hearing from my readers and will gladly answer all letters. Please write to me care of:

RWA / New England Chapter
P.O. Box 1667
Framingham, MA 01701-9998

AMANDA HAZARD MYSTERIES
BY CONNIE FEDDERSEN

THE MYSTERIES OF MARY ROBERTS RINEHART

THE AFTER HOUSE   (0-8217-4246-6, $3.99/$4.99)

THE CIRCULAR STAIRCASE   (0-8217-3528-4, $3.95/$4.95)

THE DOOR   (0-8217-3526-8, $3.95/$4.95)

THE FRIGHTENED WIFE   (0-8217-3494-6, $3.95/$4.95)

A LIGHT IN THE WINDOW   (0-8217-4021-0, $3.99/$4.99)

THE STATE VS.   (0-8217-2412-6, $3.50/$4.50)
ELINOR NORTON

THE SWIMMING POOL   (0-8217-3679-5, $3.95/$4.95)

THE WALL   (0-8217-4017-2, $3.99/$4.99)

THE WINDOW AT THE WHITE CAT
                                (0-8217-4246-9, $3.99/$4.99)

THREE COMPLETE NOVELS: THE BAT, THE HAUNTED
LADY, THE YELLOW ROOM
                                (0-8217-114-4, $13.00/$16.00)

Available wherever paperbacks are sold, or order direct from the Publisher. Send cover price plus 50¢ per copy for mailing and handling to Penguin USA, P.O. Box 999, c/o Dept. 17109, Bergenfield, NJ 07621. Residents of New York and Tennessee must include sales tax. DO NOT SEND CASH.